Lullaby for Lakeside

A novel by Beth Armstrong

Lullaby for Lakeside ©2017

All rights reserved by Beth Armstrong

Printed in the United States of America

Library of Congress Control Number: 2017903314
CreateSpace Independent Publishing Platform,
North Charleston, SC

ISBN-10 154305482X

ISBN-13 978-1543054828

Table of Contents

Acknowledgments

A first-time novelist needs help from friends who are willing to read, proof, make suggestions, find inconsistencies, and otherwise support her efforts. I am grateful to everyone who was willing to serve. They are: Andy Linscott, Buzz Brownlee, Nancy Brownlee, Sandy Chabot, Jan Hosmer, Carolyn Windham, Kathy Crowley Gardner, Deecie Denison, and my amazingly patient husband, Stewart Armstrong. I am also grateful to Charlie Ortman and Rick Cochran for publishing advice.

Author's Note:

The stories in this book are all set in a town in northern Ohio, jutting into Lake Erie, called Lakeside. Lakeside does indeed exist – west of Cleveland and east of Toledo - and still offers to families the same quirky brand of old-fashioned summer fun that it did when I was vacationing there in the late 1950s and early 1960s. My parents and I visited our Auntie Cree every summer for quite a few years. I loved the place, though we never stayed more than two nights in a summer.

Because it is now 2017, I have access to mountains of information about Lakeside (and many, many other topics) through the wonders of the computer age. I find, in doing research from the comfort of my New England home, that Lakeside was then and is now somewhat different from the town I have described herein. This is not too surprising, given the license allowed me as a writer of fiction, and given my often spotty memory. It has been over fifty years since I spent a night on the shores of Lake Erie, listening to the adults murmuring on the screen porch, or eating a mint chocolate chip ice cream cone with my father after a long ride on a tandem bike. I did return to Lakeside recently, but it was hardly an exhaustive visit.

I invite the reader to substitute the name of your favorite summer place for the word Lakeside. To call into your mind's eye the sight of the water, the heat coming off the asphalt, the scrappy ball field or cool green lawn. Recall the smell of the salt water taffy, the caramel apples, the popcorn, the hot dogs. Picture yourself when you were free to ride your bike barefoot by yourself or with the gang of kids you played with. Go to the place where you learned to swim underwater, or played kick the can until it was dark, or sang around a campfire. Where your clothes were always just a tiny bit damp in the morning. Where you tasted your first kiss. Caught a fish, brought it home, and ate it for dinner, for the first time. Got a sunburn on the beach because you read an entire book in one sitting. Smell the Noxema cream on your nose.

If you are fortunate enough to have a summer place like that, rejoice. I had more than one. But Lakeside was something special for me. I think it remains special for many others, and I am glad for them. If you have a Lakeside, take a moment to return to it before you read these stories. Smell it, taste it, hear it, even touch it. That kind of memory can warm me on a gray night in February when I can hear the sleet pinging off the window panes. Go there now. Bask in the glow. Drink in the innocence. Swim in the sweet, pure waters of unsullied youth.

Swimming Lakeside
1960

It always took too long to get to Lakeside. Her dad drove carefully and they usually had to stop at one of the many gas stations along Ohio State Route 20 to use the filthy bathrooms, fill the tank, and buy her mother a Hershey bar. Claire's mother was scrupulous about her diet and never ate between meals. She ate those sparingly, and dessert was never served at their house except on Thanksgiving and Christmas, and on the occasional hot summer night in July when she would suddenly announce, "I bought a pint of vanilla ice cream today. Who wants a dish?" But her one indulgence was a Hershey bar with almonds during a car trip. She ate it instead of lunch.

Claire just wanted the car to keep moving. She loved going to Lakeside. They had gone there every summer she could remember. Up until this year, they had always brought her Mamama with them and dropped her off for a week's visit with her best friend, Lucretia, whom everyone called Auntie Cree. This was the first summer they were going without her grandmother, because of last winter's accident which resulted in Mamama's moving to Michigan to live with her surgeon son. Even though falling down the stairs and breaking a vertebra in her neck was hardly her daughter's fault, Mamama said she felt safer living with him. Claire's mother said it probably had more to do with the fact that he was the first born, golden child who could do no wrong in his mother's eyes. Claire had worried, when Mamama moved away, that their annual trips to Lakeside would stop, but to her delight, her parents decided that they loved Auntie Cree too much not to pay her a summer visit. They never stayed more than a night or two, because Auntie Cree was getting old and having house guests might tire her out. Claire didn't care how long they stayed, just so long as they went.

Auntie Cree and her late husband, Philip Fox, were Jewish. Their religion was significant because Lakeside was a Methodist community on Lake Erie. The Foxes had been concealing their ethnic background successfully for some thirty-five years since they first bought the cottage on Fourth Street in Lakeside as a summer vacation home. Philip had been a professor of history at Baldwin Wallace College in Berea, Ohio, but had suddenly died one winter while lecturing on the War of 1812, slumping to the lecture hall floor in front of twenty freshmen. Cree had soon thereafter secured a position at the college as a house mother in a building reserved for freshmen girls. She felt it was the least she could do for these children whose contemporaries had had to deal with her husband's memorable death.

Cree felt closest to Philip when she was finished at school and it was time to move to Lakeside in late May, leaving campus the day after graduation every year. The cottage hadn't changed much from the day they bought it. It was built sometime in the 1890s, when there had been a big construction boom in the town. Lakeside was one of several Chatauqua communities that were created in the late 19th century in the United States, mostly in the northeast, for vacationers to visit, and be preached to, taught, and entertained by a variety of religious revivalists and traveling acts. The Foxes weren't in the least interested in any of that sort of thing – though they had been known to go down to the lawn in front of the hotel occasionally to take in a summer evening concert. Mostly the Foxes craved peace and quiet and simplicity in the summer, the opportunity to play cards and read books, and spend time with their son Philip and his family, who had moved into his own cottage down the street as soon as he could afford it.

Cree's yellow cottage was square, with three rooms downstairs and two rooms up. In addition to the main floor's living room, kitchen, and bedroom, there was a screened-in porch that spanned the width of the house and was deep enough to touch the edge of the road. It was on this porch that the Foxes and their friends and family spent their summers. The living room was used only when the weather was unseasonably cool or it rained so heavily that the water came inside, dampening the cards. The kitchen was tiny and cooking was done on a stove that consisted of two burners and an oven that would accommodate a pie plate and not much else. Three shelves in need of paint and the top of the small refrigerator took care of food storage needs. A scarred white porcelain sink with faded red curtains at the window over it. A small bathroom next to the kitchen that didn't have a door, only a blue and white gingham curtain hung on a long spring that was tacked to either side of the entry.

The first floor bedroom was cheerful with a double bed covered with a white chenille spread, a small blue painted dresser and a rocking chair. There was a large hooked rug covering the worn wooden floor. There were piles of books in the bedroom and on all the surfaces of the living room, mostly old hardcover and paperback novels. There was a book by Charles Goren about bridge and another about the history of Ohio. There were several different dictionaries, much in use as Cree worked multiple crossword puzzles daily, and challenged all comers to Scrabble, a game she rarely lost.

After Philip died, Cree almost never went upstairs. When friends and family visited, the two small bedrooms were used – there were two twin beds and a low painted dresser in each room. The dressers' drawers, lined in Cleveland Plain Dealer newspapers from the 1920s, stuck in the summer and smelled of moth balls. Guests were expected to make their own beds and strip them upon leaving. Claire's mother always packed some old linens from their house to make their beds, so Auntie Cree wouldn't have any extra laundry after they left.

The house seemed to sag and buckle a little more every summer. The roof line was shaped like an unused hammock; the porch always seemed to be a little closer to the ground; the front screen door, whose curlicued wooden frame badly needed paint, never seemed to fit, and banged loudly every time it closed. Cree would screech, "Don't slam the door!" to everyone as they left. The interior floors tilted and the pockmarked linoleum in the kitchen, originally a red and black checkerboard pattern, now seemed more like two shades of gray.

No one minded any of this. The bridge and cribbage games continued from early afternoon until late at night. Coffee was served on the porch in the morning; lunch and dinner were also served on the large, worn wooden table that was the centerpiece of the room. The porch walls had never been finished with the fashionable wainscoting of the era, so the wooden braces were available to be used as shelves for coffee mugs, ash trays, boxes of cards and cocktail glasses. Methodist communities discouraged the consumption of coffee and tea and all alcoholic beverages, smoking of any sort, and card playing. Even so, these were the activities that Cree and her late husband came to Lakeside to do, and nothing had changed since his death. The only person in town from whom she had to hide her habits was the pastor, who took his daily constitutional right by her porch on Fourth Street. As he passed, usually early in the afternoon, Cree would be sure to stow any incriminating objects under the chair rail and greet him with a friendly "Afternoon, Pastor, lovely day, isn't it?" to which he would reply, "Sure is, Cree, hope you're enjoying yourself." As he turned the corner, she brought the cards and ash tray back up to the table.

When their car finally arrived at the gate marking the entrance to Lakeside, Claire's dad parked it in the lot provided, and they all grabbed their suitcases and whatever gifts her mother had packed for Cree. Cars were not allowed inside the gates; everyone walked or biked everywhere in the town. Claire hoped that her dad would come back to the gate later that day and rent a tandem bike for them to ride. It was one of the things the eleven-year-old liked best about Lakeside, pedaling behind her beloved father and waving to everyone they saw. When they got near the cottage on Fourth Street, they could hear a familiar, loud voice: "Is that you, Bob Benson?"

"You know it, Cree," he boomed back, "we're a little late."

"You could have called."

"You never answer the phone when it rings."

"For you, I would have made an exception." The affection in Cree's voice was obvious.

"Here we are, you crazy old woman."

"Don't slam that door!"

"Cree, you never change," he laughed.

Carefully holding open the rickety screen door as they brought in their belongings, all three kissed Cree on her deeply lined cheek, which was soft as feathers and smelled of talcum powder. Claire and her dad carried their suitcases up to their bedrooms. Her mom held the door and closed it silently, joining Cree on the porch and lighting a cigarette.

"Margot, how have you been?"

"We're all just fine, Cree. Has it been a good summer so far?"

"It would be if your mother would come and visit. She says she can't get down here. Something about her back. If you ask me, it's just that Woody and Gini can't be bothered to drive her here."

"I wouldn't know. We have trouble getting them to visit us in Cleveland. You'd think we lived twelve hours away. We manage to drive to Jackson every year. It's only four hours." Claire's mother sounded faintly irritated.

"You might want to put that cigarette under the railing. The pastor hasn't been by yet this afternoon. I'm expecting him any minute."

4

"Are Philip and Nancy here this weekend?" Margot asked as she moved her ashtray out of sight. Philip was Cree's son; Nancy, his wife. They had a cottage of their own nearby, larger and more substantial looking than Cree's. Even so, its white paint was peeling and some of the screens needed patching.

"Yes, and they told me you should come over as soon as you're settled."

"Okay, in a little while. I need to get a good dose of my Auntie Cree first," she said affectionately.

Claire ran onto the porch and fell into a big wicker rocker with a pink and green chintz cushion on the seat. Rocking furiously, she looked around her and smiled inwardly at the bric-a-brac all around her: the 1960 calendar hanging from a nail, the small, red, tin-shaded, electric lamp over Auntie Cree's shoulder, the multi-colored plastic flowers in a green Coke bottle on a side table, the fishing poles leaning in a corner near the door, the child-sized orange life vest on the floor.

"Auntie Cree, did Uncle Philip and Aunt Nancy bring David with them?"

"He's here, child, go and get him if you want to. He's waiting for you." Cree smiled at Claire.

"Can I, Mom?"

"Sure. Are you and your dad going bike riding?"

"Yeah. I'll be back soon for that." Claire jumped up and ran out the door, forgetting momentarily about the door.

"Don't slam the door!"

"Sorry," she shouted over her shoulder.

Philip and Nancy Fox and their three children had a summer cottage across Fourth Street and over two blocks, at the corner of Walnut Street. It was larger than Cree's but just as old and weather-beaten. The first room you entered when you used the front door was a cluttered dining room. Their screened-in porch comprised the entire side of the house facing Fourth Street. Claire knocked timidly on the front door, and David came to let her in. She greeted the family who were all sitting at the table, finishing what appeared to be bologna sandwiches and potato chips for lunch. Nancy Fox asked after Claire's parents, and Claire answered her questions politely, but she was itching to get outside. Soon the two children left the rest of the family and walked amiably toward the old hotel and the lake. It was a four block walk but pleasant and easy. Children were out on bikes or roller skates or walking in pairs. Teenagers were more likely to be in large groups. Older couples walked along, sometimes

5

carrying folding chairs made of aluminum and nylon webbing. They passed two or three shops, with few customers. Mostly they passed small houses, all similar in style to Cree's: old, faded, with little or no yard, and always the large screened-in porch. Fishing poles were often leaning on the houses and bikes were tossed carelessly on the ground nearby or propped against a wall. Children's toys were everywhere. It was a perfect summer day; there was a periwinkle blue sky, with sweet sugary mounds scudding along in a light breeze.

"Where do you want to go?" asked David after they had gone a block.

"I don't care. Where do you want to go?" Claire answered.

"Do you want to go swimming?"

"Okay. But I have to go back to Auntie Cree's to get my suit."

"Okay."

They turned and walked more quickly to Cree's cottage. David was usually glad to see his grandmother, but he wished she didn't speak to him in such a loud voice, and feel so free to tell him what to do.

"David Fox, get in here this minute and say hello to the Bensons." Auntie Cree saw them coming a block away.

"I just need to get my suit on. I'll be right back," Claire called over her shoulder as soon as they entered, knowing that David would want an excuse to leave soon.

"Hi, Mr. Benson. Hi, Mrs. Benson. How are you?" asked David.

"Good to see you, Dave. How was your school year?" asked Bob Benson.

"It was fine. I'm starting a new school in September."

"Are you going out for any sports?" said Claire's dad, who was always the jovial one, always the one to ask questions, making others feel more comfortable.

"I don't know yet. I'm going into seventh grade. I don't really know what sports I can do."

"If you could pick one, what would it be?" asked Mr. Benson.

"I don't know, maybe track. I run pretty fast."

"Ever try football?"

"I don't think my parents would let me play football." David was uncomfortable with the subject. He was more interested in science than sports.

Claire appeared, having put on her suit under her shorts and cotton shirt. She was wearing dirty white tennis shoes.

"Claire, I brought your sandals," her mother pointed out.

"That's okay, Mom, these are fine. Let's go." She looked at David.

"Be back in time for our bike ride, honey," her father reminded her.

"Sure."

Claire and David left, and she remembered at the last second to grab the screen door and close it carefully.

"Good girl," said Auntie Cree.

David and Claire took off for the water. Lakeside was well named, sitting right on the shore of the big lake. The most dominant building in town, separated from the lakefront by a vast, well-groomed lawn, was the hotel. It was large, white, with green shutters, and dominated the scene. Built in 1870, it hadn't changed much since then. As David and Claire walked past, it occurred to her that the furniture hadn't changed much, either. Sagging chairs filled the side porch, made of old curly wicker and covered with lumpy, faded cushions in a floral design. Hotel guests sat on a few red, rusty, squeaky gliders, covered with the same cushions as the chairs. The hotel's front, facing the water, was all screened-in porch, used for dining. The lunches and dinners at the hotel were served cafeteria-style. When they visited Lakeside, Claire's family always took Auntie Cree to dinner at the hotel. In the city, this would have been a special evening out, but in Lakeside, it was more like a club meeting. Cree knew everyone in town and greeted them all before sitting down. Since the cafeteria at the hotel was the only restaurant in Lakeside, it was full every night with families eating pot roast, ham slices, or Salisbury steak with mashed potatoes, gravy, string beans, brown bread, and the inevitable jello and whipped cream for dessert.

The children passed the hotel and its white gazebo on the lawn, and hurried to the pier. The entrance to the pier was a long and large white pavilion with a wide arched opening. Beyond it was an uninterrupted view of Lake Erie, with its wind-tossed, white-capped, gray waves and huge boulders at the land's edge. On the horizon Claire could see a small land mass that she knew was called Kelley's Island. Other than that, Lake Erie might have been a vast ocean. Hidden from a hotel guest's view, behind the pavilion, there was a large sandy area and the beginning of an enormous, wide concrete pier that stretched hundreds of feet over the water, and then took a ninety degree turn to the left. This turn created a kind of swimming area which was divided into three distinct sections by ropes lying on the surface of the water, held up by striped buoys every so many feet. Each section signified a different water depth. Only the adults and teenagers swam in the farthest, deepest section. Claire and David were strong swimmers and knew they could handle that section, but the

7

lifeguards were careful and would never have let them in. She was glad she no longer was confined to the shallowest water, where mothers helped babies and toddlers wade around in swim fins and blue and pink inner tubes. She and David ran out on the pier, pulled off their play clothes and sneakers, and jumped into the lake, bobbing up and shaking the water out of their hair and eyes. There was a part of this section that was shallow enough for Claire to stand – the water came to her chest – and she practiced doing handstands for a while. When she came up for a rest, she noticed that David was talking to some of the other boys in the lake. They were laughing and pushing each other playfully. He noticed her and tilted his head to indicate she should join him, so she dog-paddled over slowly, wary of new kids and wishing some of them were girls.

"This is Claire," David explained to the other boys.

"Hi," said one. The others said nothing but seemed to be sharing some kind of private joke.

"Hi," said Claire.

"Want to play Marco Polo?" said the boy who was willing to speak. He directed the question to David.

"I guess," answered David.

"Okay," said Claire.

The kids seemed to know instantly how to begin. The boy who suggested the game was designated as "it." He leaned against the pier, his back to the swimmers, closed his eyes tightly and started to count to twenty. The others swam away from him and treaded water, watching him carefully. Suddenly he turned, eyes still shut, and shouted "Marco!" The others answered loudly, "Polo!" And he began to swim and dart around as fast and as unexpectedly as he could, hoping to tag another swimmer while keeping his eyes shut. He continued to yell "Marco!" and they continued to answer "Polo!" as they swam away from him and tried to anticipate which direction he would turn next. It wasn't long before he tagged another boy.

"Man, Gary, you took forever to get me!"

"No way! I was on you the whole time!"

"Hey, Steve, it's your turn," said a smaller boy.

Steve began to count at the pier. Claire was nervous about this game. The boys seemed to swim furiously and tagging looked a lot more like hitting to her. Still, she was a good swimmer and didn't want the boys to think she was afraid, so she yelled "Polo!" loudly and did everything she could to stay far away from Steve. He tagged David on his first flailing movement off the pier.

8

The game went on for another fifteen minutes or so, and Claire began to devise a plan to quietly swim away and maybe practice some water ballet moves with a couple of girls that were trying them out on the shallower side of the rope. But her escape was foiled when she was suddenly tagged by one of the boys. She didn't want to be "it" but she couldn't think of a way to say so. Rather than let the boys think she couldn't keep up, she swam to the pier, closed her eyes and began to count to twenty. At twenty, she turned and called out "Marco!" The answering "Polos!" seemed to come from every direction, but they were confusing. There was a lot of noise - kids yelling, women calling to friends, lifeguard whistles, and the laughter of the boys she was playing with. She flailed around, turned this way and that as suddenly as she could, pumped her arms, swimming toward what she thought was a voice, but not finding a body to tag. She was tired now and wanted to stop. She tried opening her eyes just a slit and there were boys everywhere, with foamy, roiling water around each of them as they kicked and swam around her, taunting and yet staying just out of reach. She was about to stop playing when she felt two hands on the top of her head. Their downward pressure pushed her under water, and didn't release.

She had not expected to be pushed under and had not taken a breath before it happened. She moved her arms and legs furiously in protest as panic began to set in. She thought she couldn't get away from those hands on her head. But then the hands let go and she kicked up to the surface, gasping, gagging, and spitting.

"Hey! Who did that?" she screamed, coughing.

"Marco Polo!" said Gary, snickering. The others joined his laughter.

"I mean it! Who did it?"

"What's the matter, you scared?" teased Steve.

"When I get dunked and I can't come up, yeah!" Claire was furious. She began to swim to the ladder at the side of the pier.

"Hey, you're still 'it!'"

"I'm done. I'm going home."

"Can't keep up with the boys, huh?" someone taunted.

"I just don't want to anymore," she answered.

"Yeah, right. Go home to Mommy," said Gary.

"You're a jerk," she spat.

Claire got out of the lake, found her clothes, put on her sneakers quickly and ran toward the exit, pulling on her shirt and shorts over her dark blue bathing suit as she hurried. It was tricky navigating the pier, filled as it was with mothers and other women sitting on their aluminum chairs, sunning, smoking, or playing cards. But there was no doubt in her mind that she was being followed. She could hear it. Turning back, she saw Gary, Steve, and David pulling on their shirts while they ran after her. They were laughing. She felt herself on the verge of tears.

She ran out from under the archway and headed toward the road that led to Fourth Street. She passed the swings and vaguely noticed that no one was using them, which was unusual for a bright summer afternoon. It was just past the sandy area on which the swing set was placed that she felt a hand roughly grab her right shoulder. She spun around and faced Gary, a nasty grin on his face. Gary was a tall boy - she guessed he was thirteen - and thin as only a thirteen- year-old boy can be. He had light brown hair, still wet from the lake, and it was shaggy and in need of a haircut. He was young for the acne that had begun to appear on his nose.

"No one calls me a jerk." Gary sneered, under his breath.

"Yeah? Well, that's a surprise 'cuz that's what you are," she tossed back with more bravado than she felt.

"Where ya goin'? To Mommy?"

"I'm just done swimming, that's all."

"Well, we think you're coming back to the lake. You're still 'it.' Unless you're chicken," Gary taunted. Steve was hanging nearby, watching and grinning.

"I'm not. I'm going home."

His grip on her shoulder tightened. "You're coming with me." And he started to push her backwards towards the lake. Claire pushed back but knew she was quickly losing ground. Gary grabbed her other shoulder and forced her to walk too fast, backward. He was panting a little. She started to feel actually afraid. She tried to kick him but he sidestepped her and laughed a little. Vaguely, she noticed Steve run toward the lake so she knew she was alone with Gary, a thought that made her feel helpless.

"Ferris, knock it off." David suddenly appeared on her right.

"Shut up, Fox," sneered Gary.

"What's your problem? She just wants to quit," David said.

"Well, she can't. Game's not over." Gary stopped pushing Claire, let go of her with one hand, and turned toward David.

"It is for her. And me," added David.

"I knew you were a pansy, Fox. Taking care of a little girl. What are you, babysitting?"

Claire noticed with the beginnings of hope that Gary's annoyance with David was lessening his grip on her. Before she had a chance to get away from him, David took a swipe at Gary's free arm. Gary released her shoulder and turned quickly to David, putting his fists in front of himself as if preparing to box. David just snorted and began to walk away.

"Fox, are you chicken? Fight me!" cried Gary.

"No way. I got better things to do than mess with idiots."

"What did you say?"

"You heard me." David was still walking, his back to his tormentor.

Gary leaped onto David's back and began pummeling his head and arms. David tried to shake him off but Gary held tight. One of his fists found its mark on David's jaw, and it was then that David yelled "Hey!" and spun around, surprising the taller boy so that he fell to the ground. Gary was momentarily stunned. David moved as if to hit Gary, but thought better of it and turned on his heels, grabbed Claire's shaking hand, and began to run, fast. She had no choice but to keep up; she had never run so fast in her life. She had the frightening sense that her body was actually moving just a little faster than her feet, and that she would soon tumble forward onto her face. Miraculously, it didn't happen, and she and David seemed to fly out of the grassy area. They passed the swing set, the shuffleboard courts, benches and flower beds. To Claire, those things were just a blur of color and sound. They never checked to see if they were being pursued, and by the time they reached Second Street, there were so many adults strolling to or from the pier, they could see that they were safe. Still they kept on running, hand in hand, quick breaths matched in speed and intensity, sneakered feet kicking behind them. They both knew the quickest route to Auntie Cree's; there was no disagreement about which streets to cross and when.

It was only when they crossed the last street, solidly on Fourth Street, that they began to slow their pace. After running one city block, they came to a stop, stooping over with hands on their thighs, panting. They were in front of one of the few empty lots in Lakeside, which was used by folks in the neighborhood as an occasional picnic spot, a pick-up baseball field, or play yard for toddlers. It was unpopulated for the moment, and without discussion, Claire and David walked to the grassiest spot on the lot, and fell to the ground, lying on their backs side by side, getting their breathing under control, enjoying the quiet, shady, private spot.

"Man, you can run fast," Claire said finally.

"I can run a lot faster than that. I was taking it easy on you," David boasted.

"I could have gone faster," she protested.

"Sure you could."

There was a silence. Neither one of them knew what to say.

"Are you okay? Did he hurt you?" asked Claire, turning to him.

"Heck, no. He's a jerk, anyway."

"Do you know him from home?" asked Claire.

"Nah, he's just been coming here since we were kids. I never liked him much."

"I thought those guys were your friends."

"Just some guys. You know," answered David.

"It looked like you were having fun with them." She couldn't get past the memory of the three boys, David included, chasing her on the pier, laughing.

"Look, I come here every weekend. I try to get along with everybody." After a pause, he said, "I'm sorry. Those guys are jerks."

After a silence, Claire said, "I should be getting back. My dad's probably got a tandem bike for us."

"You're OK, right?"

"Oh, sure," she answered.

They stood, not sure what to do next. David was rubbing the toe of his shoe in a sandy spot on the lawn. Claire straightened her shirt and tucked it into her shorts. She started to re-tie her shoelaces but thought better of it.

"Hey, David?" she said quietly.

"Yeah?"

"Thanks." She looked down at the ground, embarrassed.

"That's okay. I'll walk you back to Gramma's."

Claire looked at him, smiled tentatively. David caught her smile and returned it.

"Hey, are you telling anyone?" Claire asked finally.

"Are you?"

"Can't think why I should."

"Me, neither," said David.

They looked at each other, conspirators in a shared secret, for an uninterrupted moment, and then by silent agreement, turned and walked toward the sagging, faded, welcoming yellow cottage on Fourth Street in Lakeside, Ohio, where her family was waiting.

Selling Lakeside
1960

Harriet Slade didn't get too many calls like the one she got that April morning. She was accustomed to getting inquiries about rentals of the lake shore properties she represented in the Sandusky, Ohio region. A realtor for almost forty years, she had handled most of the properties dozens of times, sometimes more. She had sold houses and lots, farms and storefronts, but she specialized in vacation homes and rentals. She had gotten to the point of no longer needing to advertise her real estate office and its services; everyone in the Lake Erie communities west of Cleveland knew to call Harriet when they wanted a summer getaway. Harriet had never married. She had lived most of her adult life alone or living with her mother, a fact that neither angered nor pleased her. Her lifestyle, it seemed to her, was the logical fulfillment of the fact of her birth, and she accepted it without regret. As a result, the real estate business held Harriet's heart as if it were her child. She conceived it, she gave birth to it, and she nurtured it until it was successful and self-sustaining. Now the experienced parent of a well-known business, she was rarely surprised anymore, so the call that morning got her absolute attention. The smooth, cultured man's voice on the phone asked if there were a house to buy in Lakeside. Preferably three bedrooms, with a large porch and a decent kitchen. He also wanted a sleeping porch on the second floor, and he was prepared to pay cash. He introduced himself as Mitchell Edwards.

Heck (Harriet never used any stronger language than "heck" and "darn"), no one buys houses in Lakeside, she thought. They rent houses there for a week or maybe a month. Or they inherit houses, spend two weeks there with their families, and ask her to find renters for the rest of the summer. And even if someone were to want to buy a house in Lakeside, they should know that "decent kitchens" there were rare. She was sure the two porches wouldn't be a problem, but what made her slightly uncomfortable was that she didn't recognize the man's name, nor did he mention a friend or relative in town. He was a stranger. And he had enough cash to buy a summer vacation home outright. Curious but never intrusive, she asked him how he came to know about Lakeside.

"We visited there last summer for a religious retreat. We were quite taken with the place," he replied.

"Oh? Which retreat was that?" she asked.

"The Methodist regional annual meeting. It was held over Labor Day weekend. The weather was just spectacular and the surroundings made us want to come back."

"How wonderful. Did you get a chance to look around, maybe see a house or two that interested you?"

"We weren't thinking about buying at the time, but as we talk about it now, we would love a lake view, although I know there aren't very many of those. I asked several people I know in the Sandusky area whom I should call for help, and they all told me to call you." He was so smooth and well-spoken. She wished she could meet him. She trusted her own judgment as long as there was an opportunity to share a cup of coffee. She didn't want to suggest possible properties unless she had a firm sense of what would be suitable for a client.

"I don't know where you are calling from, but would it be possible for us to meet at my office, or perhaps get a cup of coffee someday soon?" she asked.

"Yes, I think that could be arranged. Let me call you back with a couple of dates. I will need to check my book. I live on the east side of Cleveland."

"That would be fine, Mr. Edwards. I look forward to hearing from you," answered Harriet, hoping she matched his formal tone.

Their coffee meeting went very well. They met a few days after the first phone call at a small coffee shop in Sandusky that the locals knew about, called Marguerite's. Harriet was as impressed with Mitchell Edwards' appearance as she had been with his telephone manner. He was dressed in a gray business suit and tie, with polished wing tip shoes

(Harriet put a great deal of store into footwear and what it said about the wearer.) His curly dark hair was cut close to the head and was beginning to gray in a most becoming fashion, and his smile felt genuine. He explained that he was married to a professor of Linguistics at John Carroll University, and that they had three children, aged two to ten. He was employed by a publishing firm, specializing in textbooks. The plan was for the family to spend July in Lakeside this summer, and possibly increase to two months in the future, depending on how the children liked it. He asked if Harriet handled rentals as well, and suggested that they would like her to rent the house for them in August. He handed her a business card with his name, company name, home and business phone numbers on it and suggested she call him with houses to visit. He could arrange his schedule easily, he assured her.

Harriet checked on the homes in Lakeside she knew were for sale, and she also notified her contacts in town who would know of others that hadn't been formally listed. It didn't take long for her to identify three properties that she thought were suitable for the Edwards family. She arranged to meet Mr. Edwards (she never called clients by their first names, even when asked to) and showed him the houses. He took his role seriously, taking multiple pictures with a Polaroid camera, asking well thought-out questions, and making notes about each cottage in a leather-bound notebook with a gold Cross pen. After just one day, he called Harriet and made an offer on a charming three-story cottage on Second Street.

"My wife and I are very happy with the Second Street cottage. We think it meets our needs very nicely. I am going to need help remodeling the kitchen, however, but if you can help me locate a general contractor, I think I would like to buy the house." Mr. Edwards sounded very pleased, indeed.

"There is a man who lives in Port Clinton who I call all the time for Lakeside work. He is very reasonably priced and works fast. I could call him today to see if his schedule has an opening." Harriet was also pleased.

"Fine. Let me know what he says and I can negotiate with him directly after that, to take over that task from you. You have been very kind. I am grateful."

Harriet and Mr. Edwards were able to negotiate a price, the seller accepted, the contractor was engaged for two weeks in early June, and Mr. Edwards met Harriet at her antique-filled second floor office to sign all the necessary paperwork. Since he was paying in cash, no bank had to be involved in a mortgage, so the paperwork was easier than usual. Harriet could recall possibly two other times that she sold a property for cash. Most Ohio vacationers were middle class and rented. If they could buy, there was a mortgage. Upper class folks vacationed in Florida or the Bahamas or the Riviera, not Lakeside. "I am disappointed that I haven't had a chance to meet Mrs. Edwards," Harriet said after they had signed the last form. She had brought in a silver tray that had belonged to her grandmother, laden with a silver coffee pot, matching creamer and sugar bowl, two cups and saucers, and a small painted china plate with delicate sugar cookies arranged on it. Harriet was considered to be one of Sandusky's best bakers, a reputation she labored to maintain.

Mr. Edwards helped himself to a cup of coffee and a cookie, which he balanced on the rim of the saucer. "I'm sorry as well. Lorraine teaches several classes and is also writing a new textbook. She will have the summer off, however, and I will be sure to bring her to meet you as soon as we can both get here. The children, of course, are in school until mid-June."

"Do they go to Cleveland schools?" asked Harriet. She was skilled in extracting personal information from clients without seeming to be nosy. It was important, she reasoned, to know as much as possible about a client in order to show the most suitable properties. Showing the wrong house wastes everyone's time, she believed.

"They attend a Catholic school in our neighborhood. St. Dominic's. When they are old enough, they will attend Shaker Heights High School. Our little girl has a babysitter who comes to the house."

"We don't have a lot of Catholics in Lakeside. The town was founded by the Methodists, you know, and the church is served by a Methodist minister, although services are ecumenical. Everyone is welcome."

"Oh, we are also Methodists. But we felt the parochial school would start the children out with a firm foundation of self-discipline."

"I think you are very wise. Sometimes I worry about young people these days. Not enough discipline and hard work. I wonder if the whole generation is a bit spoiled."

"Perhaps it is because our parents raised us during the Depression. I think they wanted their kids to have more than they had, and we are perhaps doing the same. I don't know. All we can do is hope we are giving our children solid values and every possible opportunity to get an education."

"Mr. Edwards, I think you are going to be a real addition to Lakeside."

Harriet Slade had lived in Sandusky for almost fifty years, but she wasn't really a native. She was born in Cleveland, a fact that she rarely shared with colleagues and clients. She had started life in a neighborhood that was largely populated by Slavic immigrants: Latvians, Czechoslovakians, Lithuanians, and Russians. Area bakeries sold pierogis, babka and blintzes along with bread and pies. Her family was Polish; her parents had emigrated to the United States in 1890 in search of work in the steel industry. Her father became a seven-day-a-week steelworker in Cleveland and settled in what came to be known as Warszawa, a neighborhood that surrounded St. Stanislaus Catholic Church. His wife gave birth to seven children, the first two of whom were born in the German section of Poland, Silesia. The rest, including Harriet, were born on American soil. She, the fifth of the Sladarnecki family, was christened Angelika Maria.

Her father had been so accustomed to a seven day week in the mills that when his employer, US Steel Corporation, instituted a six day week to improve the lives of its manual laborers, he was at a loss as to how to spend his unasked-for freedom, and chose a local pub for his day-off headquarters. He died while crossing East 79th Street on his way home after a particularly robust afternoon of drinking Polish beer and arguing about baseball with his cronies. By the time he saw the streetcar come around the corner, it was too late.

Angelika's mother had a cousin in Sandusky who operated a hair salon and needed help. The widow moved her seven children into a three room flat above the salon and sent them to public school while she washed towels, swept, and shampooed.

By the time Angelika had spent a month in the fourth grade at Sandusky's Mills Grammar School, she knew she was not the girl she wanted to be, and she systematically began a metamorphosis that took no more than three years to accomplish. First she asked her new friends to call her Angie. She explained that her name was Harriet Angela and that she preferred the use of her middle name. "Harriet" was a name she had just read in one of the many books she brought home from the school library, and it conjured up for her images of a blond, healthy, American girl. Both the children and the school administration eventually accepted the change, and her permanent records beginning in the seventh grade at Sandusky Junior High School listed her as Harriet Angela Sladarnecki. She got a part time job in the town library, putting books back on their shelves and dusting. She carefully saved her money and used it to buy fabric for sewing clothes that fit in with the other girls.' She was a good enough student and friendly but kept her distance from her classmates after school. No one ever visited her home above the hair salon. Her mother barely noticed the comings and goings of her children; her hours at the salon were long and her free time was spent cooking traditional Polish food which she served her family and also took to the endless festivals at Holy Angels Catholic Church. Harriet attended services there dutifully along with her siblings, but kept her distance from God, too, preferring to rely on her own wits and good judgment to ensure a happy and fulfilling life for herself.

Harriet graduated from Sandusky High School in 1918, one of ten girls to do so in a class of over 100 students. She was far from first in her class but she had no intention of dropping out before finishing. Most of her siblings had left home by that time. Her mother and one younger brother attended the graduation exercises. Harriet received an inexpensive pen and pencil set from her mother. The next day, Harriet set about finding a new home and job for herself. There was no room for advancement at the library, but she was not foolish enough to resign before finding a suitable position for herself.

She soon answered an advertisement for a typist in a local real estate office, interviewing with a Mr. Russell. She filled out the application form and called herself Harriet A. Slade, deciding to change her name once more to convince herself of her new adulthood. Her appearance was pleasing enough, she was stylishly but conservatively dressed, her typing skills were adequate, and she was available immediately. She got the job on the spot and began work the next day. She was never late, never called in sick, and did everything Mr. Russell asked of her without needing to be reminded. She paid close attention to the work he did. She found pleasure in her small contributions in helping families relocate, and gradually Mr. Russell entrusted Harriet with more and more tasks. She learned the business thoroughly and she loved it. As for her own relocation, Harriet found a room at a boarding house on the opposite side of town from her mother, within walking distance of the real estate office, which included kitchen privileges. She saved half of her salary every week and lived frugally, visiting her mother by streetcar every Sunday after church. Her mother assumed that Harriet was attending Mass before their Sunday dinners together, but in fact, Harriet was usually reading or sewing on Sunday mornings. At her mother's flat, Harriet answered to "Angelika" while she helped her mother with the weekly baking, learning from a master.

Mr. Russell began relying on Harriet even more when his health took a turn for the worse. The final months of his life were marked by hideous pain and random episodes of bleeding. Having no close family of his own, he often needed help from his devoted assistant simply to move to a more comfortable seat on the office sofa. She made tea, prepared cold compresses, and went to the pharmacy for medicines. Eventually, the doctor in town had little more to offer, and Harriet watched her employer of seven years fade away until he disappeared altogether, leaving the business to her in his will.

It was not common in those days for a business to be owned and operated by a single woman, but it wasn't unheard of, either. Harriet immediately joined the Rotary and the Chamber of Commerce. She redecorated the second floor office with heavy draperies, thick carpets, and imposing furniture to give a client the impression of a successful, enduring enterprise. She advertised tastefully in several local newspapers, including both of Cleveland's papers, *The Press* and *The Plain Dealer*, and she actively sought out wealthy Ohioans who had vacation home properties. She offered to represent their interests to families wishing to rent a vacation house. The strategy worked – it was the 1920s and the life-is-a-party atmosphere in Ohio had a positive effect on her bottom line. Harriet was scrupulously honest and she never failed to serve her clients' needs on time and sometimes without being asked. She was never late, never took a sick day, and did everything that was asked of her. Those efforts paid off and it was only a few years before Harriet Slade was able to buy her own single family home and claim her share of the American Dream.

It was the weekend of the 4th of July. Lakeside's charming cottages were decorated with American flags and bunting, and the pier was more crowded than usual, as families gathered to celebrate the holiday and kick off the official start of summer. There were children of all ages splashing in the swimming area. The pavilion that marked the entrance to the pier was covered in bunting. Signs were hung on trees and lampposts, advertising the band concert that was planned for the evening of the 4th, followed by fireworks over the water. Sailboats with colorful spinnakers and motorboats small and large dotted the unusually blue July water. Older couples strolled on the huge lawn in front of Hotel Lakeside and more athletic vacationers filled the tennis and shuffleboard courts. On Second Street, the larger and more expensive cottages that faced the water were perhaps less ostentatious in their patriotism than older, more weather-beaten houses further away, but there was plenty of activity as families gathered to picnic and play croquet and badminton.

The O'Reilly family was just arriving, carrying their suitcases down Second Street and pushing a stroller. Tim O'Reilly rented bikes at the gate for his two older children. The boys arrived at the cottage first, and tossing their bikes against the house, ran off toward the pier to check whether the water was warm enough for swimming. Tim and Gigi did not stop them. Lakeside was an unusually safe place for children. The O'Reillys had been coming to the same cottage on Second Street since before their second child was born some eleven years ago. Even though it was a rental, they considered the large Victorian two story cottage their own. It was completely furnished and filled with the summer vacation staples they needed: fishing poles, life jackets, swim fins, face masks and flippers, pails and shovels, a small Hibachi gill, aluminum webbed chairs and chaises for the front lawn, a croquet set, cards, jigsaw puzzles, old musty books and outdated copies of *Saturday Evening Post* and *National Geographic*. The two older boys shared a bedroom and the baby slept in her parents' bedroom, though there was a small room waiting for her as she grew older. They knew Harriet Slade would have made sure there was a can of coffee in the refrigerator along with some milk, bread, butter and jam. She was thoughtful that way.

As they unpacked and rearranged the porch furniture the way they liked it, Gigi noticed activity next door. Someone was setting up lawn chairs, preparing for guests, she supposed.

"I think someone finally rented the house next door. I'm glad, it needed some love, that house," she remarked.

"Really? How long has that sat empty? You think Old Man Trowbridge has finally come back?" said Tim.

"I don't think so. I saw a younger man moving furniture outside. Let's go welcome them to the neighborhood. Maybe they would like to join us for a drink later." Gigi smiled as she remembered that in Lakeside, all evidence of drinking alcoholic beverages had to be camouflaged. There was a large collection in the kitchen cupboard of rubber jackets in various colors for covering highball glasses.

"In a minute. I want to get these suitcases upstairs. I'll go over to Jenny's for food soon, too. You brought those steaks for tonight, right?"

"Yeah, they're in my beach bag. They should go in the frig. It's pretty warm out today. I think I'll go next door now, okay?"

"Sure."

Gigi brushed her long light brown hair, replaced the headband she usually wore, and straightened the skirt of her shirtwaist dress before she went next door to introduce herself to the new neighbors. She expected them to be related somehow to the Trowbridges, who had owned that cottage for decades, but hadn't been able to use it for at least five years. She knocked on the curlicued screened door.

"Hello, anybody home? I just came from next door to say hi!" she called out.

"Oh! Coming!" answered a female voice.

Gigi stepped back to allow her neighbor to hold open the screened door, allowing her access to the large screened porch that faced the lake. It was dark inside the house from her vantage point outside. She was aware of children's voices from within.

"Hi! How nice of you to come over. We haven't had a chance to meet anyone yet. Can I get you a glass of iced tea?" asked the tall, well-groomed hostess, motioning Gigi to sit on one of the two chintz covered wicker arm chairs that faced the water.

Gigi started to answer, then stopped. This woman offering her hospitality was as black as night. She stood at least half a foot taller than Gigi, with impressive posture. She wore a bright pink shirtwaist dress and a white cardigan sweater, and white espadrilles that actually made her even taller. Her glistening black hair was pulled back severely from her face and fastened in a bun at the nape of her neck. Her large mouth was open in a wide smile, showing beautiful, impossibly white teeth.

"Oh….hello. My name is Gigi….O'Reilly. My husband and I rent the cottage next door. I thought you must be one of the Trowbridge family….I'm sorry….I expected…"Gigi stammered.

"We bought the house from the Trowbridges in April. We are here for the whole month of July. It's been quite an adventure, having to furnish it quickly. We also had the kitchen remodeled. Would you like to see how it came out?" she asked.

"Um, I really don't have a lot of time. We are expecting….company…we have a lot to do to get ready….I really should go….but thank you all the same. I….I'll see you." Gigi walked quickly toward the door.

"My name is Lorraine Edwards. My husband Mitchell is around back. He will want to meet you and your husband, I'm sure. Do you have children? Did I see a couple of boys on bikes? Ours are ten and eight. They're always looking for someone to swim with." Lorraine's tone was friendly.

"Uh, sure. I'll tell them. They know a lot of kids here." Gigi opened the screened door. "Well, nice to meet you. I hope you settle in well. I have to go."

Gigi hurried next door and went inside through the kitchen door at the back of their house, the one that faced Second Street. "Tim!" No answer. He must have taken the baby for a walk to Jenny's, she thought, remembering his plan to pick up the groceries they would need to tide them over until tomorrow's bigger shopping trip in Port Clinton. She sat at the old worn oilcloth-covered table in the kitchen and stared at its checkerboard design without really seeing it. *Never* had Gigi imagined a Negro family in Lakeside. As far as she knew, there had never been a Negro *person* there. And such a woman! She made Gigi feel small and pale. And the fact that the family had *bought* the Trowbridge house! They would be staying for a *month*. Maybe in the future they would stay for a *whole summer*. Gigi wondered if the owners of her cottage knew who their new neighbors were. They should have warned the O'Reillys, she thought. We should have been told. It's not something you should just happen on. People should have a say in where they live, who their next door neighbors are. It's not right. I wonder if Harriet Slade knows. It doesn't seem likely, Gigi thought, but then I really don't know her very well, do I?

Her ruminations were interrupted by the arrival of Tim and the baby, who was sleeping peacefully in the stroller. I should put her in the crib, she decided, then changed her mind. If she is sleeping so well, why wake a sleeping baby? I don't know if I want us to stay here very long, anyway. Everything's different now.

"You won't believe what I found out," she began.

"Jenny's was out of cole slaw. Can you believe it? It's 4th of July weekend, for crying out loud," Tim told her.

"Tim, the people next door...."

"I had to get lettuce and tomato instead. Oh well, I guess that's okay. And they had cinnamon rolls for breakfast." Janie woke suddenly, and finding herself still in an umbrella stroller, began to fuss.

Ignoring the baby for the time being, Gigi said, "Tim, listen to me."

"What? Sorry. What about the people next door?"

"They are Negroes," Gigi blurted out. Janie began to cry in earnest. Gigi stood up and lifted Janie out of the stroller and held her to her shoulder. Janie continued to cry.

"What do you mean, Negroes?" asked Tim who was putting groceries in the small refrigerator.

"Negro. Black. African. Black, black."

"Really? In Lakeside? How did that happen?" She had his attention now. She began to walk the baby around the room, bouncing with each slow step.

"I can't imagine. Do you think the Trowbridges met them? Do you think Harriet Slade sold them the house?"

"They didn't buy it, did they? They're just renters like us, right?"

"Nope, they bought it. Remodeled the kitchen and bought all new furniture. Who does that in Lakeside? Nobody, that's who!" Gigi was gesturing wildly with her one unencumbered hand.

"Who did you meet? All of them?"

"No, just the wife. Lorraine. Huge black woman. Gorgeous."

"Where was the husband?" Tim asked.

"Outside someplace doing....I don't know. Something. And there's a couple of kids, eight and ten, I think. They want to play with our boys. I didn't know what to say. I don't know if we should even unpack, maybe go see if Harriet has another cottage available," Gig said. She switched the baby to the other shoulder. Janie was still crying.

"Why should we leave?"

"You want to spend our only vacation of the year living with Negroes? Seriously? And what about the kids?"

"We're not living with them, Gigi. We don't have to make friends. We can just pretend the Trowbridge house is still empty. The kids have plenty of other kids to play with. I suspect this family next door won't be back next year. I doubt they will find Lakeside very hospitable. Harriet will get to collect another commission. I don't think we should change our plans. That would just mean they win. Just live your life and they can live theirs. It's not a big problem," Tim reasoned. "By the way, what's his name?"

"I don't know. I think she said the last name is Edwards."

"I better go establish some boundaries."

"I thought we are going to ignore them."

"Well, I don't want him knocking on our door and asking for help or anything. He needs to respect our space." Tim went out the back door before Gigi could protest further. Shaking her head, she took Janie upstairs for a clean diaper.

Tim O'Reilly was a brown-haired, thin man of thirty-five who was a machinist in Toledo. He and Gigi had married shortly after high school and with hard work and plenty of overtime, he had managed to buy a small ranch house before the kids started coming. Their first son, Timmy, came as a surprise, earlier than Tim had planned, but he was such fun that they felt more relaxed when Benny came along eighteen months later. The two boys were energetic, healthy and each other's best friend. Tim and Gigi thought their family was complete, when a particularly beautiful and somewhat drunken night in Lakeside the previous summer resulted in the birth of their daughter Janie in late April. Tim, suddenly the father of three, was beginning to think he would need to moonlight in his cousin's garage to make ends meet and still allow them their two week vacation in Lakeside. He was a good father, a good provider, and a staunch member of Wesley United Methodist church in Toledo. Lakeside was a favorite vacation spot for a lot of their church friends, and despite the rules supposedly enforced in Lakeside prohibiting drinking coffee, tea, or alcoholic beverages, smoking or card playing, the Toledo Methodists had learned how to party. There was plenty of beer, cigarettes and cigars, poker games, and blessed coffee every morning. Children played together all day and late into the evening until exhaustion sent them to bed, dirty, waterlogged, and smiling. Tim had no intention of allowing some upstart Negroes to ruin the best two weeks of his year. He decided to go next door and speak to his new neighbor.

"I understand your name is Edwards. I'm Tim O'Reilly," he spoke to the tall, muscular man who was washing the windows on the back of the house, near Second Street.

"Nice to meet you. Mitchell Edwards. Lorraine told me she met your wife. It's nice to get to know your neighbors in a town this small."

Mitchell Edwards looked different than Tim had expected. He was physically powerful and well-proportioned, with short, black, curly hair. He was wearing sunglasses so Tim couldn't see his eyes but the white t-shirt he wore with jeans lay in stark contrast to dark, muscular arms. His expression was open and friendly, and he held out his hand to Tim, who shook his hand briefly.

"Look, Edwards, I don't want any trouble," began Tim.

"Trouble? What do you mean?" asked Mitchell.

"It's just that we know a lot of people here. We've been coming for eleven years. We have a big group of friends from home. And they have a lot of kids," explained Tim.

"How is that a problem?" Mitchell was confused.

"We don't really need to meet new people. You understand."

"Actually, I don't. Are you saying that our families will not be socially involved?"

"Look, the people here….you might not enjoy, um, the reception you get. I don't want to see any trouble in Lakeside. I guess I'm surprised that you decided to buy here."

Mitchell put his rag down on the back steps, buying a moment to reflect. He looked up and pulled himself up to his full height, several inches taller than Tim. "All right, Mr. O'Reilly. I think I understand. I had hoped we might have a beer sometime and get to know each other. I thought if we knew our neighbors and our kids played together, maybe all that nonsense wouldn't take hold here. Apparently I was mistaken. We will keep our distance."

"That's probably best for everybody," said Tim. He wanted to go home. This was becoming uncomfortable. He started to move toward his own rental home.

"Mr. O'Reilly," Mitchell said.

"What?"

"What would you like me to do if my son hits a ball into your yard? He is going out for baseball next spring." Mitchell's voice was lower pitched, slower, and decidedly cool.

"I just don't think he should play with my boys, that's all. Look, I wish we lived in a different world, but we have to be realists, right? You are going to find other people around here feel the same way. That's just the way it is. Nobody wants any trouble. Remember that." Tim, wishing he had never started this conversation, turned his back and went into his own cottage.

Harriet Slade decided it was time to drop in on the Edwards. She knew they had finished the kitchen and had moved in for the month, because Mr. Edwards was considerate about calling her from time to time. She took the last tray of Polish *krusczyki* out of the fryer and dusted them with powdered sugar. She put on a light dress over her solid, somewhat round body, and added a white sweater. The breeze off Lake Erie can be chilly, she reminded herself. She checked on her mother who was, as usual, in her room on the second floor, knitting.

"Wouldn't you be more comfortable on the porch? It's a lovely day, Mother," Harriet asked.

"Maybe I will go down later. I'm fine." Her mother didn't look up from the scarf she was knitting for the church Christmas bazaar in November. It will be added to the dozens she had completed since last year.

"I left you some *krusczyki* in the kitchen. I am going to work."

"On a Saturday?" Her mother sounded annoyed.

"I have to visit some new clients in Lakeside. It's a social call. Is there something you need that I can pick up on my way home?"

"We're low on Bufferin. You know it's the only one that doesn't upset my stomach."

"All right, I will get some. We will have kielbasa on the grill tonight. How does that sound?"

"Gassy."

Harriet sighed and closed her mother's bedroom door. She gathered her large white patent leather purse, her sunglasses, and a carefully wrapped package of the crispy, fried sugary treats she had learned to make as a girl in Cleveland, and got into her new Cadillac. She drove carefully, obeying all traffic laws, reaching Lakeside in the early afternoon. She parked at the gate, greeted the toll taker there, and walked to Second Street. She always enjoyed strolling on the streets of Lakeside, with its abundance of old, established trees, and old, established cottages. Cottages that had stood, largely unimproved, since their construction. Cottages that inevitably needed a coat of paint, some shoring up at the foundation, new screened doors, new appliances. Cottages that looked well loved, well lived in, and well on their way to extinction. There were few shops and few restaurants. There were no gas stations or automobile body shops, of course, but there were also no trappings of modern life like movie theaters, insurance agents, hair salons, or banks. There was one small grocery, Jenny's, a small pharmacy, a hardware store that shared space with the tiny post office, and two small gift shops that did a brisk business on things like kites, Frisbees, and postcards. Harriet passed quite a few people, most of whom were headed to the lake with towels around their necks and chairs under their arms. She turned on Second Street and made her way to the especially lovely home that the Edwards had recently purchased.

"Hello! Are you home? It's Harriet Slade, come to see how you are settling in!" she called at the front screened door.

"Miss Slade! How nice!" called Mitchell Edwards from the kitchen. He hurried to let her in the door and shook her hand warmly. "We are so glad you came. We've been wanting to show you around, now that we have it close to what we want. The boys are swimming, but Lorraine and our daughter Michelle are upstairs. Lorraine! Harriet Slade has come to visit!" he called to his wife. Mitchell was dressed in jeans and a plaid sport shirt, open at the neck. Harriet could see that he was deeply tanned, and she thought with pleasure that they must have been enjoying their first week at Lakeside very much indeed. She looked up as Lorraine Edwards came into the porch, carrying her young daughter in her arms.

Harriet was stunned by the woman and child before her. They were as beautiful as any Madonna and child one could imagine, if one were to imagine them black. Black as coal, Harriet thought, and then no, black as a deep starry night. They both seemed to gleam and shine with an inner radiance she had never seen before. She took a sharp intake of breath as the truth sank in. Mitchell Edwards with his polish and shine and cultured ways, was a light-skinned Negro. And she had never thought of it because he was so unlike the stereotype she admitted (if only to herself) she carried in her mind.

"I am so delighted to meet you finally, Miss Slade," said Lorraine, beaming.

"I have been looking forward to this as well, Mrs. Edwards. I hope you are finding Lakeside as charming as you thought," Harriet responded, regaining her composure.

"We love the town. The children are finding lots to do and we have been consumed with getting the house fixed up to our liking. We would love to show it to you if you can stay a little while."

"I would be happy to. I brought you some cookies. I hope you and the children will enjoy them." Harriet couldn't take her eyes off this stunning woman. Suddenly her favorite summer dress seemed dowdy and old fashioned compared with Lorraine's slim, white capri pants and loose fitting white sleeveless shirt, cinched at the waist with a wide, bright red belt. On her feet, Harriet noted a pair of red Keds that looked almost brand new. Wearing her own beige wedges that she used to find so stylish, she followed the tall woman through the house, admiring their taste and sophistication – and expressing her approval of the modern kitchen.

Later, the three of them settled on the screened porch which was furnished with oversized matching wicker furniture, covered with a cheerful chintz fabric. The little girl, sporting short corn-rowed hair that was punctuated with colorful, tiny barrettes, sat on the sisal rug with blocks in front of her for entertainment. Mitchell served tall glasses of iced coffee, rich with cream, and put Harriet's *kruscyki* on a white plate in the middle of the glass coffee table.

"I hope I get the chance to meet your sons," Harriet said.

"Oh, I expect them quite soon. They have been in the water since about eleven o'clock this morning. They must be ready to dry out by now."

"Have they been making friends here?" she inquired, trying not to be too pushy.

"They are so close to each other that they get along just about anywhere, " said Mitchell, smiling. "They are happy to swim every day, and they are always practicing baseball. We have been playing a lot of catch and they hit Whiffle balls for hours back and forth to each other. We hardly ever see them indoors unless it's bed time."

"Or dinner time," added his wife with an indulgent smile.

"Have you tried our hotel cafeteria yet for dinner? The food is quite reasonable and very tasty," said Harriet.

"We went there once, last week. You are right, the food is good," said Lorraine.

"I always think it's fun there. So many people go, it's like a block party," suggested Harriet.

"We don't know too many people here. We are new," Mitchell responded.

"Well, there are lots of activities scheduled every week. Shuffleboard tournaments, square dances, band concerts, Sunday services – so many different opportunities."

"We attended the band concert on the 4th," he said, quietly.

"Did you? What did you think of our little Lakeside band?"

"Very nice."

"Did you bring your children?" asked Harriet.

"Of course."

"I wasn't able to go this year. My mother was not feeling well."

"I am sorry to hear that. I hope she is better now," Lorraine said.

"Yes, thank you. Have the boys found the baseball game that always seems to pop up near the playground? It seems to me that someone is playing baseball every time I am here."

"They found it, but the teams were full up."

"Perhaps if they tried again...."

"I think they would just as soon play catch here with me," said Mitchell.

Changing the subject, Harriet asked if they had yet met their next-door neighbors, the O'Reillys. "I found this rental for them quite a long time ago and they come back every year," Harriet boasted.

"We have met," said Mitchell.

"I should think the boys would be good friends by now with the O'Reilly boys. They are close to the same age, isn't that right?"

"They have met as well. Miss Slade, would you like more iced coffee?" said Lorraine.

"No, thank you. I probably should be on my way. I need to stop at a pharmacy for my mother and start dinner. It's almost an hour to Sandusky, where I live, this time of year, at least. I want to thank you for showing me around. I had a lovely time."

"Oh, we are so glad you stopped by. We rarely have company. Please come again."

"I would love to," Harriet replied as she gathered her things and left the cottage.

Tim O'Reilly was aware that Harriet Slade was next door. He had been emptying the wastebaskets into his garbage bin when he saw her walk to the front door, and he heard voices coming from the Edwards' front porch. Gigi and the boys were at the pier, and he was staying home while the baby napped upstairs. They were expecting two other families to join them for steak and a game of Kick the Can later and he wanted to clean up and make room for the trash and all the beer bottles he was expecting to have to take to the trunk of his car the next day. However, he was currently more interested in the conversation taking place in the house next door. His hope was that Harriet was politely suggesting that the Edwards might be more comfortable in another vacation community. He was a little worried about this evening's lawn game; it might spill over onto the neighbor's front yard. It's hard to enforce boundaries in a game when no physical barriers exist. All the lake-facing yards in Lakeside were connected in one continuous lawn, encouraging vacationers to enjoy their time together, both children and adults.

Tim decided to try to approach Miss Slade with his concerns, so he went upstairs, scooped his sleeping baby up in his arms, put her in the umbrella stroller kept in the back yard, and looked up to see Harriet waving good-bye to the Edwardses and walking between their cottages to Second Street.

"Hi, Miss Slade, remember me? Tim O'Reilly," he greeted her as he fell into step beside her.

"Of course, Mr. O'Reilly, I never forget a client. How is your lovely family? I gather there is a new baby? Is this...?" She bent over the stroller and smiled at the peaceful child.

"Yeah, Janie was born in April. I finally got a little girl. She's great. We're all doing good."

"How lovely. Please pass along my congratulations to Mrs. O'Reilly," said Harriet.

"Will do. Uh, may I ask you a question?" ventured Tim.

"Of course."

"About the family next door? Do you think, I mean, will they....do you think they are exactly Lakeside types?"

"The Edwards? They are a lovely family. They love it here. I am so pleased they found us. I believe it was at a religious meeting last summer. They fell in love with Lakeside. I have always said, we just need to get people to visit and we would never have an empty room," smiled Harriet.

"But, Miss Slade? Do you think they will make friends here? Don't you think they would be happier somewhere else? Maybe Cedar Point would be better. I was wondering if you might suggest it," Tim continued, trying again.

"Mr. O'Reilly, I really can't imagine why I would want to do that. Where someone lives is a matter of personal preference, don't you agree?"

"Yeah, sure, but what about their kids? Who are they going to hang out with?"

"I thought perhaps your boys and theirs would be a natural. I understand the Edwards boys are quite passionate about baseball."

"My boys have all the friends they need."

"Mr. O'Reilly, it has been my experience that no one ever has all the friends they need. I am sorry, but I must hurry now. My mother is expecting me home. I hope you enjoy the summer." Harriet walked slightly faster toward the gate and her Cadillac. She was angry, which was an emotion she was unaccustomed to dealing with, and she wanted to be alone to cool off.

Tim watched her walk away from him. Her back was as straight as a tree, he thought, and her old-fashioned dress clung to her round body like a shield. He had always found her to be a little ridiculous, with her huge handbags and thick-soled shoes, her wide face and overly coiffed, obviously dyed blond hairstyle, and her formal speech patterns. She was probably the only human who always called him Mr. O'Reilly. Yet there was something strong in her that reminded him of his grandmother, Maeve, who had come to the United States from Ireland. She had been of peasant stock and never lost that solid, care-worn wisdom brought from home. Tim wondered if Harriet Slade had come from peasants far away from America. Slade, he thought, what nationality is Slade?

His thoughts were interrupted by the sound of children yelling. He was walking past a vacant lot on Maple Avenue where kids sometimes gathered for pick-up baseball or soccer. He became aware of two boys rolling on the ground, trading punches and grunting, surrounded by a large group, yelling and gesturing. As he watched for a minute, he slowly recognized his own Benny was one of the fighters. He had some difficulty pushing the stroller into the grassy, bumpy lot, but managed to grab both boys and pull them apart, kicking and squirming, leaving Janie, who had awoken, to watch.

"What the hell do you think you're doing?" he shouted at his son.

"He started it!" yelled Benny, to a chorus of supporting yells and unintelligible words.

"Who are you?" asked Tim of the other boy, whom he did not recognize. Tim had to work hard to keep the boys from hitting each other.

He kept one palm on the chest of each boy and held his arms straight out from his sides.

"Who wants to know?" taunted the other, clearly older, boy.

"I do. Cut the crap and tell me what this is all about," snapped Tim.

"That's Gary Ferris," said Timmy, who had pushed through the crowd to stand next to his still-writhing brother. "He did start it. He said some stuff he shouldn't have. Benny got mad. We all got mad. Benny was just doing what we all wanted to do. You shouldn't get mad at him."

"I did not raise my boys to fight. You know that. Now what started all this? Come on, let's get this settled. And Timmy, go get the baby. " Tim looked at the whole group of kids.

Silence. Gary stood still with a slight grin. Benny scowled at him, saying nothing. Timmy, his hand on the stroller, looked at Benny.

There was a commotion at the outer edge of the group and Tim looked up. There was a boy, a good-looking Negro child, approaching Tim, with obvious reluctance.

"I guess it's my fault, sir," said the slim child. He was dressed in a baseball-style t-shirt and jeans and sneakers. "I tried to join the game. I'm sorry." Another boy who was right behind him shook his head.

"Why shouldn't he join the game?" asked Benny. "Gary was the one that tried to stop him."

"We don't need no more players," Gary stated.

"Why not?" said one of the boys.

"Just don't," said Gary.

"Yeah, well, I say we do. I've seen this guy pitch. He's good," snarled Timmy toward Gary's infuriating smirk. "You can always use a pitcher, right, Dad?" asked Timmy.

"I want to know if you guys are OK. Anybody hurt?" asked Tim.

"No," said Benny.

"Nah," said Gary.

"In that case, boys, you come home with me this minute. We will talk about this at home. The rest of you, do the same. Gary, you especially."

"You're not my dad," answered Gary defiantly.

"True. Lucky for you. Let's go, guys."

Tim walked the boys home fast. Timmy pushed the stroller while Tim kept his hand on Benny's shoulder. Tim's feelings about Benny and the fight were mixed up and he wanted time to think about them.

"Where's your mother, anyway? I thought you went swimming," he asked as they walked.

"She's still at the pier. She's playing cards with some women. She said it was okay to play. Dad?" asked Timmy.

"What?"

"What were we supposed to do? Gary is such a jerk and he called Jason a bad name," he said.

"Who's Jason?" asked Tim.

"Jason Edwards. Jeez, Dad, he lives next door. You know him."

"Next door? Oh, yeah, him. I didn't think you guys knew each other."

"Pretty hard to miss when a couple of guys are playing baseball right in front of your face. They're really good, too. We've been playing at the lot for a couple of days now. I thought you knew that."

"A couple of days? Really? Where have I been?" asked Tim.

"I don't know. Playing with the baby. Cleaning the grill. Fishing. Stuff."

Entering the kitchen through the back door of the weather-beaten cottage, Tim studied his older boy's face. There was no trace of accusation there, only the simple fact: Tim hadn't noticed who his kids were playing with. The thought flashed through his mind – what would he have done if he had seen his boys playing with the Edwards boys? He honestly didn't know. He turned to the younger boy, who had grabbed an apple off the counter and was eating it in huge gulps.

"Benny, why did you fight that kid? He's bigger than you. Did you think you could take him?"

"I don't know. I didn't think about that. I hate him, is all," said Benny, hanging his head.

"Look at me, boy. Why do you hate him? We don't like to hear you say that about anybody." Tim spoke more gently to the child.

"Because he called Jason a..."

"A what?"

"A nigger," Timmy stepped in and answered for his younger brother. "That's a bad word, right, Dad?"

"Riiiight....yeah, that's a bad word, guys. Real bad."

"So Benny did the right thing, didn't he, Dad?"

"I don't know. I don't want you fighting. It never fixes anything and always makes the other guy madder at you. These things just get worse, guys."

"But what should we have done different?"

32

Tim searched for an answer that was honest and still compassionate. He wanted his boys to live in the real world, even though he knew it was a flawed one. "Do you really think it's a good idea to play with Jason and – what's his brother's name?" asked Tim.

"Scott."

"What's wrong with them?" asked Benny, looking up at his father, his dirty face fresh and young and trusting.

"I guess....well....there's nothing wrong with them, it's just, um, I...." Tim honestly didn't know where to go with this.

Gigi walked in the kitchen door at that moment and immediately spotted a growing bruise on her younger son's cheekbone.

"Oh, my God, what happened?" she asked, lunging for Benny.

"I'm okay, Mom, jeez."

"Did you fall?" she asked.

"He got into a fight. He's okay," Tim tried to reassure her.

"A what? Benny doesn't get into fights. That's ridiculous!"

"Mom, it's okay, no big deal. Benny just did what every guy out there wanted to do. He's a hero, my kid brother," said Timmy, looking at Benny.

"Why? What happened?"

"We were playing ball on the lot when Jason from next door showed up and asked if he could play, and Gary Ferris, he said no and everybody else said okay and Jason, he didn't know what to do and then Gary called him a bad name and then Benny jumped Gary. It was actually pretty cool. Nobody got hurt. Dad showed up real soon," Timmy blurted out.

"You showed up? I thought you were here with Janie," she asked, turning to Tim.

"Janie and I walked Harriet Slade to her car. I wanted to talk to her. I was only gone a couple of minutes."

"Sounds to me like a lot happened in a couple of minutes. Guys, go upstairs and take showers. Benny, I'll put ice on that cheek when you're clean. Go on, I need to talk to Dad." The boys, glad to be free of the drama, ran up the stairs. "And change your clothes, too!"

"He's okay, honey," Tim began.

"I know. But what happened out there? Why were the boys playing with Jason Edwards?" Gigi took Janie out of the stroller and went to the small refrigerator to fix her a bottle. Janie was babbling happily.

"I guess they have been with the Edwards boys before. They're friends. They play ball together."

"Since when?"

"Since we haven't been paying attention. For a couple of days."

"Well, that stops now," said Gigi.

"You know what? I'm not so sure."

"Are you kidding me? Our kids friends with....."

"With who? What were you going to say?"

"You know what I mean."

There was suddenly a knock on the screened door. "Hoo hoo! Anyone home? It's Harriet Slade."

Tim and Gigi looked at each other in surprise. Holding the baby and the bottle, Gigi went to the porch. "Hi, Miss Slade. Come on in. Would you like some iced tea? Sorry I'm not really dressed. I just came home from the pier, and the boys got into a little scuffle so we're a little disorganized."

"Oh, heck, I don't care about that. I just wanted to talk to Mr. O'Reilly for a minute," said Harriet.

"Hi, again, Miss Slade. I thought you had to get home," said Tim, coming into the porch from the kitchen.

"Well, you know, I was, but I got to thinking and I just had to come back to speak to you for a moment. Oh, by the way, Mrs. O'Reilly, congratulations on the lovely new baby. She is just adorable."

"Thank you," said Gigi.

"Would you like to sit down?" asked Tim. Gigi, waving, took the baby back to the kitchen to feed her.

"No, I really mustn't stay. I just wanted to ask if you and Mrs. O'Reilly would like to look at a lovely rental I have at Cedar Point. It's a three bedroom with a sleeping porch and I thought it would have a bit more room now that you have the three children. You might be more comfortable there. There are lots of people from Toledo, and good fishing, too. And the Cedar Point rental is available next year for the same two weeks you like to vacation. I think it is quite suitable for your family. I'm sure the children would enjoy the amusement park. You know, the new roller coaster is supposed to be the biggest one in the whole country. Isn't that something! Well, I will leave you to think it over. You know how to reach me, right? Next time, I will have that glass of tea. Bye, bye, now." And she turned and left the O'Reilly cottage.

Tim noticed that she walked rather more slowly and if possible with an even straighter back than she did before. He watched her until her solid figure was out of sight, thinking. He was thinking about what kind of world his children will inherit. He looked through the screen at the house next door. It's only a house, and they're only a family, he thought. It's not a big deal. None of this is a big deal. The kids seem to know that, he thought, and so does a little old lady like Harriet Slade. Why should anything else matter? He went into the kitchen and watched his pretty wife as she fed applesauce to little Janie. What does Janie care about this stuff? Do I want her to care about this stuff? Would she be better off if she did? Slowly, Tim sat down at the kitchen table and put his hand on his wife's arm. "Honey, I have a suggestion," he said to Gigi.

"What?"

"Let's ask the Edwards to join us tonight."

"Excuse me?"

"I mean it, Geeg. This is silly. They live next door. Their kids are friends with our kids. We have the same real estate agent. He drinks the same brand of beer as me, I've seen his trash. What the hell is wrong with them? Come on, let's give it a shot."

"You really want to? What'll our friends say?"

"I don't know. I guess we'll find out. Okay? What do you say?"

Mitchell Edwards never did hear about the fight at the vacant lot. Jason came home that day and they played catch in the spacious yard that separated their house from Lake Erie. When Scott came home from grocery shopping with his mother, he joined them. They added a little batting practice, careful to hit toward the yard in front of the currently empty cottage on the other side of theirs. They had a standing rule against hitting balls into the O'Reilly's yard. After a while, they noticed people arriving at Tim and Gigi's house, carrying lawn chairs and coolers. There were four adults and six children, none of whom looked familiar to Mitchell. However, his sons waved to one of the boys, who came loping over.

"Hey," said the blond, athletic looking boy.

"Hi," said Jason. "What's going on?"

"Party next door. You coming?"

"I don't know. Dad, are we going next door tonight?"

"Not that I know of, son," said Mitchell.

"Guess not," said Scott to the other boy.

"Well, can we play some ball here?" he asked them.

"Dad?"

"Of course, you know that's fine. We have some bases on the porch if you want to set up a diamond."

"I'll go get Timmy and Benny and the other guys."

Tim O'Reilly was setting up the Hibachi grill on some cinder blocks in the front yard when he noticed his sons and three more boys had started a ball game next door at the Edwards'. He sat back on his

35

heels and watched as the boys chose up teams and seemed to unanimously choose Jason to pitch for both sides. Gigi came outside, carrying a tray of napkins, plates, and stainless utensils, headed for the picnic table in the yard. She stopped behind Tim and followed his gaze. She watched for a long time, saying nothing. He knew she was standing and looking but chose not to comment. He didn't see her shake her head, but he heard her long sigh.

Mitchell Edwards was watching the game from a lawn chair he had brought outside. Tim had a beer in one of the covered tumblers from his kitchen. He went inside and poured another one. He carried it over to Mitchell, along with a folding chair.

"Mind if I join you for a minute?" he asked.

"Suit yourself," answered Mitchell. Tim offered him the beer, and after a slight hesitation, Mitchell accepted it.

"The guys look good out there. That Jason's got a hell of an arm."

"Thanks. He works hard at it."

"Hey, Edwards, we wondered if you and your wife would like to join us for hamburgers tonight. It looks like the boys are already partying together. What do you say?"

Mitchell Edwards looked at Tim for a long interval. "Yeah? You sure?"

"I asked you, didn't I?"

After another interval, Mitchell stood up. "Let me go get Lorraine. I think she has a blueberry pie in there."

"Sounds good. See you soon."

That night, the baseball game lasted until the stars came out, and Kick the Can lasted until the moon reached its zenith over the calm waters of Lake Erie, sending an uninterrupted, quiet column of light from Kelley's Island to the O'Reilly's front lawn. The laughter lasted even longer. Tim knew he would have to make two trips, taking the trash to his car tomorrow, and he was going to need a lot of coffee for breakfast.

Sailing Lakeside
1961

With my luck, it will rain all weekend, Margot thought, looking out the car window as they pulled out of the driveway of their Shaker Heights house. Lakeside can be dreary in the rain, and I'll be stuck inside with Bob, Claire and Auntie Cree in the living room, where there isn't much to do except for the ubiquitous jigsaw puzzle on the card table. I hate jigsaw puzzles, she mused, so many little pieces, they all look the same, and in the end, you just have another picture of the Grand Canyon or the Parthenon or something. What a bore. She was already getting accustomed to watching TV around dinner time. It was a good way to get the news and there was usually some kind of variety show afterwards. Funny how something so new to us can get to be a habit. We've only had a TV for what, five years? And now the thought of being indoors in an old-fashioned summer community without the little round screen was faintly depressing, like knowing Christmas dinner wouldn't include pumpkin pie because your grandmother was on a diet.

The drive to Lakeside should take about two hours, but this was Labor Day weekend, and it seemed as if the whole east side of Cleveland was driving somewhere west that day. They drove so slowly that by the time they got to Lakeside, it was almost dark, but at least the rain had let up. And sure enough, as they walked toward the dilapidated yellow cottage on Fourth Street, Cree was on the porch, wearing a heavy sweater over her day dress, playing solitaire and smoking. Margot was relieved that they didn't have to walk in the rain; there was nowhere to get her hair done in Lakeside and they were planning to be there for three days this time. Bob had suggested the longer visit; it wasn't something that Margot would have considered, as they typically only stayed for one night. But Bob pointed out that Auntie Cree was getting on in years and their annual visits to Lakeside were probably numbered. Margot protested that they might tire the old woman out, but he said, on the contrary, they might be able to help her with some small jobs around the cottage, and they would take over the meal preparations, and give Cree a break from housework.

"I'll bring a few tools. There's bound to be some way I can help her out," Bob said.

"She is a proud woman. I don't want to insult her."

"Margot, I'm not going to insult her, I'm going to give her a hand. She lives in that old, run-down place all by herself, without a husband or anyone to help."

"She has Phil. He's just a couple of blocks away," Margot reminded him.

"Phil only shows up on weekends and seems more interested in improving his tan than helping his mother, in my opinion," Bob pointed out.

"Phil is a great guy. You have never liked him," said Margot.

"Maybe because you dated him in high school."

"Ancient history, for God's sake."

"Even so, he is worthless when it comes to anything that resembles work, and you know it."

"I thought we were going there to spend some time with Claire before she starts school next week," Margot reminded her husband.

"There's plenty of time – we've got three days."

"Don't remind me. What the hell am I going to do for three days?"

"Oh come on. There's the pier, and shuffleboard, and miniature golf, and the cafeteria, and there might even be a movie playing that we want to see. And if Nancy is around, I bet we can play some bridge. You'll be so busy, the weekend will fly by."

"Yeah, that's how it's going to go."

"Let's just finish getting packed up. I have to go into the office for a couple of hours but we should be able to leave by three."

Claire brought enough comic books to pass the time in the car, but just barely. She loved Lakeside and was excited they were going to stay for the whole weekend. Everything about Auntie Cree's cottage was delightful to her: the bedroom drawers that smelled of moth balls mixed with someone else's past; the jigsaw puzzle that was always halfway done in the living room; the old *National Geographic* magazines where she could read about remote African cultures whose women posed for the cameras with naked breasts; the wicker rocking chair on the porch where she could rock and read while the grown-ups talked and played cards; the bathroom that had a curtain where there should have been a door; dinners cooked on an old charcoal grill in the yard; meals usually consisting of hamburgers and corn or barbequed chicken and potato salad. And Auntie Cree herself was one of Claire's favorite people. She was somewhere in her mid-eighties, and had always looked the same to Claire; tall, broad-shouldered and wide of torso, she stood straighter than most people a generation younger than herself. She had impossibly long snow-white hair which she braided every morning and twisted in some kind of figure eight onto the back of her head, holding it there with hair pins. Claire was fascinated by this process, and Cree allowed her the privilege of watching. Auntie Cree's eyes were bright and deep blue, with lots of tiny laugh lines at their corners, and although she rarely laughed out loud, they twinkled when she was amused, which was often. Her skin seemed to be made of the thinnest, softest velvet, and Claire loved to touch her hand or cheek. Cree spoke loudly and directly to everyone. She was intelligent, well read and articulate, and quite sure of what she expected from those around her - and she was rarely disappointed.

They arrived at the cottage in time for dinner, which Cree had already fixed. After they unpacked their things and put them away in the upstairs bedrooms, the adults had cocktails while Claire went into the living room where it was warmer. Margot knew her bookish daughter would pull a *Life* magazine off the shelf, curl up into an overstuffed upholstered chair, turn on the floor lamp, and begin to read. She was dozing off when they called her for grilled cheese sandwiches and tomato soup.

"Oh, Claire, I meant to tell you. An old friend has arrived in Lakeside for the weekend on his catamaran and wonders if you would like to go for a sail tomorrow, to Kelley's Island," Auntie Cree announced as they ate. "His name is Alec McCrae."

"What's a catman?" asked Claire.

"Catamaran. It's a sailboat with two hulls. They are supposed to be more stable than most sailboats, meaning they aren't as likely to capsize."

"Capsize?" she asked. Claire had never been on any sailboat.

"Turn over," explained her father.

"I'm not too interested in turning over!"

"That's why I feel comfortable sending you out on a catamaran. When you see it tomorrow, you can decide if you want to go," said Auntie Cree.

"Bob, you go with her," said Margot.

"I have too much to do here for Cree. And I'm not that crazy about sailing, you know that."

"Well, I can't sail," said Margot, "and I don't think Claire should go alone."

"She won't be alone. Alec will watch her. Will there be anyone else on board, Cree?

"Oh, I am sure there will. Alec is very sociable."

The next day started out gray, damp and dreary, but by nine a.m. the sun had burned off the haze, revealing a day that was perfect for sailing, or any summer activity. The light reflected off the lovely old community with its Victorian hotel, streets filled with antique cottages and strolling vacationers. There was a light breeze that carried with it the scent of late summer flowers: tall purple coneflowers, majestic pink and white phlox, round clusters of asters and the last of the hydrangeas. Huge old trees were just beginning to warn of impending hibernation with a few oak leaves and acorns dotting the streets and the sprawling lawn in front of the hotel. Claire was excited about swimming; it was her favorite sport and too soon the opportunities would be gone. She put her suit on under her clothes when she woke up and gazed through the small window of her bedroom in the cottage. She loved to see the neat rows of old worn houses. She liked imagining the children in the upstairs bedrooms up and down the street. Adding sneakers to her outfit, she bounded down the stairs and found Auntie Cree alone on the porch.

"Don't you ever sleep, Auntie Cree? You're always on the porch," she greeted her dear friend with a kiss to the soft cheek.

"The older I get, the more I don't want to miss anything, child," answered Auntie Cree. "Go get yourself some breakfast and come and join me."

Claire ran into the kitchen and poured some Rice Krispies into an orange Fiestaware bowl. She added milk and grabbed a banana from a bunch on the counter and joined Auntie Cree at the porch table. They watched the town wake up while she ate. A few bikers passed them, getting some early exercise. A neighbor came out in his shorts, barefoot and shirtless, and picked up children's toys from what passed in Lakeside for a front yard. Sea gulls and swallows competed for air space, diving and swooping around each other in the quiet of the morning. Somewhere a baby wailed.

"Should I get you more coffee?" Claire asked.

"The pastor is likely to walk by any minute. He doesn't want to see me with a coffee cup in my hand. Better wait."

"What's wrong with holding a cup of coffee?"

"Oh, the Methodist church kind of owns this town, you know. They founded it back a long time ago, and they still run the convention center, where all the meetings are. You know, the tent revivals and all that. Anyway, Methodists aren't too keen on drinking stimulating beverages of any kind."

Cree turned toward the street. "Morning, Pastor Flynn. It's going to be a beauty," she called through the screen to the white-haired gentleman, who was taking a brisk morning walk.

"Morning, Cree. Not many more of these weekends left this year, eh?"

"I'm afraid not. I actually have to leave this week. Classes start on Thursday. Phil will drive me home on Tuesday."

"Well, I am sure we will see each other here next year, the good Lord willing," answered the pastor.

"From your lips to God's ears," smiled Cree, as the pastor moved along the street, greeting others on their screened porches. Claire took Auntie Cree's coffee cup from the shelf hidden under the chair rail where it was out of sight of passers-by, and refilled it from the percolator on the stove. She poured in some cream and added a small spoonful of sugar, and carried it carefully onto the porch. Her mother had just sat down at the table.

"Good morning, my dear," said Margot to Claire.

"Morning, Mom. Do you want coffee?" asked Claire as she handed the cup to Auntie Cree.

"Well, thank you. That would be lovely."

When Claire came back with her mother's coffee, her father had joined them.

"Hi, Daddy."

"Good morning, sweetie. Sleep well?" her father hugged her to him after she had put the coffee down.

"I always sleep well here."

"I didn't sleep well at all," said Margot.

"I thought you were pretty restless," said her husband.

"You were snoring so loudly I thought you would wake Claire and Cree."

41

"Sorry. You should have told me to turn over."

"I did. You would snore again two minutes later. It was hopeless."

"Oh, well," said Cree, "I didn't hear a thing. No harm done."

"Well, at least you got some sleep," Margot muttered.

"Daddy, can we go for a bike ride today?" Claire asked Bob.

"Tandem?"

"Of course!"

"Well, we better do it early. I have to fix Cree's screen door and see if I can figure out what's going on with the kitchen faucet."

"And Claire has a sailing date, don't forget," added Cree.

"When am I going sailing?"

"When Alec shows up. But he's something of an early bird; I would expect him pretty soon. You best go bike riding now. Bob, grab a bite of breakfast and go rent that tandem. They are pretty popular and this is likely to be a busy weekend, it being the end of the summer."

"I'm on my way," Bob smiled. He was neatly dressed and already shaved.

"What am I supposed to do while you two are on the tandem bike?" asked Margot.

"You never want to ride a bike," said Claire.

"But I don't want to be bored!"

"Why don't you work on the puzzle?" asked Cree.

"Is there a crossword?"

"Only if Bob goes and gets a Plain Dealer from the newsstand."

"Bob, I need a paper."

"Okay, like I said, I'm on my way. C'mon, Claire, let's go get a paper and a bike."

Later that morning, Alec McCrae showed up at Cree's cottage. He was a pleasant-looking man in his forties, Margot guessed, rather small of stature and just starting to gray. Cree explained that he worked at the college where she was a house mother. She had introduced him to Lakeside when she learned he had a sailboat. He walked with Claire to the beach. Lakeside is not known for its beaches; the grass grows to the water line, and the only separation between land and water is usually huge boulders. But the town council had long ago seen the necessity for a beach for swimming, in order to attract families to the town for more than classes, demonstrations, entertainments, and religious services. They built a huge concrete pier from the shore hundreds of feet out, to encourage fishing, and then turned the pier at a ninety degree angle to the west to partially enclose a swimming area. On the east side of the pier, near water's edge, there was a place one could pull up a sailboat if it had a retractable centerboard, as did Alec McCrae's catamaran. As Alec and Claire walked through the gateway of the pavilion, she saw the sailboat pulled up on the rocky shore.

"Is this it?" she asked Alex.

"This is it! What do you think?"

"It's smaller than I thought it would be."

"It's big enough to sail across the whole lake, and go to Canada, if you like."

"That's okay, I don't think we should be gone that long."

Alec laughed, and then looked up and greeted another couple approaching.

"Claire, this is Susie and Dan Hotchkiss. They are joining us today."

"Hi," said Claire.

"Hi!" replied Susie. "Are you an experienced sailor?"

"No. I've never gone sailing."

"Well, you're in for a treat. We brought goodies!"

"Like?" asked Alec.

"Like stuff you don't see too much of in Lakeside!" Susie's voice was sing-song and a little too enthusiastic for Claire's taste.

"Well, it's five o'clock somewhere!" answered Alec.

Claire followed instructions as they prepared to launch. There were terms she had never heard but both Alec and Dan were patient as they explained the strange words and showed her how she could help. The most important task was to keep out of Alec's way as he rigged the catamaran, tying ropes, moving boxes around and tightening all kinds of equipment she had never seen. Claire was bewildered.

"Never say 'rope' on a boat," Dan told her. "They are either sheets or halyards. This big sail is called the mainsail and the smaller one in the front, I mean the fore, is called the jib. Your job is going to be to hold the jib sheet, and to let go of it when Alec tells you to. Also you will have to learn how to come about, which means moving from one side of the boat to the other, keeping your head down and trying not to get knocked into the lake by the boom."

"That sounds hard," she said, hesitantly.

"Not too hard, you'll get the hang of it quickly," he assured her.

Before long they were underway, Alec at the tiller, sitting next to Dan on the port side, Claire and Susie on the starboard side. Claire decided to remember that "port" means "left" on a boat, so she made a point of noting that both words had four letters. She was holding the jib sheet, wrapped once around the palm of her hand, loosely, as Alec had shown her, so it could slip easily as it needed to respond to the puffy, changeable winds common to lake sailing. Alec had turned the tiller over to Susie for a few minutes to help with that lesson. He sat next to Claire on the hard seat and put his right arm around her back, grasped her hand, and looped the sheet around it. He pulled to show her how she could tighten the jib against the wind, and how to loosen it and let it flap. He showed her how control of the jib actually affected not only the speed of the catamaran, but its direction, and he tried to explain how he, as the skipper, could figure out what was needed, and what he would say to her when he wanted her to do something.

"Did you wear your bathing suit?" he asked her as he resumed control of the tiller, and Susie slid back to her seat next to Claire.

"Yeah, it's under my shorts."

"Well if I were you, I would take my clothes off and wear my suit in this beautiful weather. It might be our last chance this year."

"Okay," she answered slowly. She let Susie take the jib sheet long enough for her to remove her t-shirt and shorts, bundle them and stash them under the seat. She was vaguely aware that her clothes probably wouldn't stay dry under there and wished she had brought some kind of duffle bag.

The sailing was beautiful. They were able to clear the Lakeside area, skillfully avoiding the pier and the many lines attached to fishing poles all along it. When they reached open waters, Alec told Claire to haul in the jib closely, Dan moved to her side of the boat, and suddenly they were scudding over the top of the gray endlessness that is Lake Erie. Claire was excited. She was also nervous. How fast should we be going, she wondered, and what if we lost control of this thing? Shouldn't we all be wearing life vests? She knew there were enough vests on board for them all, but they were stowed under the foredeck. What if we need them in a hurry?

"Are we going to go any faster than this?" she called out to Alec, her long brown hair flipping back and forth across her face.

"Scared?" he laughed. He was holding a can of Budweiser beer in his left hand, the tiller in his right.

"No. Not scared. Just wondering, that's all."

"Hey, Dan," Alec said. "Take the tiller for a while."

Alec climbed over Susie and slid over onto the seat next to Claire when Dan had gotten control of the tiller. His body provided more warmth than Susie's. Claire was staring out at the horizon and the increasing presence of Kelley's Island as they sailed farther north. Her upper body was actually cold and she wondered if she could let go of the jib sheet long enough to retrieve her t-shirt. She could feel Alec's breath on her neck and that made her feel even colder. When she turned to ask him, she was surprised to find him so close to her that she could have touched his nose with hers.

"Oh! I, uh, was thinking I could get my t-shirt from under the seat."

"It's probably pretty wet by now. It won't warm you up."

"Oh well, that's okay. I'm fine."

"The best way to get warm is skin to skin contact, you know."

"I'm really fine. Honest."

"Suit yourself," Alec said as he opened another can of Budweiser.

They continued to sail with Dan at the tiller. Claire found herself hoping that Alex would take over again, but Dan seemed to enjoy being in charge, and clearly knew what he was doing. After a time, he noted that they had slowed down, and he wanted to change direction.

"Okay, Claire, we're going to come about. Remember what I told you about keeping your head down. And let go of that jib sheet!"

Dan suddenly shouted, "Hard alee!" as he shoved the tiller as far away from its center position as he could. The catamaran turned quickly, the boom and mainsail seemed to fall across the width of the boat, and the jib flapped madly in the wind. Claire and Alec ducked and climbed over the centerboard to the port seat, Dan sat far aft on the combing, near Susie, and leaned out over the water for balance. Alec reached over Claire, grabbing for the jib sheet on the port side, finding it and hauling it until the jib was again under control. The sailboat righted itself and suddenly they were sailing faster than ever towards the west. Alec was concerning himself with straightening out the length of the jib sheet and he needed two hands to do it. His arms were encircling Claire who sat between him and the jib sheet block. She tried to shrink herself so that he wouldn't have to lean on her. But it seemed that they couldn't avoid being in close contact.

"One thing you have to learn about sailing, it's pretty close quarters, and everybody has to be friendly, right, Dan?" said Alec as he turned to the aft to help himself to another beer.

"Okay if I stay at the tiller, Alec?" called Dan.

"You're doing great. This is fabulous!" Susie answered.

"It's fine with me. How about you, Claire?" Alec asked.

"I don't care. It's okay. Are we going back soon?" Claire wondered.

"You ready to call it a day?" he said.

"Maybe. I've got some stuff to do for Auntie Cree."

"Okay, we head for home. Captain, change course, please," he directed Dan.

"Aye, aye, sir," Dan answered, with a sharp salute.

On the way back to the east side of the Lakeside pier, Dan had to come about twice more, involving everyone's scrambling back and forth over the centerboard. Claire was bruised on both shins and her forearms ached with the strain of holding the jib sheet. Alex sat close to her on the seat and supervised her sailing, his breath smelling more and more of beer and his voice sounding low and throbbing in her ear. She was aware that she was unable to move without rubbing up against him. She was chilled throughout her body, but whether from the cool wind on her skin or the weird feeling of being surrounded by a strange adult man, she couldn't tell. Dan got the catamaran to within thirty feet of the landing area. Suddenly Alec took the tiller, lowered the mainsail, instructed Claire to let go of the jib sheet, pulled up the centerboard, and expertly guided the boat to its sandy berth. Claire grabbed her clothes from under the seat, and despite the clammy sensation on her skin, put them on. She jumped on the combing, stepped over the rub rail, and splashed into the shallow water.

"Thanks for the sail. I learned a lot," she called over her shoulder, and then scrambled up a pile of boulders in her hurry to get out of the lake, and headed for Fourth Street.

"You're welcome anytime, sailor!" cried Alec, grinning at her departing back.

Margot was playing solitaire at the big weather-beaten porch table, and thinking about pouring herself a sherry, when Claire banged in the screen door.

"Hi, honey, how was it?" she asked her daughter who was moving quickly toward the stairs.

"Fine. I need to change. Be down soon."

Claire changed her clothes slowly, drying herself vigorously with the beach towel she had slung over the doorknob. She brushed her hair, trying to see herself clearly in the cloudy mirror that hung over the short old dresser. She was disturbed by the sail she had just gone on, by Alec. She had felt uncomfortable, vulnerable, childish and unprotected, and she didn't really know why. Nothing bad had happened to her on the boat. No one had said or done anything wrong. She was home and she was safe.

But she felt irritated and guilty. She had no idea why. And she knew she did not want to talk about it with her mother.

Bob came in the back door, through the kitchen, to the porch at the front of the house when he heard the screen door screech. "Damn," he thought, "I still don't have that thing oiled enough." He wondered if Claire had come back from her sailing adventure.

"Was that Claire?" he asked his wife when he joined her on the front porch.

"Yeah. She's upstairs, changing," Margot answered as she slapped a card on a long pile.

"How was her day?"

"She didn't say much. Seemed to be in a hurry."

Bob started to reach for the 3-In-One Oil to lubricate the offending hinge, but thought better of it. "I'll just go up and check on her," he said.

"Why? She's fine. Leave her alone. She's a big girl now. She'll be down later."

"Because I want to talk to her. What's wrong with that?"

"It's what you always do. I think you hover too much. Give her some space."

"What do you mean by that? I'm at work all day. This is my vacation and I want to spend some time with my daughter. I don't know why you always criticize."

"I thought you wanted to fix that kitchen faucet."

"Done," he snapped.

"Well, you could sit down and spend some time with me. You haven't done anything with me all day. I've been doing crosswords and playing solitaire. It's my vacation, too," she pouted.

"Margot, I can't get anything right with you. I'm supposed to help Auntie Cree, I'm supposed to spend time with my daughter before she starts school, I'm supposed to entertain you because you're bored. I'm damned if I do and damned if I don't."

"Bob Benson, go upstairs and tend to that child of yours," roared Auntie Cree from the living room. She walked onto the porch. "I am tired of listening to you two bickering. Margot, if you want something to do, I have a short grocery list. You could go to Jenny's for me and pick up a few things. And you can visit Nancy who needs a fourth for bridge this afternoon. And the three of you usually enjoy playing a round of miniature golf. They say it will rain tomorrow, so I suggest you strike while the iron is hot, and stop wasting your time and my energy with your whining and complaining. Besides, I need that deck of cards for double solitaire. Now skedaddle out of here." And with that, Cree sat on her favorite chair and reached for the cards. "And while you're up, get me an iced tea from the refrigerator."

Bob knocked lightly on the closed bedroom door. Claire opened it tentatively. "Oh, hi, Daddy."

"May I come in?"

"Sure." She walked to the bed and sat cross-legged on its sagging mattress. He recognized the faded, flowery bedding. Margot had brought it from home so they wouldn't saddle Cree with extra laundry.

"How was the sailing trip?"

"Fine."

"Fine? That's it? What was it like? I've never seen a catamaran. Is it big? Does it go fast?"

"It's not too big. I guess we went pretty fast," Claire answered.

"Well, how many people were on board?" Bob persevered.

"Four."

"You, Alex, and who else?"

"Some people named Dan and Susie. Adults. I was the only kid."

"It doesn't sound like you enjoyed it. Was it scary, honey?"

Claire paused until he thought she wasn't going to answer. "Daddy, is it okay for me to not like somebody that I just met? For no good reason?" Claire asked, seemingly changing the subject.

"Who don't you like?" asked her father.

"Alec," she almost whispered.

"Why not? Tell me what happened."

"Nothing happened, I just don't like him, is all."

Bob looked at his daughter as if for the first time. She will be thirteen on her next birthday, he thought. Not a baby, not even a little kid. She was entering the unknown world of adolescence. He had grown up with two brothers and Margot was the only woman he had seriously dated in his life. What he didn't know about girls was a lot. But he sensed that Claire was struggling with something, something he had never experienced.

"Do you want me to call your mom up here to talk?" he asked gently.

"No. I'd rather talk to you," she answered quickly.

"Tell me about Alec."

Claire hesitated. She didn't really know what to say. But she tried. "He sat next to me. He taught me how to hold the ro- I mean the sheets. He let Dan steer most of the time and stayed with me. That's okay, right?"

"Right. Did he say something that hurt your feelings?"

"No. He – he didn't really do anything. But, uh, he – well, he was so close to me, I could hardly move. I could smell his breath. He sort of – he -"

"Did he touch you, Claire?"

"It wasn't like that. He was just – too – um – physical? Do you know what I mean? He was right next to me all the time. I - just didn't like it, Daddy. I feel guilty about it, but I - I - just don't like him. Is that all right?"

"Yes, it's okay. Honey, you're a smart girl. I trust you. You'll figure it out."

Claire leaned toward her father and rested her head on his shoulder. They sat in that position without talking for several minutes. Then her father broke the silence with two words: "miniature golf?"

Claire and Bob went into the tiny kitchen to see if they could find any lunch. To their surprise, Margot was in there, frying bacon. The rich, salty odor was beginning to permeate the little cottage. Margot had taken bread, mayonnaise, tomatoes and lettuce out of the small refrigerator. She even had pulled a bag of potato chips off the top of it.

"Mom! BLTs for lunch? Cool!" exclaimed Claire.

"Well, you must have worked up an appetite on that boat," said her mother.

"I am hungry!"

"Me, too," said Bob, giving Margot a squeeze around her shoulders.

"After lunch, want to play miniature golf, Mom?"

"Okay, why not?"

"Should we invite Auntie Cree?" she asked her parents.

"I don't think Auntie Cree does that anymore, honey," said her father.

"Who says I don't?" called out Auntie Cree from the porch. Bob made a mental note to remember that despite her age, Cree had amazing hearing.

"Okay, old lady, I'll take you on. Penny a putt?" he called out to her, grinning.

"I never take bets. But I can still putt. All those years on the golf course have to count for something."

"Cree, do you want a BLT with us? There's plenty," called Margot.

"I have already eaten enough for the day, but thank you," she replied.

Claire took her plate and went out to the porch to join Auntie Cree. Her parents followed soon after and Margot put a glass of milk in front of Claire. After lunch and a quick clean-up of the dishes, all four of them walked to the miniature golf course, about two blocks away. Cree led them as they walked, tall and straight, eyes forward, moving with speed and determination. Watching her, Claire wondered if it was possible to play miniature golf wearing a shin-length cotton dress and leather high top shoes. They passed families playing catch in the street; the lack of cars made Lakeside streets safe. They passed people walking to the lake, carrying coolers, beach towels, pails and shovels, and suntan lotion. The miniature golf course was close to the tennis and shuffleboard courts, and was surprisingly empty for a holiday weekend. The game was fun. They all cheered when someone made a hole in one, and all the adults felt it necessary to teach Claire some of the fine points of putting, which she found vaguely irritating. But she was glad they were all together, enjoying their afternoon, so she let the negative feelings go. As they turned in their putters and balls and began the walk back to the cottage, they were surprised to see Alec McCrae approaching them. He was wearing white shorts and a navy blue polo shirt, and loafers without socks. He was tanned and athletic-looking, and he was smiling at Auntie Cree.

"Cree, so great to see you twice in one day," he greeted her.

"Alec McCrae, you look like a tennis pro," she responded with a twinkle in her blue eyes.

Bob turned to look at Alec, realizing who this stranger was.

"This must be Claire's parents," said Alec. "I had the pleasure of sailing with your daughter this morning. She was a really good sport. I think she may have the heart of a sailor."

"I heard," said Bob, slowly, taking in the younger man's face, memorizing it.

"Claire, good to see you. I'm planning another sail tomorrow - Kelley's Island is my destination. Are you up for it?" he smiled at her.

"I – uh – don't know. We might have plans," she stammered.

"I'm sure you can go if you want to, dear," said Margot. "We don't have any plans that I know of."

Bob intervened. "Claire and I have lots to do tomorrow, sorry." He sounded irritated.

"Bob, don't be silly. We come here with nothing but time. It's up to Claire. She can go if she wants."

Claire looked at her father, pleading with her eyes to help her get out of this situation.

Cree looked at Claire carefully.

50

"Alec, it's time you found someone your own age to sail with. There are plenty of young women running around for you to annoy. Go talk to them and leave my family alone," she said, teasingly.

"Cree, don't be so mean to Alec. I think Claire might enjoy seeing Kelley's Island," said Margot.

"I really need to get home, Margot. Alec, nice to see you." And Bob, taking his daughter's hand in his, began to walk toward Fourth Street.

"I apologize for my husband, I don't know what's gotten into him," said Margot.

"Margot, I need to get home. Please come with me," said Auntie Cree.

"All right, Cree. So nice to see you again, Alec. Maybe you want to stop by later for a drink. You know where to find us."

"Actually, Alec, we may be at my son's tonight for dinner," said Cree quickly.

"That's okay, I have plans myself. Nice to see you all," said Alec.

Cree and Margot walked at a distance behind Bob and Claire. Margot was actually concerned that Cree walked so slowly, after her brisk walk to the miniature golf course. Margot peered at Cree to see if there was something wrong, but Cree's face was unreadable, eyes staring straight ahead. Suddenly Cree stopped walking and turned to face Margot in the gathering dusk.

"Margot, you are a good woman, raised by a good mother. But sometimes I think you don't pay attention to the clues all around you."

"I can't imagine what you…."

Cree hushed her with a raised eyebrow. "Your husband and daughter were clearly trying to get out of a bad situation. I don't know what happened on that boat, but Claire was not happy about it, and wants nothing to do with that man. Now, I know that without anyone telling me anything. Why don't you?"

"She said her sail was fine."

"A twelve-year-old girl goes sailing for the first time, and then reports that it's 'fine?' And that's it? I've known that girl of yours for her entire twelve years and the last time she used one word in a sentence, she was shy of two years old. That child is a talker. She comes in from an adventure and uses one word to describe it, and you don't think that's odd. Why do I know your daughter better than you do?"

"Well, you don't. Sorry, but…."

"And your husband. He is a lovely man who is trying to do right by his mother-in-law's friend. He brings tools with him in case I need something." She ticked off on her fingers: "He cooks hamburgers. He buys you the paper. He makes drinks. He cleans up the kitchen. He gets his daughter to tell him what is going on. He is a keeper. And all you can do is whine. You know better than that; your mother and I raised you better. Is there some reason that you have ceased to appreciate the best thing that ever happened to you?"

"No," said Margot, chastened. Embarrassed. She was aware that Cree's loud voice could be heard throughout the quiet neighborhood. She wanted to go home. "Cree, can we walk home now?"

"Yes, we can. You will go home, you will apologize to your husband and daughter for being so self-centered that you didn't see what was in front of your face, and you will kiss them both and tell them what you and I know is true, that you love them more than anything in the world."

"But.....okay," said Margot. She said, "Thank you."

"You are welcome. Now let's go." And Cree suddenly began to walk purposefully toward her summer home.

When they reached the cottage, the afternoon light had faded and long shadows surrounded the little yellow house. Claire and Bob were inside, in the kitchen, but they had turned on the lights on the porch and living room. Cree went into her bedroom and slammed the door loudly. Margot lit a cigarette while standing on the porch, gazing without really seeing the sleepy town as it began to settle down for the evening. She turned with a shake of her head and went into the kitchen which was lit from a single bulb hanging in the middle of the room. The center of the room was in a glare and the corners were shadowed. Claire, her back to her mother, was making a salad at the little battered table in the corner.

"Claire, are you all right?"

"Sure, why?" said Claire.

"You didn't tell me much about your sail today. Did you have fun?"

"It was okay. I think I maybe don't like sailing that much. You get really cold and wet. And....."

"And what?"

"And I guess I didn't really like Alec too much."

"Why not?"

"I don't know. He acted kind of.....well, he made me feel.....I was uncomfortable."

"Did something happen?"

"No, not really. I just thought he was too close to me sometimes. He touched me a lot. It was by accident, but…."

"Claire, not every man who sits near you or touches you by mistake has designs on you. You need to try not to overdramatize things so much. Save your discomfort for the really bad things that happen." Margot went to the refrigerator to find the sherry bottle.

"I didn't think he had designs on me, Mom, that's not what I said."

"You're getting older. There are going to be plenty of men. There's no reason to make a soap opera out of every encounter." She poured the sherry into a drinking glass. The ginger colored liquid shimmered in the too-bright light.

"I didn't think that's what I was doing."

"Well, it sounds to me like you're making a mountain out of a molehill. I think we should drop it."

"Fine with me."

Bob came in the back door. "Hamburgers are done. Are we ready to eat?"

"I'll set the table on the porch," Claire said. She went to the shelves and took down the mis-matched dinner plates and carried them to the porch. Bob looked at Margot inquiringly.

"She makes too much of little things," Margot said, and took a long swallow of her drink.

"Maybe…. Find out if Cree wants some sherry, okay? And call her to dinner?"

Dinner was quiet that night, each lost in their own thoughts. The moon that had been visible over the lake had disappeared as clouds began to gather at the horizon. Only a little starlight peeked through on the summer-weary town whose slide into autumn had begun. Soon the mists of winter would envelop Lakeside and grant it a well-deserved nap. But for tonight, summer memories and winter plans marched hand in hand across the overcast sky, and somewhere a gull screamed.

Wishing Lakeside
1962

There are times when it's hard to be an only child, thought Claire as she was trying to go to sleep. Most of my friends have sisters – or even brothers – they can play with. Going to the movies, they can sit together and not just with their parents. After school, they can talk about the other kids they know while doing their homework. Sometimes they have mutual friends. I just have me. Oh, there are benefits, too, she thought. I can watch what I want on TV if my parents aren't around. I can stretch out on the back seat of the car and read when we go on trips. There's always plenty of food to go around and I don't have to share with anyone. And some of my friends' siblings are just plain annoying. But what I wouldn't give to have had somebody around today.

Claire had had a tough day. It was early August and a lot of her friends and the kids in the neighborhood were gone at camp or on a family vacation. It had rained all day, contrary to the weatherman's prediction of "partly cloudy," so she couldn't go for a long bike ride. Her mom had been focused on house cleaning and enlisted Claire for scouring bathrooms, so she had to do all three of them by herself. Now her hands smelled of bleach and three fingernails were chipped. She thought about turning on the light and getting an emery board and some hand cream, but stopped as she remembered doing manicures when she slept over at Cindy's house last week. Doing her nails by herself just felt like another chore tonight. She rolled over in her small twin-sized bed, smoothed the wrinkled white sheet under her, and thought about how much she hated the liver and bacon that her mother had made for dinner. Then she thought of Camp Firebird, where she had spent the month of July, and how she loved the food there. Claire loved going to Firebird; this had been her third year and she was pretty sure it would be her last. She was starting seventh grade in the fall and most of the campers were younger than that, but she would miss it.

One of today's frustrations had been going with her mother to a local department store which was the sole source of school uniforms. Claire had serious reservations about the school she was going to attend in September. She had finished the sixth grade in her local elementary school and most of her friends would be going to the local junior high, but her parents had decided she should go to a private girls' day school instead. And this school required uniforms in the junior high years. They had bought two brown jumpers, four alarmingly bright gold short-sleeved shirts, a thin leather belt, half a dozen white crew socks, and worst of all, a new pair of white-with-brown saddle shoes. There also a pair of brown "bloomers" for gym class. These were baggy shorts whose bottom hem had been threaded with elastic so it looked like each thigh was encased in a small brown inner tube. Her mother had allowed her to buy a brown cardigan sweater, which Claire planned to wear every day to cover up as much of that horrible gold shirt as possible, and some cable knee socks in a variety of colors. She wondered whether she would get a better education because she had to wear a uniform. She doubted it. Claire fell asleep, thinking of saddle shoes and campfires and clean bathrooms.

But things brightened up. At breakfast the next day, unusual because both her parents were at the table, Claire's father said, "So how about we go to Lakeside next weekend?"

"Seriously?" asked Claire, dropping her spoon into her cereal bowl and sitting up straight.

"Well, the paint plant has to be cleaned and most of the guys will be involved with that, so I see a chance for maybe four days' vacation. And we need to check on Auntie Cree. She's not getting any younger. Are you up for it?"

"Have you checked with Cree?" asked his wife, pouring a second cup of coffee from the percolator on the stove. "She doesn't like surprises."

"No, I thought I would call right now. That is, if Claire can stand a couple of days at Lakeside."

Claire giggled. "I think I can force myself. How early can we leave on Thursday?"

Her mother said, "Wait a minute, before you call. We've never gone to Lakeside for such a long visit before. Do you think that's going to work? What'll we do all that time?"

"Well, I was actually thinking we could bring our clubs and play the Sandusky course Phil has been talking about. What do you say to that?"

"Okay, that might be fun. But should we leave Claire with Cree that long?"

"Mom, I'm twelve years old and I've been to Lakeside, well…..maybe, what, ten times?"

"Hardly."

"Well, close. I know my way around. I'm a good swimmer. I passed every level at Firebird – the next level is getting my WSI so I can be a lifeguard, for heaven's sakes. I can swim without you watching me, and they have lifeguards! I don't need a babysitter. I'll be fine."

"I know, honey, but I wondered how much fun it would be without a friend. I was thinking you might want to invite Cindy to come with us."

She hadn't thought of that. "Are you kidding me? That would be fantastic! Can I call her?"

"I have to call Cree first," said her dad. "Then you can call her."

"Cool!"

The ride to Lakeside was considerably shorter, it seemed to Claire, with her friend in the car. Claire felt the need to tell Cindy every detail of the little summer community she could think of so Cindy could feel comfortable there. She told her about the small shops on Second Street, the white gazebo in front of the hotel, the once-a-week movie showings of out-of-date films, the tandem bikes, the shuffleboard courts, the waterfront and the pier, the snack bar. She described Cree in minute detail, because Claire loved Cree with all her heart. Her mother chimed in with stories of her own teen years in Lakeside, when she and her brothers used to visit. They had been free to wander the town and find other kids while their parents played bridge and laughed on Cree's porch, and on Saturday nights, she said, there was always a big dance in the hotel ballroom with a live big band orchestra from Sandusky or Port Clinton. There was a sweet tone in her voice when she spoke of the dances; Claire's mother loved to dance and it seemed everyone her age did, too, in the mid-1930s. There were always plenty of dance partners, plenty of root beer, and there was always the thrilling possibility of a little summer romance. Claire thought, not for the first time, that she would have loved to have lived then.

After they stopped for gas and ate Hershey bars for lunch, which Cindy thought was a good omen for the weekend ahead, they drove through small town streets until Claire exclaimed, "We're here!" as soon as she could see the town gate. There were several cars lined up before them. "We pay the fee, then we park the car and carry our stuff to Auntie Cree's house. Remember I told you there aren't any cars here?"

"I remember," answered Cindy, straining to see any glimpse of the town. "Where's the lake?"

"It's just a couple of blocks, you'll see."

It really didn't take long to walk to Cree's little yellow cottage on Fourth Street. The girls had each brought just one suitcase, filled with shorts and tops, sandals, two bathing suits, a beach towel, a sweater and shortie pajamas. They had each brought a book as well. With junior high looming, they had summer reading lists to finish.

Cree's cottage was right on the street, its front completely screened in, and cheerful window boxes filled with red geraniums perched on the edge of the sills. There was a small shed attached to one side of the house, while on the other side, the next cottage was so close, there was nothing but a thin dirt path between the structures. There was a second floor, Cindy could see, with white ruffled curtains pulled back on each side in the dormer windows. The roof of the house sagged a little, and the porch door squeaked when Mr. Benson opened it. He was yelling and laughing at the same time as he called for Auntie Cree.

"I'm coming, for heaven's sakes, give me a minute! You don't need to yell, I haven't lost my hearing!" a voice called from the inside.

"There you are!" said Claire's father, wrapping a tall, white-haired woman in a big hug.

"Bob Benson, let go of me! I need to catch my breath. Where is Margot?"

"Right here, Auntie Cree. Here I am," said Claire's mother.

"Well, let me look at you. Yes, you look fine. Just fine. A sight for sore eyes, that's what."

"Hi, Auntie Cree. How are you?" asked Claire, who had just come in the big porch.

"Oh, my stars, it's Claire. You're practically a young woman. Just look at you," said Cree, smiling a little and crinkling her bright blue eyes.

"Auntie Cree, this is my friend Cindy. She and I are going to sleep upstairs in the room with two beds. That's how I knew there was room for her. I hope you don't mind."

"Cindy? Hello, young lady. Of course, you are welcome in my little house. I am glad you will be here to keep Claire company. I can't keep up with her anymore. I tell you what, why don't you girls take your things upstairs and unpack. I don't know if the beds are made but you can handle that if they need it. Are you all hungry?"

"We're all fine, Auntie Cree," said Margot, as Claire and Cindy ran through the living room and up the worn staircase to the bedrooms. "I'm so glad to see you. You look lovely today."

"No, I do not. I look old and creaky. But I'm still here and I'm still managing on my own, thank you very much." Cree, wearing a faded, light cotton dress that hung down to her shins, and a once-white cardigan sweater over her shoulders, eased herself into a chair by the screen. A pack of cigarettes, an ashtray, and a book were on the large, worn table next to her.

"Well, we knew that," said Bob Benson, patting her hand and sitting on a chintz-covered wicker armchair next to his favorite old lady. "But I brought a few tools and I thought you could find something around here that I could fix for you."

"You're a dear to think of that, but you know Phil lives right down the street. He keeps me pretty well fixed. And by the way, as I recall, you don't really know how to use those tools very well, anyway, so you can just stop showing off."

"I'm going upstairs to see how the girls are doing. Can I bring something down for you?" asked Margot.

"No, dear, nothing up there interests me anymore. But thank you."

Margot picked up a brown paper shopping bag she had brought from home, filled with sheets and towels, and went upstairs to help the girls make the beds, which she well knew were not made.

She found Claire and Cindy sitting on their beds, bouncing a little, and laughing. "What's so funny?"

"It's the smell. The mattresses on the beds and the dresser drawers and the air, I guess, it all smells like Lakeside to me. Cindy thinks I'm weird," said Claire. Cindy laughed.

"Well, the mattresses are made of horse hair and have been here at least since I was not much older than you, and the drawers have moth balls to keep the moths away from the sweaters and blankets. And the air, well, that's just old and stuffy. Let's open the window and get some fresh air in."

They made the beds with the sheets Margot had packed and put their clothes in the drawers. Each bed had a worn gray Army blanket folded at the end and a heavy, lumpy pillow. Claire loved every detail. Before going downstairs, she showed Cindy the other bedroom in which her parents would sleep. Her mother was making that bed.

"Mom, when you used to come to Lakeside, where did you all sleep? There were five kids in your family and there's only two bedrooms."

"Well, there are three bedrooms, because Auntie Cree sleeps downstairs. My parents slept up here and I slept in your room. The boys all had to figure something out downstairs. But I doubt there were ever more than one or two of them here at a time. Lakeside was my favorite place, but they were always busy doing something else, as I remember."

"Mrs. Benson, how is Auntie Cree related to you?" asked Cindy.

Margot Benson perched on the edge of her bed. "Well, Cindy, you know, she really isn't. Auntie Cree and her husband Phil were my parents' best friends. They were together so much while I was growing up that I thought of them as family; I guess we all did. Their son Philip is my age and we played together when we were little. After a while, I don't remember when exactly, they bought this cottage in Lakeside. They were from the west side and Lakeside was less than an hour from their house. But we visited even though it took more than three hours to get here from East Cleveland. Sometimes my parents came here for a weekend without us. The four of them would play cards all day and night. Bridge, cribbage, even a little poker, I think. Every night they would walk down to the waterfront and enjoy the view of the lake before they went to dinner in the cafeteria at the hotel. They just loved it here, all of them. And so did I."

Claire and Cindy were finally free to head down to the lake. They had made polite conversation with the adults, but Claire could tell Cindy was getting bored, and she wanted her friend to love Lakeside as she did, and that meant getting out on their own and having some fun. So they put on bathing suits under their shorts and tops, and walked the four short blocks to Lake Erie and the Lakeside waterfront. On the way, they saw an ice cream parlor with stainless steel stools lined up at a stainless steel counter, the Auditorium, and a couple of small churches, but mostly cottages, large and small, typically old and weathered, almost all occupied with families. Houses were so close together that it was often difficult to know where one ended and the next began. The girls passed an empty lot on Third Street where a disorganized group of boys were engaged in a noisy game of baseball, although Cindy couldn't see any bases. They turned off of Second Street at Central Avenue and in front of them was the lake. There was an enormous green lawn between them and the water, but they were drawn to the vast expanse of bluish-gray water. They quickened their pace. They had to go through a wide gateway to get to the sandy waterfront. It was an arched opening in what Claire called the pavilion, a long narrow building, on top of which people could sit and watch the waterfront. Inside on ground level, there was a small snack bar. There were bike racks on the street side of the archway, all filled today. Cindy and Claire walked through the entry and onto the long concrete pier stretching out into the lake and forming, with its ninety degree turn, a swimming area. The nearest section was a sandy beach and shallow water, perfect for mothers with young toddlers and babies. There were two other delineated swimming areas, created by stretched ropes and buoys, indicating deeper and still deeper water. Claire led Cindy to the deepest section. Stripping down to their bathing suits quickly, they found space on the pier to put their beach towels, shoes, and clothes. Claire was the first one in the water, jumping in feet first and calling to her friend when she surfaced. Cindy was more cautious and sat on the edge of the pier, dangling her feet into the water, checking the water temperature.

Cindy was, at twelve, a remarkably pretty girl. Her blonde hair was even more so after two months of time spent outdoors. She liked to put lemon juice in her hair when she was sunning, and both she and Claire were convinced that it lightened her hair color. Cindy was slender and delicate-looking, which belied a competitive spirit and graceful athleticism. She loved clothes even at this young age and always wore the latest styles. She didn't seem to be aware of the attention she commanded, particularly from boys her age and much older. Claire looked nothing like her friend. She tended to overeat, which showed, and her hair was a dark shade of brown. She wore it short and straight, often pulled back on one side with a pastel-colored plastic barrette. She chose her clothes with one criterion in mind: their ability to make her look thinner. Today she was wearing a navy blue one-piece swimsuit with a short pleated skirt at the hips. There was a jaunty red anchor embroidered on the left shoulder strap but otherwise, it was plain and unremarkable. She spent most of her time while swimming, in the water, where Cindy was more likely to sit at the edge of the pool, wearing a two-piece white suit that emphasized her dark tan.

Cindy slid into the lake and shivered at the temperature, then dove under and swam to Claire. "We're gonna have to wash our hair after!" she gasped as she shook the lake water off of her head. They both began to swim in strong, silent strokes from the pier to the outer edge of the swimming area and back. There were few other swimmers in the deep section that afternoon and the girls had the luxury of being able to swim laps without having to swim around other people. After a while, they both grabbed the pier with their fingertips, panting.

"Who's that?" asked Cindy, pointing to two boys who were lying on the pier on towels.

"I don't know. Why?"

"They weren't there when we got here."

"So?"

"I don't know, I just wondered if you knew them."

"I don't know people here. I only come once a year and usually hang out with my parents. Where are you going?"

Cindy had easily pulled herself up on the edge of the pier and had found her towel. Claire watched from the lake as her friend dried her hair and finger-combed it into shoulder-length waves, sat down on the towel and reached into her beach bag for suntan oil. Reluctantly, Claire got out of the water and joined Cindy. She dried her hair and legs and sat down on the pier, looking around at the people on the pier. "Are you done swimming?" asked Claire, seeing no one who looked familiar.

"For now, I think. Is that okay?"

"Yeah. Sure. Are you hungry? I brought some money for the snack bar."

"Maybe later." Cindy folded a second towel into a pillow and lay down, bending her legs at the knees.

"Okay." Claire had neglected to bring a second towel and, finding the concrete pier uncomfortable, rolled over on her side and hoisted herself up on one elbow. "What do you think of Lakeside so far?"

"The lake is great. Once you get used to the cold. I was thinking we could try shuffleboard. Can we?"

"The courts are almost always full, but we can try. I don't really know how to play."

"My grandparents play. I can teach you. It's more fun if you have teams."

"Well, we can play against each other, right?"

"I guess."

Claire said, "There's also miniature golf. Maybe my parents would come with us. Dad loves it."

"Okay."

"Hey, you girls new around here?" said a tall, white-blond boy. Claire was startled by the voice. She hadn't seen him get up from his nearby towel and walk to their side of the pier.

"Hi," said Cindy. "I'm new but Claire has been here before."

"Hi, Claire. And what's your friend's name?" he smiled at Claire but indicated Cindy with his elbow.

"I'm Cindy," she answered before Claire could form the words. "Who are you?"

"I'm Bill and my buddy over there is Donny. We've been around since the first of August. My family has a cottage on Second Street." He sat down next to Cindy.

Donny was sitting up, squinting through the bright sun to see what his friend was up to.

"My grandmother's best friend lives here, on Fourth Street. We're just visiting for the weekend," Claire said, finding her voice. She sat up and hugged her knees to her chest.

"Mind if we join you?" asked Bill, beckoning to Donny, who seemed uninterested.

"It's a free country," said Claire, at the same time Cindy said, "Okay."

The four of them shifted around somewhat awkwardly for a few minutes until they were sitting more or less in a circle on the pier, with Donny somewhat behind. His eyes stayed on the water. Bill sat between his friend and Cindy and devoted his attention to her. He asked questions about her home and family and school and soon they were wrapped in a conversational cocoon, leaving Claire and Donny to watch and listen.

"Do you fish?" Claire finally asked Donny, who was shorter than Bill and had dark blond short hair and an athletic build, unusual in a boy so young. He didn't look at her when he answered, "Yeah, some."

"Have you caught anything this year?"

"Some bass. We had 'em for dinner last night."

"That's cool. Are they hard to catch?"

"Not if you know the right bait."

"Did you clean them yourself or did someone else do it?"

"Myself."

"Yuck. That's the main reason I don't want to fish. My mom won't clean them and my dad says fishing is his idea of nothing to do."

"Too bad. It's pretty fun.

"So whose family has the house here?" asked Claire, changing the subject since the fishing topic seemed to have run its course.

"Bill's."

"Are you here with him the whole month?"

"Nah. Just for this week."

"How do you like it?"

"It's okay. Look, do you mind if I go swimming? It's pretty hot out here."

"No, that's okay." Claire watched as Donny stood with surprising alacrity, pulled off his t-shirt, dropped it on the pier, and ran to the edge, diving in and swimming with an athletic crawl to the far end of the swimming area. She turned back to Cindy and Bill to see whether they wanted to join him but they, too, were standing up. They put on their tops over their suits while Claire watched. "Where are you guys going?"

"Come with us. We're going to see if we can play shuffleboard," Cindy said with excitement.

"What about Donny?"

"Hey, Donny, we're going to check out the shuffleboard!" shouted Bill.

Donny waved and nodded but showed no interest in getting out of the water and joining them. Claire hesitated, wondering whether she had some obligation to be especially polite to Donny and wait for him, or whether it was okay to just leave him alone. Remembering that he had shown little enthusiasm so far, she decided to join Cindy and Bill. She hurried to put on her clothes and join her friends. She had to run to catch up, leaving her out of breath when they approached the courts. There was one vacant court and no one sitting on the benches waiting.

Cindy told them what she knew of the rules and added, "girls against boys." By the time the girls had finished their first round, Donny had joined Bill. There was a good deal of good-natured arguing over scoring, and both teams took more pleasure in knocking their opponents' pucks out of the way than in strategic placement of their own. Eventually the game ended when the lure of the snack bar became too great. The afternoon ended when Claire caught sight of a clock on the casino wall. "Man, we have to go. My parents are gonna be mad."

"See you tomorrow?" asked Cindy, looking at Bill.

"What about tonight? Wanna see what's playing at the movies?"

Claire said, "I saw a poster. It's *Please Don't Eat the Daisies*. I've seen it. It's okay."

"What time?" asked Donny.

"It's always at 8:00. The theater is a riot. You never saw one like it. But the popcorn's good. And the show is free," Bill answered him.

"We have to ask," said Claire.

"Well, ask. We'll walk with you and wait to see what they say."

Claire wondered later if that qualified as her first double date. Well, her first date, period. Probably not, she thought, although it might have been Cindy's. Donny didn't seem too enthusiastic about the whole evening and he didn't even sit next to her in the theater. Bill and Cindy talked a lot during the movie and made it hard to hear, but she had seen it already and hadn't liked it enough to care. She concentrated on her popcorn and smelling the musty, dusty old theater, and wondering if her mom had gone to the movies with boys in the '30s. Bill suggested a walk on the lake path after the film ended, but Claire said they really had to go home; her parents were waiting with their eyes on the clock. That probably wasn't true, she knew; they would be so wrapped up in a bridge game with Phil and Nancy Fox that they would hardly notice. Bill shrugged and the boys walked home in the opposite direction from the girls.

Later, in their cottage bedroom upstairs, propped up on their twin beds with the lights off and the stars visible between the faded white window curtains, Cindy told Claire that she really liked Bill.

"What do you mean, like him?" asked Claire.

"You know, like. He's cute, don't you think?"

"I guess so. He's pretty old, isn't he?"

"He's 14."

"Is he in high school?"

"Starting 9th grade in September. He lives in Rocky River, on the west side."

"You sure found out a lot. I didn't hear any of that."

"What about Donny? Do you like him?" asked Cindy.

"I don't know. Probably not. He's kinda boring."

"Too bad. We could double."

"I thought we just did."

"I mean, again." Cindy giggled. "We could play miniature golf, maybe. Or go swimming in the dark."

"You can't go swimming in the dark. There's no lifeguard. My parents would kill me."

"Don't you *ever* break the rules? We could get out of here without anybody even knowing."

"No, well, maybe a few times. It isn't worth it." After a pause, Claire asked, "How could we get out of here?"

"Just go downstairs after everybody's in bed."

"First of all, they would hear us. The stairs creak. And also, they don't go to bed early. They play cards and drink until late."

"Well, how about the porch roof? Outside this window?"

"Are you crazy? That's right over their heads! And how would you get down?"

"There's a drainpipe on the corner of the house. You could shimmy down it. It would be easy. You just hold on for a few feet, then drop to the grass. I'll help you."

"No way. You'd have to go alone. And then I'd get in trouble for not stopping you."

"Okay, scaredy cat. Then let's ask if we can go for a walk. That wouldn't even be a lie. It's so safe here, I bet they'd let us."

"Well, yeah, that might work. But if they say no, that's it. Maybe we should wait a couple of days."

"What for? We've only got a weekend, and then Bill goes back to Rocky River and I go back to Shaker Heights and I might not ever see him again. C'mon, you only live once!" Cindy was on her knees, bouncing with excitement. It was hard to resist. "Maybe tomorrow night," Claire said, "but tonight I'm too sleepy."

The next morning, Claire's parents announced their intention to play golf in Sandusky with Phil and Nancy. They asked the girls what their plans were.

"Probably swim. And now that we know how to play shuffleboard, we might do that again," answered Claire. "Can we have lunch at the snack bar? We're gonna need some money."

"Here's five dollars. You gotta make it last, okay?" said her father.

"Thanks, Dad. We will."

At breakfast on the porch, Auntie Cree asked the girls what their plans were. "We'll go to the pier, okay? Do you need us to help you with anything?" answered Claire.

"Could you go to the store for me this morning? I need some groceries from Jenny's and you can stop at the post office to check my box. Then it's off to the pier with you."

Claire and Cindy went to the post office and picked up a letter and a magazine for Auntie Cree, then went into the old grocery store on Second Street called Jenny's. The weathered wooden floors slanted, and the small wheeled carts sometimes balked at floorboards that had lifted a little over the years. Cree had given the girls a short list and as they waited at the butcher counter for a pound of ground beef, Claire saw Bill come into the store with an older man.

"Check it out over there," she whispered to Cindy.

"Oh my God! Where is he going?"

"The other way. Frozen foods and bakery. Stay cool. He'll show up."

Bill turned the corner and spotted the girls. He said something to the man he was with, and pointed their way. Both of them smiled and approached the butcher counter.

"Hi. This is Cindy and Claire. This is my dad, Mr. Hoffman."

"Hello, ladies. Bill told me you all went to the movies last night. How was it? Should his mom and I check it out tonight?"

"It was okay if you like Doris Day movies. It's nice to meet you, Mr. Hoffman," said Claire.

"Nice to meet you two," he smiled. "Especially since our vacation has just been cut short."

"What do you mean, cut short?" asked Cindy, looking at Bill.

"Dad has an emergency at work. We're leaving tomorrow morning. We were supposed to stay until next week."

"Oh, that's too bad," said Claire. She really didn't feel that strongly about it, but she could tell Cindy was disappointed.

"Maybe we can get together later or something," said Bill. "With Donny."

"Yeah, let's try," said Cindy. "We're supposed to go swimming after we leave here."

"Dad, is it okay if we go swimming?" said Bill.

"Yes, after you help me with the trash and mow the lawn."

"Maybe we could meet you at the snack bar at noon?" asked Bill.

"Okay. See you then. Bye."

The crowd at the pier was bigger than before and it was hard to actually swim in the lake, so after making a half-hearted attempt to get some exercise, the girls gave up and lay on their towels on the hard concrete. Claire had remembered to pack an extra towel for a pillow. Cindy smeared baby oil all over her arms and legs, and they listened to someone else's transistor radio playing top twenty hits. Bill and Donny never showed up, to Cindy's disappointment. At noon, the girls got dressed, brushed their hair and went to the casino snack bar. Their five dollars didn't go far, but they could get a sandwich and a candy bar each. After lunch, they walked along the lakefront, stopping at a wooden bench near the granite-enclosed bell and watched the boats on the lake. They talked about the beginning of the school year and agreed that going to different schools was going to be strange.

"What's going to be the weirdest part, do you think?" asked Cindy, who was wearing a bright pink sleeveless blouse over white shorts.

"Not knowing anybody in my classes." Claire felt dowdy and wished she had found something more interesting to wear than navy blue shorts and t-shirt. The contrast between her and her friend added to her misgivings about the coming school year. What if everybody at the new school looked and dressed like Cindy?

"You know Linda."

"Yeah, but not very well. I don't even know if I like her. What about you? Are you excited about school starting?" asked Claire.

"Sort of. This has been a weird summer. I usually think summer flies by, but this year, it's been really slow."

"Are you bored?"

"Not bored, exactly. I can't explain it. Every time I sit down to read the summer book list, I lose track of what I'm reading and end up calling somebody or trying on makeup or watching TV with my sister. I can't concentrate on anything. Where the heck are Bill and Donny?"

"Who cares? Let's go see the wishing well. I haven't taken you there yet."

"I care, that's who." But Cindy followed her friend away from the lake and toward the far end of the town, away from the gate. They walked along Second Street for a while, turned south on Elm Street, then along a dirt path that took them into a woodsy area where no houses had been built. At one end of the clearing there was a concrete slab with picnic tables covered by a wooden canopy. Near that, there was a small playground for young children and a few families were there, pushing kids on swings and supervising a large sandbox. Past that, the path went into a thick stand of trees, opening up into a clearing. At the back end of the clearing stood a huge weeping willow tree with branches that hung so low they formed a secluded spot within of cool semi-darkness. Next to the tree was a quaint stone wishing well, complete with crank and oaken bucket.

"Cool! Can we make a wish? Do we have any money left?" asked Cindy.

"We have about forty cents."

"That oughta be enough. I have a lot to wish for. Can I have half?"

"Sure. Here's two dimes." Claire laughed.

Cindy ran to the well and leaned over the edge, peering down into the mildewed, dark interior. Claire had made multiple wishes over the years in the wishing well and was aware that none had come true yet. She didn't feel like doing it again. She hesitated, unsure what she wanted to do, but turned when she heard a sound behind her. Bill Hoffman walked into the clearing.

"Hi," said Claire. "I didn't think we'd see you today."

"Sorry. My parents made us do so many chores, and Donny wanted to go fishing one more time, so we had to get out some stuff from the car, and then we have to put it all back later, and it just got nuts. I decided to take a walk and this is my favorite place in Lakeside. I didn't expect to see you, either. Where's Cindy?"

"Over there, at the wishing well."

Bill, no longer interested in Claire, walked to the well. Claire decided to go back to the playground and see if she could push some of the children on the swings. She loved playing with little kids, and she thought Cindy might like some time with Bill. Claire had been surprised at how miserable Cindy had been at lunch when Bill and Donny hadn't shown up, so she figured she would be doing her friend a favor if she got out of the way.

There was only one child on the swings, and after asking permission of the obviously bored mother if she could watch the child for a while, she pushed the little boy on a swing and then helped him twirl around on the merry-go-round, enjoying the child's whoops of laughter. Claire sat on the triangular board in the corner of the sandbox and made sand castles with her new little charge and helped him dig a hole to China. When he finally tired of sand games, his mother, who had been reading on a nearby bench, thanked her for her help and took him home for a nap. Claire remembered she hadn't seen or heard from Cindy and Bill.

Claire took the path to the clearing, and seeing no one, walked toward the wishing well. Just as she could see the air-brushed outlines of the weeping willow tree, she heard a scream and the furious rustle of leaves, followed by indistinguishable whispering, rapid and intense. Her heart thrummed furiously in her chest, but she froze. "Hey? Is that you, Cindy? Are you okay?" She wasn't sure whether she preferred that Cindy answer her or not. Part of her wished the scream had come from a stranger and she would merely suffer with embarrassment when she saw the people next to the tree. Currently, they were hidden by the cascade of willow leaves that hid the trunk and anyone next to it. There was no answer at first, but whispering, sometimes loud, sometimes hushed. "Cindy? I'm coming in to find you. Ready or not...." she cried with less assurance than before.

She walked slowly and looked all around her as she approached the tree. She separated the strands of leaves as she heard what sounded like loud crashing about in undergrowth and then she was sure she could hear someone weeping quietly. Now she hurried to wave the leaves away. At first she saw no one, but then a bright pink caught her eye on the far side of the tree trunk and she dropped to her knees on the ground when she knew it was Cindy lying in the leaves.

"Oh my God, are you okay?" Claire cried in alarm.

"I'm okay," sniffed Cindy. Her face was hidden from her friend because it was covered by her crooked arm. She was lying on her back.

"What happened? Where's Bill?"

"I don't know. He left."

"Just now?"

"I guess."

"Cindy, what happened?" Claire asked again.

"Nothing."

"I don't think nothing. C'mon. Tell me."

"He kissed me."

"You don't sound too happy about it. I thought you liked him."

"No. I don't."

"Did he push you down?"

"Maybe."

"Are you hurt?"

"No….. I'm glad you're here." Cindy took her arm away from her face. There was a bruise on her cheek, already showing up, yellow and ugly. She sat up in the leaves.

"Geez, did he hit you?"

"I guess so. Anyway, he's gone, so we can forget it."

"Can you walk okay?"

"Sure."

"Then let's go home."

When Claire and Cindy got to the little yellow house on Fourth Street, there was no one on the porch and no one answered when Claire called out. They went to the kitchen. Claire went to the freezer to find ice cubes, wrap them in a dish towel, and give the pack to Cindy to hold against her bruised cheek. The two girls sat at the worn kitchen table. Auntie Cree suddenly appeared at the kitchen door.

"Auntie Cree! I didn't think anybody was home," said Claire.

"I was taking a nap. I thought I would see if I could offer you girls a snack. But it appears you need medical attention, not food." Cree was talking to Cindy.

"I'm fine. It's just a bruise. Nothing to worry about."

"And how did you come to be bruised?"

"I fell. It was silly."

"You fell on your face?"

"Sort of."

Cree looked at Claire. "I have the sense that I am not getting the whole story. I would like to know how my new friend and houseguest has injured herself. Will you be the one to tell me?"

"We were at the wishing well. We – met a friend there. He and Cindy were talking but I was sort of babysitting a little boy. I didn't see anything. You have to convince Cindy to talk to you."

Cree turned to face Cindy. "Cindy, my dear. You have nothing to fear from me. I pride myself in showing my guests a good time in Lakeside, and I don't like to think they might get hurt. Tell me about your young man and you at the willow tree. I have been there many times so you don't need to describe the setting. Only the incident."

Cindy turned and looked at Auntie Cree's face. It was large and wrinkled but there were the most brilliant blue eyes and they were totally focused on her. Cree was still standing near the doorway, straight and calm, and her hands were folded at her waist. They were covered with brown spots but the fingers were long and surprisingly smooth. Cree's demeanor broadcast both serenity and generosity. She did not seem to be in any hurry and waited for the girl to feel safe to tell her story.

"Do you want to sit down?" asked Cindy, nearly whispering.

"All right, I will." Cree chose the third kitchen chair, sitting up straight, hands folded quietly in her lap. She waited. They could all hear the ticking of the black and white cat clock on the wall, whose tail moved relentlessly back and forth, marking the passage of time. Cindy stared at Auntie Cree, then finally began to talk.

"We met these two boys, Bill and Donny, yesterday."

"Yes, I remember."

Cindy spoke slowly, reluctantly at first.

"Bill is – cute. I liked him right away. I wanted to see him again. We saw him at Jenny's this morning, shopping with his dad. We made plans to meet them at the pavilion for lunch but they didn't show up. So we went to see the wishing well and the tree. Claire says it's her favorite place in Lakeside. I love the well. I made a wish. I wished Bill would come and join me there. It was cool and shaded and the tree is so big and I don't know what I wanted to happen but it just seemed like the best place."

"I can well imagine. Go on."

Cindy began to talk faster. Some kind of barrier seemed to have been broken.

"Claire left to go play with some kids and I was alone and then Bill did show up. It was like the wishing well really worked. I was so excited. We talked for a while. I didn't like the conversation as much. He was talking about the parties he's going to go to now that he's in high school and how he's going to drink beer and there will be girls and dancing and he didn't make it sound fun, just kind of out of control and – I don't know, I didn't like it. I wanted to talk about movies or school or something. He kind of got closer to me while he was talking and I bumped up against the tree and he just kissed me really quickly before I knew he was going to. I wasn't ready and I didn't really like it. He was pushing me too hard and his teeth pushed against my mouth and it hurt and I think I kind of twisted my head to get away and he didn't like that and he grabbed my face so it wouldn't move and he kissed me again,

70

harder, and I think I pushed him away and said something like "don't" and he said "why not there's nobody around this is what you wanted anyway" and I didn't want it...... and I wanted him to go away and I pushed him again and he kind of grabbed my arms and pulled me away from the tree and there were a lot of leaves and roots and stuff and I kind of tripped and I think he laughed... and I fell down and hit my face on a root and he jumped down next to me and I got scared and then I heard Claire call my name and say she was coming in, ready or not, and he stood up and kind of kicked me and ran away from the tree in the other direction from her so when she showed up I was on the ground and he was gone and she was worried about me but I'm okay. Really. I'm okay." Cindy looked at Auntie Cree, and then at Claire. She took a deep breath and sat back on the chair. "Really..."

Claire took all this in and slowly realized that the situation she had encountered and interrupted was one that was way over her head. She had no frame of reference for understanding a situation in which a boy demanded more from a girl – physically – than she was willing to give. Claire didn't know that that kind of intimidation even happened. What she understood was that she had interrupted something she wasn't supposed to see, that Cindy didn't enjoy her time with Bill, and that Cindy had been hurt in a fall. Now her mind was reeling with questions she had no answers for.

Cree sat quietly, never taking her eyes off of Cindy. There was a long silence as each of the three females held her own thoughts, questions, and fears.

"Cindy, has anything like this ever happened to you before?" Cree asked gently.

"No. I only kissed a boy once before, and that was at a party, because of a game."

"Claire, how about you?"

"No! I've never even been on a date, unless going to the movies with Cindy, Bill and Donny, last night, counts. But I don't think it does."

"Well, you know I work at a college, right? I'm a dorm mother. I have sixty college girls living with me every year, and if they have personal problems, sometimes they come to me for advice and suggestions. And I'm a woman. So I might be able to help you both with this story. I have told it to some of my girls, too." Claire and Cindy encouraged her with their silence.

"When I was a young wife, I had a best friend. She had grown up in a very wealthy family and she was given every advantage. Beautiful clothes, the best tutors, music lessons, a huge impressive house. She lived

71

with her mother, her sister and her grandparents. Her mother and father were divorced, quite the scandal at the time. Eventually her mother remarried and her new husband came to live in the big house with all of them.

"After a time, my friend's stepfather began to take a special interest in my friend. He shared books with her, took her to concerts, read out loud to her in the evenings, complimented her new clothes. She was about your age when this started, I think. And then he came into her room one night and started to kiss her, very hard and repeatedly. My friend was shocked and she hated it, but in those days it was something very difficult to talk about and she didn't want to hurt anyone's feelings, especially her adored mother's, so she kept it to herself. The stepfather tried again and again to force his attentions on her and my friend knew it was wrong. She finally figured out how to be in her sister's room at certain hours of the evening and eventually coerced her grandfather to provide her with a lock to her door. Then she begged her mother and grandparents to send her abroad to boarding school. They complied, although they probably didn't understand her real motivation. Her sister went to the school, too. By the time they had grown up and their education was completed, they felt safe enough to come home and resume their lives in Ohio. And about that time, her mother divorced the stepfather, so he was out of the house. My friend didn't know what caused the marriage to break up; she was just glad it had.

"When we were in our thirties, my friend went through a very difficult time. She was happily married with three sons and another baby on the way. She had everything she had ever wanted – no money to speak of, but she had learned how unimportant that is – but she felt suddenly terribly sad. She wanted to stay in bed all day and didn't enjoy the children's comings and goings as she had. She felt sick with headaches and stomach troubles and she was always tired and wanting to sleep. I was so worried about her – we all were.

"One day I was with her at her house. I think I was watching the children for a while and maybe making some soup for everybody. She came into the kitchen. It was naptime and we were alone. She began to talk. She told me all about her childhood, more stories than I had heard before. I realized I hadn't heard much of her childhood memories; we tended to focus on my stories instead. But that day she talked and talked. And when she got to her teenage years, her stories were told through tears. She told me about her stepfather. I didn't even know she had one. She told me all about him and what he had tried to do to her. And how she had hated and detested him from that day forward and how she had worried about her sister and protected her, and later how difficult it had been for her to love her husband completely and well for many years, because she was afraid to trust him. And how patiently he had waited and helped her through it. And how grateful she was for that.

"My friend got better. She had a doctor's help and of course she had me, and mostly she had the best husband. She had two more children and a wonderful life...."

Cree stopped for a moment and her blue eyes clouded over as she stared at her own hands. Then, straightening her back, she continued.

"....and I miss her every day. But I learned so much from her that day, and I have been more aware of the struggle some women face than I would have been if she hadn't confided in me. Girls, I hope your parents agree with me that you are old enough to know that sometimes men expect women to submit to their physical demands, whether they want to or not. Some men think they have the right to ask for and get what they want from women. Now, I hasten to say that this is not true of all men, not at all. But since time began, there have been men who have tried to take advantage of women, and because men are usually stronger than women, they unfortunately succeed all too often. But the worst thing that women can do is to stay silent. We may not be physically stronger, but we have the power of words. We can and must ask for help, we can and must tell what happens to us, and we must learn to trust ourselves and our beliefs.

"Cindy, what happened to you today was not acceptable. Bill tried to force you. And you escaped before you were seriously hurt. But the worst thing you did today was try to deny that anything of consequence actually happened. I hope that you will go home on Monday and tell your mother the whole story. Don't leave anything out. Let her help you, and learn to trust yourself, too. Please. This is very important to me. It's the same thing I tell my girls at the college. Speak up. Get help. Be aware. Will you do that for me?"

"Okay, I will, Auntie Cree.... Is it okay if I call you that?" Cindy smiled at the old woman.

"Oh I would dearly love it. Claire, this story was for you, too. We women have experiences that can only properly be shared with other women. I hope you count me as one of those you can turn to."

"I do. Was that woman my grandmother?"

Cree gestured with a dismissive wave of her hand. "Oh, you know, it doesn't matter who it was. It was a long time ago. Let's not get too maudlin about it all. You know, I am a little hungry and I want to sit on my porch. Claire, would you bring me a small piece of that coffee cake we had for breakfast? The one from Jenny's? And a little glass of milk, too. Thank you, dear."

And Cree stood, using the back of the chair for a little support, and walked slowly through the living room and onto the porch. There was a baseball game going on down the street, and the shouts of children could be heard. The girls heard the scratch of a match as she lit a cigarette. Cindy put the ice pack back on her cheek and sat back on the chair while Claire rummaged in the tiny refrigerator. By the time the Bensons came back from their golf game, she and Cindy were doing a jigsaw puzzle in the living room while Cree had started the cocktail hour.

Buying Lakeside
1966

Harriet Slade spread out the enticing, glossy brochures on her desk at the office and sighed. She noted the luxurious bedrooms, elegant dining rooms that included large parquet dance floors, pictures of enormous buffet meals that stretched beyond the confines of a photograph, and beautiful young couples leaning on railings, arms around each other's waists, enjoying a spectacular sunset on the endless silver sea. She looked up, gazing at nothing in her all-too-familiar surroundings, and tried to put herself into one of those fairy-tale shots. The mental image would not form. Intruding on her fantasies was the memory of the tremulous voice of her mother, calling her. "Angelika!" Her mother always called her by the name she had been christened with. Harriet had changed it long ago, but her mother refused to acknowledge it. "Can you hear me? I want some more hot tea." Harriet sighed again and put the brochures into her top desk drawer, closing it slowly and silently. All those years of buffing, sanding and oiling the antiques pays off, she thought.

She stood and went to the bay window opposite her desk. Looking out between the heavy velvet drapes at the streets of Sandusky, Ohio, she noted with some satisfaction that the view had not changed appreciably in the forty years she had occupied this office. The real estate business was located in a Victorian mansion that was surrounded by others of the same period, with carefully tended yards and city-owned tree lawns fronting the elegant homes and well cared-for foundation plantings. Driveways led to detached garages that usually echoed the style of the houses. Lately people had been starting to paint exterior detailing of the houses with bright colors – greens, purples, reds, and golds – that made the whole neighborhood seem to preen like a teenage girl who had just gotten her first new outfit of the season. Maybe I should spend the money painting the trim on the house instead of gallivanting off to some European port with a bunch of strangers, she said to herself.

The phone rang and interrupted her musings. Knowing her secretary was at lunch and she was alone in the office, she let it ring the customary two times, then answered, "Harriet Slade Realty. May I help you?"

"May I speak to Miss Slade, please?"

"This is she."

"Miss Slade, my name is Howard Myers. I am an attorney in Cleveland. I am calling in regard to a legal matter involving your late brother, Roman Sladarnecki. I am hoping I can come to Sandusky and meet with you at your convenience."

"My late brother? Roman is dead?"

"Oh, I am so very sorry. I assumed you knew."

"No, I didn't. How did he die? And when?"

"It would be best if we discussed it in person. I would also welcome your visit to Cleveland, if you would prefer. Perhaps you will be visiting family to make arrangements?"

"I never visit family. I haven't been to Cleveland in many years."

"Then I will be happy to come to you. Would it be all right if I intruded on this unhappy time with a visit?"

Harriet hesitated. "I can't imagine what you might have to say to me that involves my brother, Mr. Myers, but I suppose there is no harm in your visiting. Let me look at my calendar for a moment...." This was an unnecessary step – Harriet always knew exactly what her calendar contained - but stemmed from years of habit: trying to make customers realize what a busy woman they were talking to. "Both Wednesday and Thursday mornings look open at this point, Mr. Myers. Shall we say ten o'clock? And do you need directions to my office?"

"No, thank you, Miss Slade. I will be able to find you. I will see you on Wednesday at ten o'clock. I look forward to meeting you. And again, my sincere condolences on your loss."

"All right, I will see you then. Good bye." Harriet ended the conversation rather abruptly, for someone who prided herself on perfect etiquette. It was not a quality she had learned in her mother's home, but she had decided early in her teenage years that she would rise above her family's status and create a persona that was above reproach. She had watched upper class women who came into the real estate office when Harriet was starting out as a typist, and she had memorized their speech patterns and way of walking until, imitating them, she could no longer be characterized as a working-class Polish immigrant. She had learned to sew from her mother and had found ways to recreate their elegant fashions from remnants, and had carefully cultivated a reputation as a stylish woman as a result. As the years went by, she worked even harder to maintain that image, even now when her clothes were store-bought. She had off-the-rack items meticulously altered to fit perfectly, and knew which fabrics, skirt lengths, and accessories were the most becoming to her rather short, stout, yes, matronly figure. She knew her success at real estate could be traced to many different factors, but didn't shortchange the less obvious ones.

Harriet tried to imagine what legal matter Mr. Myers could possibly have to discuss with her. She knew relatively little about her late brother – actually she knew little about all of her siblings, most of whom lived in the Cleveland area. One sister, Marta, lived in Sandusky, and Harriet only saw her at Marta's monthly visit to see their mother at Harriet's house. She hadn't been to Marta's apartment for years and they rarely spoke between visits. Theirs had never been what one would call a close family. But Roman – what had he done for a living? He worked for some mill or factory, didn't he? He had married young but his wife had died in childbirth, back before Harriet had graduated from high school. He took his baby and moved to the south side of Cleveland where a former classmate had told him there was work. But he hadn't been able to work 60 hours a week, as the job required, and care for a baby, so he had allowed his sister-in-law to adopt his daughter. After the baby's adoptive family had re-located to Pittsburgh, he had gradually lost track of the child. He figured she was better off in a household with a father, a mother, and two other children. But what happened to him after that? He worked, he had bought a small house in Parma, he went to church. That's about all she knew about him. Well, it's not as if he made an effort to see his own mother, she said to herself. It's not all my fault. We would get a Christmas card. He signed it, "Merry Christmas and Happy New Year, Roman."

The phone rang again. After two rings, Harriet answered.

"Are you coming home soon?" her mother asked.

"It's only one o'clock, Mother, I will be home as usual at five," she answered patiently. This was becoming a daily phone call.

"But it's dinner time."

"No, not yet, dear. There is chicken soup in the refrigerator from last night. All you need to do is heat it up in a saucepan for your lunch. Have you had a nap?"

"I'm not tired; I'm hungry. When are you coming home?" her mother persisted.

"Soon, I promise. I need to stop at the market to get some eggs and cabbage. Is there anything else you need?"

"Can we have ice cream?"

"All right. Strawberry, right?" Harriet smiled.

"Why can't we have chocolate?"

"We can. I thought you liked strawberry best."

"I like chocolate. You should know that."

"All right, Mother. Chocolate. I'll be home soon. Why don't you have some of that chicken soup?"

"I don't know where the pot is."

Harriet sighed. "I'll get it out for you tonight. Then you can heat up the soup tomorrow. Okay?"

"I wish you would come home."

Harriet decided she would close up the office and do just that. It was becoming more difficult to care for her aging mother and she knew the time was approaching when she wouldn't be able to handle it by herself. Not if she wanted to continue working. She shook her head with uncertainty. She wrote a detailed note to her secretary, Estelle, describing what had transpired in the office that morning, and the few chores left to be done. She added a suggestion that the office could close early that afternoon, giving the woman a few unexpected hours off. Then she shrugged on her black blazer, picked up her large black patent leather purse, locked her office door, dropped the note on Estelle's desk on the ground floor, and left. She got in her Cadillac and drove to the supermarket nearby. She picked up the food she needed and got in line at the checkout counter. While she waited, she idly read the headlines on the covers of the movie magazines prominently displayed where she could see them. At the last minute, she decided to buy one that featured an article about Sophia Loren, Harriet's idea of a beautiful woman.

At home, Harriet parked her car in the driveway and entered the house at the side door that led to the good-sized kitchen. There was a slot in the wall next to the door, with a sliding door on each side – outside and in – that was used every three days by the milkman. She would leave a note in it with her order and the delivery man would fill it and include an invoice. Today she took out a bottle of milk, a smaller bottle of cream, and a pound of butter, and carried them to the refrigerator. She grumbled to herself, as she almost always did, wondering why her mother couldn't perform this simple task, allowing the dairy products more time in the cold. But nothing she said persuaded her mother to bring in the milk, and so far, they hadn't gotten ill from whatever food poisoning seemed inevitable. She was grateful for the thick stone walls that enveloped the old house, figuring they held the cool temperatures better than the shingled walls of the newer, less sturdy houses people were building now.

Harriet had bought her house in the 1930s, when perfectly good houses came on the market because their owners couldn't keep up with the mortgage payments. She had felt vaguely guilty about cashing in on others' misfortunes but she reasoned that no one else would buy the house and it would eventually fall to a developer's wrecking ball. She lived alone at that time and since she was self-employed and she had been saving almost half her earnings in a safe in her office since she started working, she wasn't out of a job. Besides, Harriet was willing to live in the house without remodeling, and she only needed to furnish the living room, kitchen, and one bedroom. She was patient and extremely frugal, sewed her own clothes, walked or took the streetcar to get to work, and worked seven days a week if necessary. Her firm established a reputation as the first place to call when one needed housing. She would work tirelessly to find suitable rentals for down-and-out families as well as companies needing to downsize. She also was willing to spread out to surrounding towns in north-central Ohio, including farming communities and lake shore vacation towns.

By the time the country entered the war, Harriet was the go-to realtor for a hundred miles around. As the war ended, earnings increased, and people began to have expendable income. She found more and more of her business involved finding vacation rentals in towns like Cedar Point and Lakeside. Her commissions were steady if not sizeable, and her home gradually began to reflect her carefully cultivated taste. The stone walls were clean and well-pointed, the double front door included stained glass inserts, the grass was thick and green and led to large azaleas, rhododendrons and hydrangeas covering the huge foundations. The stone garage began to house a series of always sparkling clean late-model cars. Unlike her neighbors, Harriet rarely hired outside help, preferring to spend her money on the tools she needed to maintain her house herself. Weekends were spent – when not at the office – tending the lawn, sweeping the driveway, and watering the small flower garden beds in the back yard. Indoors, it was much the same – she dusted and vacuumed weekly, washed and waxed all uncarpeted floors, washed windows with crumpled newspaper and vinegar twice a year without fail, and rotated and flipped her mattress each time she changed the sheets. Of course, unlike her neighbors, she lived alone, without children or animals creating messes and she was meticulous in her personal habits so it was rare that a mess was created in the first place.

All that changed in 1955, when her mother's youngest child, Harriet's fifty-year-old brother Jan, finally found a wife, a job in Indiana, and an apartment, all in the space of six months. Harriet helped her mother, Celina Sladarnecki, move out of the flat she had rented for almost fifty years and brought her to her own house, which had, after all, five bedrooms. Her mother's furniture all fit in one of the larger bedrooms, which Harriet quietly found rather pitiful. The eighty-year-old woman was still healthy and strong. She had worked in a series of hair salons since she moved to Sandusky as a young widow. Starting out sweeping and laundering, she had eventually learned to shampoo, cut and color hair, and worked six days a week until the day she moved to her daughter's house. It seemed to Harriet that Celina's strength and mental clarity started to deteriorate that day. Lately it had slipped more rapidly as if the energy needed to stay alert had been turned down like a thermostat.

Celina had joined Holy Angels Church when she moved to Sandusky back in 1908 and she remained steadfastly loyal. She was a member of the women's auxiliary, she took her turn polishing the wooden pulpit, altar, and pews, baked countless batches of Polish dessert treats, and knitted basketsful of scarves and mittens for the poor. Harriet was now, to her annoyance, called upon to transport her mother to Mass every Saturday evening. She felt obliged to stay through the services and drive her home as well. She had managed to avoid the church of her childhood since she graduated from high school, and she was well pleased with that arrangement. There was something so illogical about Catholicism in the twentieth century, she thought. But her mother wouldn't hear of it. Harriet did have to admit she enjoyed helping Celina with the baking responsibilities, but she would have liked to just drop the bowtie cookies, babkas, and gingerbreads at the door of the parish hall and retrieve the pans after work on Monday afternoon.

Harriet had a tea tray ready for the Cleveland attorney. She always used her grandmother's precious silver implements when she had important client meetings. Somehow Celina had managed to keep the tray, coffee and tea pots, creamer and sugar bowl all through the move to America, even after she was widowed and during the hard times of the Depression. She allowed Harriet to use them in her business because she knew her daughter would care for them properly. She had made a batch of *kruscziki* the day before, so Harriet included them on the tray. Howard Myers was a little early for their appointment; he said the drive from Cleveland didn't take as long as he had planned.

"What can I do for you, Mr. Myers?" Harriet began after they had settled on the long sofa with their tea and cookies.

"Again, I want to apologize for breaking the sad news to you over the phone. I just assumed someone would have called you."

"My family is not close. I have called all of them since I heard from you. No one had been informed. When did Roman die?"

"Just last week. I wanted to be sure I had all the paperwork I needed before I talked with you."

"Why wasn't my mother informed?"

"I am so sorry, I was under the impression that Roman's mother was deceased." The lawyer was flustered with embarrassment.

"Well, she is very much alive. She lives with me. It would be a good idea for you to speak with her."

"Is she healthy?"

"Strong as an ox."

"May I assume she and her son were also not close?"

"My mother had seven children. They live all over the Midwest, but only one of them besides me sees her. We are not a close family. We get Christmas cards, maybe an occasional letter. We didn't know Roman was ill."

"Actually, he wasn't, until a couple of weeks ago. At his annual checkup, his doctor found a mass. It turned out to be stage four pancreatic cancer. He was gone in ten days. He wasn't in any pain until the last few days or so. His suffering was brief. You can take comfort in that."

"Thank you. My mother will be relieved."

"There is another matter that brings me here." Howard reached into his briefcase. He handed Harriet a letter in a sealed envelope.

"What is it?" asked Harriet.

"I don't know its contents, but your brother asked me to give it to you after his death."

Harriet looked at him quizzically but then went to her desk, took a letter opener out of a drawer, sat at the desk, opened and read her brother's letter.

'Dear Angelika, I hope this finds you well. I am dead. I want you to have my things. You are a good business woman and a good daughter. You can sell my house and keep whatever you want in it. I made a will and gave everything to you. Your brother, Roman.'

Harriet read the letter again, then looked at Howard Myers. "This is quite a surprise. He is giving me everything – his house and its contents. Permission to sell the house. Do you know where it is?"

"In Parma. He lived in it for forty years. We always met in my office – I don't know the condition of his home."

"Well, it's not likely to be much. If it's not in reasonably good condition, I may have to arrange to have it demolished."

"You might want to go through it carefully first."

"Why?"

"Miss Slade, how long has it been since you have seen your brother?"

"Oh, years and years. At least fifteen, maybe more. I've never been to his house."

"I have his will here, naming you as the sole beneficiary of his estate. I also have bank statements and I have a list of the contents of his safety deposit box and the key, which is now yours. He made arrangements for me to have all this as soon after his death as possible..... your brother was a wealthy man."

Harriet stared at him. The words could have been spoken by someone in the next room or on the street, wafting in through an open window. "How – I mean, what do you – uh, excuse me. This is rather unbelievable. Are you sure?"

"Quite sure. Roman was a gambler, did you know that?"

"No."

"Well, typical of many gamblers, there are days when you strike it rich and other days when you lose everything. Although he lost more than he won, he developed the habit of putting half his winnings in the bank. And he was, from time to time, quite lucky. He knew the horses, he was a good poker player, he even tried the lottery. Every time he thought he had it made, and was starting to look for a new house and car, he would find himself broke again, but he never forgot to make a deposit. Just before he became ill, he hit the jackpot at the race course and put that money in his safe deposit box. He kept me informed; he needed a lawyer to get him out of trouble from time to time. He was one of my more colorful clients."

Harriet shifted in her seat and took a deep breath. "Mr. Myers, there seems to be one fact you have missed. Roman had a daughter. Did you know that?"

"Roman told me that when he found out he was sick. Naturally, I was taken aback."

"Shouldn't she be the legal heir to his estate?" asked Harriet.

"Roman tracked her down. He had always known pretty much where she was. She had never married and was working in a hospital in Pittsburgh. She died a few months before he did, of complications of diabetes." Howard asked. "I take it you didn't know?"

"Of course I didn't know. I told you, I haven't been in touch with my brother. I had no idea about his daughter."

"Well, although I am sorry to deliver so much bad news about your family, she is no longer an issue for these purposes. The money, the house, it's all yours. I have papers to show you and we will need to meet again so you can sign the necessary ones. You might want legal representation. We are talking about quite a lot of money – over a million dollars. And the sooner you come to Parma to see the house and decide what to do with its contents, the better. You might want to sell it. I will leave you now with these papers," he said as he reached into his briefcase for a large pile of file folders, "and I recommend you read them all slowly and carefully. Write down any questions you have and call me at this number and I will do my best to answer them." He handed her a business card.

"Thank you, Mr. Myers. I appreciate your coming all this way to see me. This has all been quite a shock. I just don't know what to think." She stood up. "Don't forget your coat. Would you like to take a few cookies home to your wife? Are you sure? Well, drive safely. I will call you soon."

Harriet Slade took the glossy brochures out of her desk drawer and began to write notes on a legal pad. It was the dead of winter in Sandusky and there isn't much that is drearier, she reflected. The weather in northern Ohio is influenced greatly by Lake Erie. The lake effect can reduce the severity of a winter storm - but it can also do just the opposite and cause more snow to drop on shoreline areas than the rest of the state. It can make the winds so strong that walking across a road requires the strength that only the young possess. Streets can be reduced to parallel ruts that stripe the gray, crunchy, sandy stuff that fell originally as fluffy whirlwinds of snow. Sitting in her warm paneled office, Harriet preferred to look at the travel brochures than outside, as the weather deteriorated to a combination of snow and rain pelting diagonally past her bay window.

It had been six months since she learned the news of her brother's death and her inheritance. The months had been so filled with appointments, trips to Parma, and phone calls, that she had hired another realtor to handle clients at work. He was working out all right, she thought, although she found his manner a little too casual for her style. She had fixed up a large storage room for him to use for an office but she was displeased with the décor he had chosen for it. It involved a simple table instead of a proper desk, several metal filing cabinets, whose drawers didn't always close completely, an upholstered desk chair for himself and a pair of orange molded plastic chairs for clients. Orange plastic, she thought, how is that comfortable or welcoming? She shook her head. She must insist on furnishings that reflect the kind of business she had worked her whole life to establish. She would order new furniture herself.

The fact was, the business practically ran itself, with a staff of two realtors besides herself and one absolutely indispensable secretary. She was grateful for this fall and winter because it had taught her that she didn't have to hover like an anxious new mother over every call, every property, every client. Most of the business these days was rentals in vacation communities, and Estelle, her secretary of almost twenty years, knew all the returning clients almost as well as Harriet. She could make the necessary calls, create the necessary forms, hire the necessary contractors and get the necessary repairs made, without much help. Harriet had more than once suggested that Estelle take the real estate exam, but Estelle protested she was happy doing her work sitting at her desk, talking on her phone. She didn't really want to drive all over Ohio looking at houses and apartments and chatting up prospective tenants.

So, almost convinced of her firm's stability without her daily input, Harriet focused on her new status as a woman of means. She prudently chose a financial firm to invest the vast majority of her inheritance. She found nothing in Roman's depressing little house worthy of saving. It was a two bedroom cottage with faded shingles and a carport. She hired an odd-jobs man to help her go through the house, looking for anything of value or use and came up empty. She then put the house and property up for sale. A local developer called her within a day and made an offer of $12,000. She readily agreed, and within a few weeks, the house was demolished, with all its contents, and the lot was added to a new housing project going up all around it. She spent over half of the $12,000 in junk removal, legal fees and real estate transfer fees, not to mention the odd-jobs man.

However, there was plenty of money. More than she ever imagined having. It was a heady feeling, but it was also worrisome. She didn't tell anyone in her world about the money, not even her mother. The conversation with her mother about Roman had been difficult. "Mother, we need to talk about something. Put down your knitting, please."

"I can knit and talk at the same time."

"I know, dear, but this is serious and I want your full attention."

"Oh, all right. What is so important?"

"I had a meeting with a lawyer from Cleveland today. His name was Mr. Myers. He represented Roman."

"Why would Roman need a lawyer? That's ridiculous – he must be a crook."

"No, Mother, he wasn't a crook."

"How do you know? Mrs. Kowalski at the church was taken by one of those men. She lost everything and has to live with her niece. They look fancy and all, but they'll take everything you've got if you're not careful. I wouldn't invite a lawyer inside my house."

"Mother, listen to me. Mr. Myers told me that Roman is dead."

Celina stopped shaking her head and looked at Harriet with empty eyes. "What do you mean?"

"Mother, he had pancreatic cancer. He wasn't sick very long. He didn't suffer. He's gone, Mother."

"Pancreatic cancer? Does that hurt? Did he have an operation?"

"No, no operation. He was only sick for a couple of weeks. There was no time. He didn't hurt, Mother, he didn't even know he was sick until it was too late to be treated. I'm so sorry."

Celina's voice tapered to a thin, barely audible sound. "He was my first."

"I know, Mother. If you want, we can go to Parma and see his grave. We'll have to wait a little while for the headstone to be engraved, but I'll take you if you want to go."

"Roman? He was such a big man. Always so strong….. I'm getting old, aren't I?"

"We're all getting older, Mother. There's something else I want to tell you."

"Did another one die?"

"No, no one else has died. But the lawyer told me that Roman left everything he owned to me. There was a letter from him. I read it. He had some money and a house. I need to go to Parma to see if it's a house I can sell and to take anything I want out of it. Do you want to come with me?"

"And see his house........? No, I don't think so. He never invited me to see it while he was alive, why would I want to see it when he's dead?" Celina pulled a once-white handkerchief out of the cuff of her once-white cardigan sweater and dabbed at her eyes. "What's for dinner?" she asked her daughter.

March in Sandusky has little to recommend it, except for those rare days in which the odor of spring surprises with its warm, earthy undertones. Aware of the upcoming change of seasons, Harriet had begun to consider what it would be like to take a real vacation, something she had never allowed herself to do. One quiet Friday afternoon in late March, she picked up the phone, hesitated, put it down again. With new resolve, she picked up the receiver and dialed the number of the travel agency listed at the bottom of one of the glossy brochures she had been keeping in a dark corner of her desk drawer. When she hung up half an hour later, feeling breathless and a little lightheaded, she had booked a trip on a passenger ship to the south of France. All her life she had dreamed of the blue waters of the Mediterranean, the beaches of Nice, and the splendor of Monaco. She would be leaving in a month from New York and landing in Cannes. She knew she faced hours of phone calls to get ready, but the first was to her sister, Marta, who lived in nearby Lorain. It took some doing to get Marta to agree to let Celina come and stay with her and husband for a month. The couple was persuaded only after Harriet promised to pay all the expenses involved.

Harriet stood up from her desk, realizing she had been sitting down for close to two hours without a break. She went to her small anteroom and put a saucepan of water onto a hot plate to make tea. She busied herself with tea bags, warming the china teapot, taking cream and lemon out of the small refrigerator. When the tea was made, she carried her cup and saucer out to the main office and gazed out the bay window. The streets were drying from a morning rain and the moisture, added to the old snow still on the ground, had turned everything gray. The snow banks were a charcoal gray, verging on black, the pavement was a dark, streaked gray, the tree trunks and branches were a dull metal gray, the sky was overcast into a pale granite wall of unremitting gray. Even the evergreen branches were more like, well, "evergray." She smiled bitterly as she noted her own gray sweater and skirt; she hadn't realized she had dressed to match the city today. She turned back to the desk and picked up one of the brochures spread like playing cards on the desk. Provencal: a cultivated green hillside, lying at the feet of burnished mountains, and split by a deep blue snake-like stream, beckoned her to dream of faraway places that featured color, warmth, and light. She knew she had made the right decision.

The phone interrupted her thoughts. After two rings, she answered, "Harriet Slade. How may I help you?"

"Hello, Miss Slade. My name is Philip Fox. I am calling you because I have a cottage in Lakeside to put up for sale, and I am hoping you will handle it for me."

"Certainly, Mr. Fox. Are you by any chance related to Mrs. Lucretia Fox?"

"Yes, I am her son."

"Oh, how lovely. I am very fond of your mother. I hope she is well."

"Well, unfortunately, she is not doing as well as we would like. I have had to move her into a nursing home. She will no longer be able to manage her summer home in Lakeside. That's why I am calling you. It's her cottage that needs to be sold."

"The yellow one on Fourth Street? I can't imagine it without Mrs. Fox sitting on the porch. She's been there for how many years now?"

"She and my dad bought it in 1928. I grew up coming to Lakeside in the summer. I have my own place nearby."

"My, that is a long time. It will be strange to see others use it. Still, there are so many happy memories there, the new owners can't help but feel lucky."

"Thank you. That's a real nice thing to say. Can I meet you there some time to talk over what needs to be done to get ready to list it?"

"Of course. In the meantime, you can begin by removing as much of your mother's personal things as possible. These houses often sell furnished, but no one wants to see knickknacks or photographs or that sort of thing. Do you need references for people who can help you?"

"No, my kids and I can handle it - after I get permission to bring in a truck, but I plan to clear it out this weekend. Can I meet you there next week sometime?"

Harriet and Phil Fox made an appointment for the following Monday morning. The day dawned brightly, and although she was a few minutes early, she drove her Cadillac to the parking lot outside the gates, parked, and walked the four blocks to the Fox cottage. Even though cars were generally prohibited from Lakeside streets, in March, hardly anyone was around and no one would have noticed, but Harriet felt like walking. The yellow house on Fourth Street was similar to the other Victorian-era cottages surrounding it; square, two story, a brick chimney, a large screened-in porch facing the street, with a screened door on the side. Overgrown hydrangeas and yew bushes covered the sides of the house and some of the porch as well, and she noted a well-established wisteria vine crawling over the top of the porch and onto the roof. She could picture its pale purple blooms in May and June, and how they drip from the roof like fat bunches of grapes. Phil Fox arrived a few minutes later and together they went inside to look around. Harriet pulled her camel hair coat closer around her neck. There hadn't been any heat in the cottage since Labor Day Weekend. Even the sun shining brightly that day couldn't penetrate the interior rooms. There were a fireplaced living room, a bedroom, a kitchen and bathroom on the first floor, in addition to the large porch. Up the narrow staircase, there were two small bedrooms and a small dark hallway. There was a tiny back yard behind the kitchen with a clothesline stretched between two poles. It was clear that the Fox family had already removed books from bookcases, dishes from shelves, and toiletries from the bathroom. The porch had a large center table and two chintz-upholstered wooden rocking chairs, but the corners, although cobwebbed, were empty of fishing poles and life jackets.

"You have been working hard, Mr. Fox. I am impressed. I know this must have been difficult for you."

"A lot of memories, Miss Slade. Do you think this furniture is worth keeping?"

"It is best to let the buyers decide that. They may request that you remove more things as a condition of sale, but sometimes they are grateful to not have to buy so much at first."

"All right. Have you seen what you need to see? I am hoping we can sit down at Archie's in Port Clinton for coffee and you can tell me how to proceed from here. It's just too cold to do it here."

"That sounds fine. I will meet you there in half an hour."

Harriet and Phil reached an agreement about price and other considerations later that morning. She called her office from the café's pay phone and spoke with the secretary about starting the process of listing the little cottage. Deciding that everything she could do that day was done, she uncharacteristically decided to leave work early and go home.

"Mother? I'm home early," she called as she came in, trying not to alarm her mother.

No answer. "Mother? Are you upstairs?"

Still no answer. Harriet hung her coat on the peg in the kitchen entryway and went into the quiet house. Hearing nothing, she went upstairs. "Mother?" She went to her mother's closed bedroom door and knocked lightly. Silence. "Are you in the bathroom?" She knocked on the closed bathroom door. She could hear nothing. She went back to her mother's bedroom door and opened it. The room was dimly lit by the weak sun of a March afternoon. Usually there was a lamp lit next to her mother's rocking chair where she often spent her afternoons knitting, but no light was on. Harriet peered into the gloom. Seeing nothing, she walked in farther. After her eyes adjusted to the darkness, she saw something beyond the double bed. Approaching tentatively, she realized with a lurch in her heart that her mother was lying on the floor. "Mother! Can you hear me? Are you all right? Did you fall?" She fell to her knees next to her mother's face and noticed with relief that Celina was breathing.

"Can you hear me, dear? Can you open your eyes?" There was no response. Harriet was afraid to move her mother in case a bone was broken, so she stood up and grabbed the phone on the nightstand and called the doctor. "My mother is unconscious on the floor. I think we need an ambulance!" Assured by the nurse that an ambulance would be there soon, Harriet hurried downstairs to let them in. Although it felt like longer, the emergency crew arrived within five minutes and took her mother to Memorial Hospital on a stretcher. They assured her that Celina would be well cared for. She followed the ambulance to the hospital.

Harriet spent an anxious afternoon and evening in the emergency room waiting area. She read every magazine that had been left on the tables, but couldn't have said later what they were or what she had learned. Finally a surgeon came to speak to her.

"Your mother seems to have suffered a serious stroke. We have to perform surgery to ease the pressure in her brain from the bleeding. It is a delicate procedure and her age makes it somewhat more dangerous, but it is her only hope, I am afraid. We will need your permission to operate."

"You have my permission, doctor. When will she have the operation?"

"In about thirty minutes. It may take quite a while before we know if it was successful. After you fill out the paperwork, I would recommend you go home and get some rest. We will call you as soon as we know something."

The reality of Harriet's mother's death took some time to sink in. Although Celina and she had a relationship that could hardly be termed warm, and although Harriet had found her mother often to be irascible and demanding, still they had lived under the same roof for over seven years. Before Celina moved into her house, Harriet had visited faithfully every Sunday afternoon. She had learned to cook and sew and knit from her mother, skills she appreciated having. What parts of their Polish heritage Harriet had absorbed had come from her mother. It was hard to grasp the reality that once more she was living alone, no longer responsible for any life other than her own. She went through the motions of notifying her siblings, making funeral arrangements, buying a burial plot at the Holy Angels Church cemetery, and disposing of her mother's clothes and other belongings. She needed to take a leave of absence from the real estate business and noted with some discomfort that it continued to thrive without her daily involvement.

One early April afternoon when the sun suddenly felt warm, effectively changing the world from winter to spring, when the gray mounds of dirty snow were gone from every space except the most shaded ones, when crocuses had pushed their way through to the light of day, adding purple, yellow and white accessories to the neighborhood's light green dress, and when the smell of mud mingled with the scent of new grass, Harriet felt the call of Lake Erie, and decided to take a short drive. She added a warm cardigan sweater to her day dress, instead of her heavy winter coat, and took a drive to Lakeside. She had always enjoyed strolling the streets of the vintage Chatauqua community, where the vicissitudes of modern society seemed to bounce off the hedges and fences and disappear back to where they came from. Charming cottages, old, gnarled trees, the large and rambling Victorian-era hotel, wide lawns sloping to the sparkling lake water – it all seemed like a cherished childhood bedtime story. She wanted to think about where the rest of her life was heading, and the clarity of the day seemed to her to be a good omen for the clarity of thought she craved. When her mother died, Harriet had reluctantly cancelled her travel plans, and since that day had been living one day and one task at a time. Today was the day to shake off the cobwebs she had been festooned with, and take stock.

Harriet found herself on Fourth Street and stopped in front of the little yellow cottage with her company's For Sale sign sitting at a precarious tilt on the strip of mud in front. She straightened the sign and looked in the porch windows. Nothing seemed to have changed since the last time she was here. She thought of Cree Fox who had sat on this porch every summer day for the last thirty-seven years. Such a wonderful woman – straight and tall, beautiful in an almost masculine way and blessed with the most glorious white hair – and well known as a forthright, opinionated person who could be counted on for a disarmingly honest response to any question worth answering. Harriet knew she would miss Cree whenever she passed this house. She wondered whether anyone had seen the cottage yet – she was uncomfortable with how far out of the business loop she had become. Was there something they should do to show the house better? She decided to contact a landscaping contractor to tame the shrubs and wisteria, now that spring had begun. Her thoughts were interrupted by a woman's voice.

"Hello? Are you interested in looking at the house? I can get you in touch with the agency," the woman said as she approached Harriet. "It's a darling cottage. I am sure you would like the inside. I live next door."

"Oh, I am so sorry. My name is Harriet Slade. It is my agency that is handling the house. I was just passing by and got curious. I didn't mean to disturb your afternoon. It's such a lovely day."

"Oh, of course! I should have recognized you. I'm Ida Green. I have seen you in town before but we've never met." Ida was taller than Harriet, and slimmer. She was wearing well-tailored khaki slacks and a simple navy blue blouse, and had added a navy cardigan over her shoulders for warmth. On her feet she wore navy leather flats, Harriet noticed, thinking they were probably expensive, and looked brand new.

She had an engaging smile and a glorious head of gray-sparkled thick dark brown hair. She had a short apron tied around her waist. "I was actually in the midst of making bread when I saw you walking around the cottage. I am so glad you gave me an excuse to come outside. What a stupendous afternoon!"

"You are here early in the season. Do you live in Lakeside year round?" Harriet asked politely. She was accustomed to learning about the people she met; it was part of her success in real estate.

"No, I live in Cleveland Heights most of the year. But I have been coming to Lakeside earlier and earlier the last few years. It is the place where I am truly happy, so I wonder, why put it off until Memorial Day?"

"Do you have family with you?"

"Not any more. My children have grown up and left Ohio; my husband died three years ago."

"I am so sorry to hear it. You must miss him terribly," said Harriet, sincerely. There was something about this woman she liked. Ida's dark brown eyes sparkled in the sunlight and were surrounded by creases that deepened when she smiled, a wide, welcoming smile.

"Oh, thank you, but I am used to it now. To tell you the truth, living alone seems to suit me. I can do exactly as I please, eat what I want when I'm hungry, and sleep until I wake up. I keep very busy with all kinds of projects, see friends when I can. It's actually a good life. What about you, Miss Slade? Do you live nearby?"

"Please, call me Harriet." She was surprised to hear herself say it. She had always maintained a kind of formality in relationships and rarely encouraged anyone to call her by her first name. "I live in Sandusky but I do a great deal of business here, so I spend more time in Lakeside every year. I am quite drawn to it. When I smelled the spring air this afternoon, something told me to drive here."

"Well, Harriet, I am glad you came. Listen, would you like a cup of tea? I need to punch down my bread dough and I would love some company on this lovely day."

She hesitated. She had little experience with casual friendships, having been almost consumed by her business since she started it in the 1920s. There were acquaintances through work, especially at Rotary and Chamber of Commerce functions, and her mother's circle of friends at church, and of course neighbors who stopped to chat sometimes on a Saturday when everyone was outside doing yard work. But Harriet had little time, she thought, for the kind of friend you call when you want to go out for dinner or to a movie. "That would be charming. Thank you for asking," she answered, thinking maybe it was time to relax and see what having a friend felt like. Maybe it was time to give up the constant diligence at the office; maybe it was time to spend some of the money she had inherited on entertainment and adventure just for herself. Maybe that's what she was supposed to figure out on this sunnily optimistic day in this quaint, out-of-this-world little town.

Harriet and Ida chatted comfortably for more than two hours. Harriet had never spent an entire afternoon with someone who had nothing to do with business or family, and found the experience to be nothing short of exhilarating. They found many areas of common interest, and Harriet laughed easily at Ida's stories of the eccentricities of the town she had been keenly observing for years. Quirky residents. Tourists looking for the kind of vacation you can find at, say, Disneyland or Coney Island, and their surprise when they found Lakeside instead. Older residents dealing with some of the more rambunctious children. The way so many residents cleverly concealed their drinking of alcoholic beverages so the Methodist minister could remain blissfully ignorant of such goings-on. It was a delightful afternoon and she was reluctant to say good-bye to this fascinating woman, but didn't want to overstay her welcome.

"Good-bye, again, Ida, and thank you for such a pleasant visit. I can't remember when I have laughed so much," she said at the door.

"Oh, I enjoyed it so much. I wish you would come back and visit again soon. Oh, wait just a minute! I want to share some of the bread with you. It's just done."

"How wonderful. I would love to visit again," said Harriet, hoping she didn't sound too pushy.

"How about we make a date for later this week? Can you stay for dinner? I love to have someone to cook for," said Ida.

"Well, I would love that. My calendar is open. What night would work for you?"

"Wednesday?"

"Wednesday it is. Shall I come at 6:00? And I will bring some wine. White or red?"

"We'll no doubt be having fish. White would be perfect."

And thus began a series of increasingly lengthy visits between Harriet Slade and Ida Green, usually in Lakeside. Their friendship deepened quickly as they found it easy to talk about a wide variety of topics, and a mutual love of walking through the town in spring weather, when it wasn't terribly hot and the number of people was relatively few. Harriet woke in the mornings now with a sense of expectation that carried her through the spring days with a newfound feeling of pleasure. It was a feeling that was so new to her, she didn't have a name for it. She only knew that she looked forward to her next date with Ida and her pulse quickened when she thought of it. One day in mid-May she called Estelle at the office.

"Harriet Slade Realty. May I help you?"

"Hi, Estelle. It's Harriet. I have a question," Harriet began.

"Oh, hello, Miss Slade! I am glad to hear from you! How are you doing?"

"Very well, my dear, thank you. I want to know whether anyone has made an offer on the little yellow house on Fourth Street in Lakeside."

"No, Miss Slade, but several people have asked to rent it out."

"Mr. Fox wants to sell."

"I know, but it needs a lot of work, and so far no one has been willing to take it on. Do you know a prospective buyer?"

"Actually, I can't believe I am saying this, but I am thinking of buying it myself."

"Really! What a great idea! I can see you living in Lakeside; you have always loved it there," cried Estelle, who was surprised to her core. She had always believed there was nothing remotely spontaneous about her employer.

"Can you please line up an appraiser and a building inspector to come to see it with me? I need to find out what I would be getting myself into," said Harriet.

"Sure! Let me know what they say," said Estelle, before hanging up.

Harriet decided to officially retire. She needed time and energy to renovate and re-model the house in Lakeside, which had not been updated for more than thirty years. It needed a new kitchen, a new bathroom, new floors, new plumbing and wiring, a heating system beyond a drafty fireplace, and comfortable furniture. She wanted it to be insulated and the foundation needed shoring up. The back yard needed new sod and a small flower bed, and she wanted new window boxes all along the front porch so she could indulge her pleasure in growing annuals like zinnias, petunias, alyssum and lobelia. Ida helped her shop for household items and together they created a space that suited Harriet more than her house in Sandusky ever had. At least it suited the new, modern Harriet, the Harriet who opened windows wide every morning to let in the fresh, clean air, the Harriet who hummed while she did chores inside or out, the Harriet who was learning to cook savory soups and stews and wonderful combinations of fresh vegetables, the Harriet who seemed suddenly to prefer bright floral fabrics and crisp, pastel blouses, and the one who had discovered the comfort of wearing slacks instead of dresses. Everything about her seemed lighter and more casual.

She spent so much time in Lakeside that eventually she closed up the Sandusky house and planned to stay away until the weather forced her out of her summer home. The Lakeside house was mostly livable while the contractors worked, and when it wasn't, she went next door to Ida's. They always had a jigsaw puzzle to work, they played gin rummy on the porch, they cooked together, teaching each other new dishes and creating better meals than could be found in many Ohio restaurants. Ida introduced Harriet to other women – and some men – in the little town and they joined their friends on the pier some hot afternoons for cards and conversation. They even swam in the lake once or twice, although Harriet was hardly a strong swimmer. Still, the water was refreshing when the weather was hot and humid, and Ida always made her feel that whatever she did and however she did it, she was good enough. Better than good enough. The summer days were long and lazy, and filled with their companionship.

By August of that summer, Harriet wanted to be with Ida every day, and she usually was. It was the best summer of her life so far. She wanted it to last forever. Her house, when it was finished in late August, made her giddy. She often stopped in the midst of a room for no reason, just to look. Almost every decorating decision reflected Ida's influence. Her kitchen was now designed for a serious cook, even though it was still small, and the bathroom was bright, modern, and included a large shower stall.

The only room she hadn't completed by the first weekend in September was her bedroom. There was a double bed and a small dresser, on a hooked rug, that Cree Fox had used. Harriet decided one sultry morning to shop for bedroom furniture. She carried her coffee cup to Ida's porch, checking to be sure the pastor wasn't coming down Fourth Street on his morning constitutional. Methodists disapproved of coffee, among other beverages.

"Morning! I'm on the porch!" she cried out to announce her arrival.

"Hi, be right down!" answered her friend from the bedroom upstairs.

"May I warm up my coffee?"

"Of course, I always make enough for both of us."

Harriet went into the cheery kitchen, decorated with red and white gingham curtains and a rooster motif carried out in canisters, dishes, ceramic figures, and even the wallpaper border around the top of the walls. As she went to get more coffee, she gently touched the terry cloth apron hanging on the oven handle. It felt soft and strong at the same time, she thought. The rooster design on the front was faded from years of laundering but it was clean. Harriet looked at the percolator but didn't really see it as she let her mind focus on this humble apron. Soft, strong, well-used, cheerful, clean. Just like Ida, she thought. She picked it up and held it to her cheek, her eyes closing. She took a deep sniff. It smelled of spices and detergent, a pleasant smell. This is how happiness feels, she said to herself. This is how contentment smells. Ida came into the kitchen and gazed at her friend for a full minute before speaking.

"Good morning," she said gently.

"Oh! I didn't hear you come in. Good morning." Harriet put the apron on the stove top, flustered.

"There are some cinnamon rolls from Jenny's on the table. Help yourself."

"You are trying to make me even fatter! I had an egg, I'm fine."

"You are not fat. I think you look perfect just as you are. That blouse is so becoming on you."

"Well, thank you for your dishonesty."

"What shall we do today?" asked Ida, gesturing dismissively.

"Well, I think it's time I finally do the bedroom. I'm thinking it's time to go to Toledo and buy a bedroom set. Want to come with me?"

"Oh, goodie! Let's go soon. We can have lunch at that new Italian place."

Harriet and Ida spent the day happily shopping. They tried to think of everything Harriet would need so that they wouldn't have to spend another day away from their beloved town. The days were getting noticeably shorter and they were all too aware that the summer would end sooner than they wanted. It was exhilarating, Harriet thought, to be able to order everything you wanted for a room and just write a check, knowing there was enough money. For a woman whose girlhood had been spent in poverty and whose early working years had been made frighteningly uncertain by the Great Depression, having money was a new experience for which she had no training. She had never explained her financial windfall to Ida, whose own lifestyle indicated similar good fortune. Perhaps she should take Ida into her confidence about money, she mused. By late afternoon, all the purchases they could think of were completed, and they got into Harriet's Cadillac to drive back to Lakeside. Deliveries were all scheduled for the next day, but they had plenty of bags of smaller items to put into the car's spacious trunk.

"Whew. What a whirlwind. I hope we thought of everything," said Ida, sinking into the plush leather seat and leaning her head back on the headrest.

"Me, too. I think the room is going to look beautiful. Thank you for your help. I couldn't have picked out such nice things without your very good taste."

"Oh, I think we make a good decorating team, don't you?" smiled Ida.

"I do, indeed. The only thing I still worry about is that bed. Are you sure it will fit in the room? It seemed so big to me."

"Harriet, we measured, remember? It's going to be fine. And so comfortable. You will thank me later, I promise you. Queen size beds are the newest thing. If you ever decide to rent the place, tenants are going to want a queen size bed. It just makes sense."

"You're right. I'm being silly. Gosh, this traffic is heavy."

"It's rush hour. And a Friday. Everybody in Toledo is trying to get away to the lake for Labor Day Weekend. We'll just have to relax and sit it out….. At least we're together," said Ida, looking fondly at Harriet.

Harriet returned her gaze. "Sometimes I can't believe I have only known you for four months. It feels as if I have known you almost all my life."

"I know. Was it only this past April?"

"The third."

"Yes, the third. It was the most heavenly spring day. You were peeking in the windows of the Fox place."

"It's the Slade place now."

"Right you are. And it is so lovely, I want to visit every day. What a transformation!"

"We did it together. I never could have managed alone. What a treasure you are to me…"

"We're next door neighbors. Who would have believed?"

"It's the best thing that has ever happened to me, and I mean that," Harriet said solemnly.

"And to me. I pretended I wasn't lonely. I almost had myself convinced, but then I met you and our friendship has filled the void. I feel completely content," said Ida, smiling at her.

"I love having a friend."

"I love having you as a friend."

"I love you."

Ida turned to her and just looked. A silence. Harriet kept her eyes on the road ahead, though the cars were scarcely moving. Her heart was pounding in her ears and her mouth was completely dry. She didn't know whether she was hungry or slightly nauseated but her stomach felt the way it did before she had to recite in school, years ago. She wanted to look at Ida but was afraid of what she would see in her dear friend's eyes.

"Do you mean that?" Ida asked quietly.

"Yes."

"Like a sister?"

"No."

"Like a best friend?"

"More."

"More?" Ida repeated.

"Much more," Harriet answered, daring to glance at Ida.

"Are you sure?"

"Yes." Harriet could hardly breathe.

"I love you, too," whispered Ida.

"Oh, God, I don't know what to do," Harriet whispered back.

"Keep driving. I want to go home. With you."

After a pause, Harriet said, "Dearheart, have you ever been to the south of France?"

Missing in Lakeside
1966

Little Janie O'Reilly's disappearance lasted for one terrifying afternoon. It started out as most Lakeside summers did; by Memorial Day weekend, houses were welcoming their summer occupants, long-time neighbors were greeting each other and filling each other in on news, the sound of hammers signaled that owners were doing small repair jobs in preparation for tenants. Window boxes were filled with fresh, new flowers that would last the summer, like cheerful red geraniums mixed with reliably white Dusty Millers. Fishermen filled their tackle boxes with ties they had been fashioning in their garages and dens during the gray winter months in northern Ohio. Volunteers in organized patrols swarmed over the small town on clean-up duty, bagging the winter's debris and mulching the public gardens. A group of Trustees had formed a committee to re-paint the Convention Center's windows and trim. There was a palpable bustle and hum around the town. Summer had returned and Lakesiders were getting ready.

Tim and Gigi O'Reilly usually came to Lakeside for two weeks including the Fourth of July holiday, a vacation they had been sharing with Toledo friends, for some ten years now. Their children, Timmy, Benny, and Janie, were all in school since Janie had reached kindergarten age. But this year, Timmy had a part-time job after school and in the summer in Toledo. They decided to try coming instead for the three main summer holiday weekends: Memorial Day, Fourth of July, and Labor Day. Gigi had her doubts that three-day weekends would make her feel as refreshed as a two-week vacation always had. But she wasn't about to leave Timmy home alone, even though she was proud he had taken a job as an assistant to a Certified Medical Technologist at the University of Toledo Medical Center. There was also no chance that they would stop vacationing in the little Chatauqua community. Although it was not far from their home, it felt like stepping into the past, sepia tinted and comfortably worn. Tim and Gigi were able to be less rigid with the children. The whole family relaxed.

Of course they had to rent a different house than the one they were used to, and they had to change houses from one weekend to another. But any of the Victorian-era, usually run-down cottages in Lakeside were acceptable – they were all furnished and equipped for a family summer vacation on Lake Erie. Tim and Gigi had friends nearby everywhere they rented. The town was very small. Everybody knew everybody after a couple of years. That's one of the reasons they kept coming back.

When they arrived for the Fourth of July weekend, they were pleased with the house they had rented. It had four bedrooms upstairs and a large sleeping porch. It had both a glassed-in porch on the street level and a screened-in one. It had a larger kitchen than they were used to in Lakeside, and there were bathrooms on both floors, a real luxury. The furniture on the main floor was suitably shabby. Nothing matched. But there were enough chairs for them all to use in the living room and a wonderful swing that hung in the screened-in porch. There was a small front yard and an even smaller back yard, but Lakeside was filled with play spaces of all kinds, and children were free to go wherever they wished with no fear. Parents allowed their children to roam freely, knowing that the town boundaries were walled and gated, the swimming area at the lake was staffed with lifeguards, there was plenty to do, and someone was always watching the children. Parents often found out what kind of trouble their kids got into before the kids showed up for dinner.

Timmy and Benny rarely caused their parents much grief. They were good boys, brought up to obey family rules and treat others fairly. They loved Lakeside. They never wanted to do anything that would jeopardize the annual vacation there. They enjoyed swimming and fishing, pick-up baseball games on various empty lots, riding their bikes through the sleepy streets, and even shuffleboard, which was a favorite game of Lakesiders of all ages. The day the O'Reilly family arrived, after carrying suitcases and bags of groceries into the house, Timmy and Benny jumped on their rented bikes and with barely a backward glance, took off for the lake. The house was on Fifth Street, four blocks from the water. Everything was so close together in town that four blocks hardly mattered. The entire town was barely one mile square, and laid out on a grid. It was virtually impossible to get lost. Tim and Gigi had plenty to do to set up the cottage to their liking – moving furniture, wiping down the porch tables, putting fishing equipment in the corner of the porch, putting food away in the refrigerator, cupboards and shelves. Gigi had baked coffeecake for the next morning and she had carried it in carefully from the car. Tim made several trips back and forth from the town's parking lot at the entrance gate until he had brought in everything. He found Janie eating a snack of grapes and crackers at the kitchen table.

"That's everything, I hope," called Tim to Gigi, who was upstairs making beds with the linens she had brought from home.

"Thanks, honey. Listen, can you take Janie out for a walk? She didn't sleep in the car. Maybe some fresh air would tire her out and she would take a little nap."

"Okay. Isn't she getting kind of old for a nap?"

"I don't care. I'm not ready for her to give it up. It's the only peaceful time of my day," Gigi called out.

Tim looked at his daughter at the table, deep in concentration over her food. "Hey, monkeyface, how 'bout we go for a walk?"

"Okay, Daddy. Can we go to the lake?" said the little blond girl, brightening.

"Maybe later we'll all go down and see how cold the water is. But let's wait for the boys to come back. You and I can go see the wishing well, whaddaya say?"

"Can I make a wish?"

"You betcha. Do you need to go potty before we leave?"

Janie obligingly used the little bathroom off the kitchen while Tim cleaned up her snack. They left the cottage holding hands and walked south toward the woods at the outskirts of town. They passed cottages built so close together that one could reach out a window and touch the neighbor's wall. Most were occupied, a few still closed up as in the winter. There was the high-pitched sound of young children laughing and shouting. An elderly couple, coming back from the lake, stepped carefully, arm in arm. The man was carrying a small paper bag with handles, that had the word "Jenny's" on the outside, which is how Tim knew they had just come from the small market in town. "Afternoon," he said, nodding to them. They smiled and stopped to speak to Janie.

"Hello, there. Are you going for a swim today?" asked the woman.

"Maybe," said Janie softly, leaning closely against her father's leg.

"Well, have fun!"

After the couple had moved beyond hearing distance, Tim decided to make a suggestion to his cherished daughter. "Honey, the next time someone speaks to you, I want you to look them in the eye and say 'How do you do?'"

"Why?" asked the little girl.

"It's just good manners. And it will help you feel less shy. You look them in the eye and say 'how are you?' And if I or Mommy introduces you to them, you use their name. You say, 'How are you, Mrs. Jones? Or 'How are you, Mr. Brown?'" Janie giggled at the high pitched voice Tim used to pretend he was she. "That way, you will remember their name the next time you see them. And when you do see them again, then you say, "Hi, Mrs. Brown, it's nice to see you today."' And Mrs. Brown will tell everybody that Janie O'Reilly is just the nicest girl in Lakeside. Which I already knew. I just want everybody else to know it, too."

"Okay, Daddy." Janie looked doubtful.

Father and daughter walked – well, Janie mostly skipped, practicing a newly-mastered skill - to the outskirts of the town, where there was a park used for picnics and parties. Near the edge of the woods, at the bank of a small stream, there was a huge weeping willow tree that for decades had offered shade and a cozy backrest for people reading a summer novel. Near the tree, there was the old wishing well. Tim imagined that it had once been a working well for use by picnickers in the early Victorian days of the summer community, but these days it was mostly empty. The bottom of the well, which could be seen if the rays of the sun were shining at just the right angle, sometimes held a few inches of rainwater. But what was more easily visible were the thousands of coins, mostly pennies, glinting copper, silver, bronze and black at the bottom of the well. Janie asked her dad for a penny.

"Sure, honey. What are you going to wish for?"

"Timmy says I shouldn't tell. He says my wish won't come true if I tell. Like on my birthday cake."

"Well, that's right. Timmy told you right. Don't tell me. Just close your eyes and wish real hard. Then throw in the penny."

Janie tossed the penny so hard it went over the well and into the long grass behind it. "Oh, I lost my wish!" she cried.

"Here's another penny, pumpkin. No problem," said Tim, reaching into his pocket.

"No! I need that one! Or my wish won't come true!" Janie ran behind the well to search for the lost coin. Tim looked up to see a group of people walking into the park. Obviously there was a planned event for the afternoon. Tim spotted and waved to one or two long-time Lakesiders that he knew, although the group was mostly older than he. He suspected that they were all members of the same church and had come to the picnic grounds for some kind of religious service. Lakeside often hosted religion-based groups; indeed, the town was founded for just that purpose. The O'Reillys were members of their local Catholic parish but not regular in attendance. They came to Lakeside to vacation, and that was all.

Among the group was a couple that had lived a few houses down from Tim and Gigi the previous summer, Paul and Patricia Prosser. They had been pleasant neighbors, Tim remembered, but were rather serious and straight-laced. They took the Methodist-inspired "rules" of the town literally, and there was no drinking of alcohol or caffeine at their cottage; no card playing, either. They went to bed early and were easily annoyed by loud partying. Tim and Gigi had decided to have their parties at friends' cottages that summer. But there was no avoiding them now; Tim greeted them warmly.

"Nice to see you guys. Are you in the same house as last year?"

"Yes. It's just perfect for us. I'm surprised to see you. We thought you weren't coming this year," said Patricia with a smile.

"We're over on 5th street. We could only come for the long weekend. Timmy has a job this summer and we didn't want to leave him home alone," explained Tim.

"Good for you. I hate to see kids with too much responsibility when they aren't old enough to handle it. Not that Timmy is immature, he's just young, that's what I mean," said Paul.

"Timmy says he wants to go to medical school, so he's going to need to get used to working hard – and helping with his tuition," Tim explained with a laugh. He noticed a young man with a guitar was setting up under the trees at the shady side of the picnic area. He had an amplifier and some kind of generator, so Tim figured there was going to be some hymn singing soon. He decided it might be a good idea to get home. He turned to the wishing well to get Janie.

"Hey, monkeyface, where are you?" he called out.

Tim walked to the well and went behind it, looking for his little girl. But he didn't see her anywhere. "Janie? Honey? Where'd you go? We should get back now."

He walked around the willow tree and looked into the woods beyond. Turning back toward the picnickers, he searched the group for any sign of a five year old. There were no young children in the congregation so he figured she would be easy to spot. "Janie?" he called out. A few people looked up at him.

"Lose somebody?" asked a middle aged man, his red face and shiny forehead a contrast to his white golf shirt barely tucked into madras plaid Bermuda shorts. The shirt had evidently been bought when he weighed twenty pounds less than he did today.

"My daughter, Janie. She's around here someplace. I need to get her home and out of your way. Are you guys having a church service?"

"Yes, we're on retreat this weekend. What is she wearing? I could help you look."

"Thanks. She's wearing, uh, shorts, I think, and some kind of t-shirt. I honestly don't remember. She's just a little kid. The only one here, it looks like. Janie! Where the heck are you?"

A few other congregants stopped their conversations and looked at Tim with friendly curiosity. The minister, identifiable because he wore a white clerical collar under a black short sleeved shirt, called to Tim, "Can we help?"

"Has anyone seen a little blond girl? She was just here a minute ago. Her name's Janie. She's my daughter."

There was murmuring among the people. Some of them walked into the area surrounding the picnic grounds and began to look around. Occasionally a voice called out "Janie!" The group fanned out wider and wider, but no one spotted the child. Tim was aware that his heartbeat was faster and he was beginning to perspire heavily. Where was that kid? Tim walked quickly all around the perimeter of the area, looked down into the wishing well and the stream more than once, looked up into the branches of the willow tree, and then went crashing into the dense woods. Although the air there was ten degrees cooler, he felt only the heat and the sweat on his face. He called out Janie's name every few seconds and stopped to listen for a response. Nothing. He could picture Gigi, happily resting in a comfortable chair on the screened in porch, enjoying the respite of a house with no children in it. What would she say if he came home without their daughter? What would he say if this had happened while Gigi was in charge of the girl? Tim returned to the picnic grounds. Most people had sat at picnic tables by now and were preparing to listen to the pastor, but when they saw Tim, they looked concerned.

"Have you found your little girl?" asked an elderly woman, wearing a large-brimmed hat to shield her face from the sun.

"No, I haven't. I'm sorry to interrupt but I think I could really use some help here," said Tim rapidly.

"Let's fan out and search the woods. Let's try to get organized so every area is checked. She could have fallen and hurt herself," said one of the men. At least ten men joined him. They quickly chose the area each of them should cover, and struck out to comb the woods for Janie. Tim felt some relief and enormous gratitude at their willingness to help find his daughter. He spoke to the pastor.

"I'm really sorry. I know you have a service to conduct," Tim said, although he wasn't looking at the cleric's face; he was scanning the area for a glimpse of Janie.

"Well, it can wait a while," he replied, "and we certainly want to help if we can. I'm sure she's not but a few feet away from here. Maybe she's hiding from you, for fun."

"Maybe," said Tim, with doubt in his voice and his heart. Janie wasn't that kind of kid. A father knows his children.

Gigi O'Reilly was already enjoying her vacation. At home in Toledo, she was the busy mother of three active children and also a teacher's aide in the local elementary school. She gladly took the job when her little girl started kindergarten, mostly because she wanted to keep an eye on Janie. Janie was a kind of surprise child; Tim and she had thought they were finished having children after the birth of their second son, now fourteen. Her obstetrician had warned Gigi against having more children after Benny was born. He had to be taken by Caesarian section and the labor and birth had been very hard on Gigi. However, birth control was frowned upon by their local priest and was hard to come by in any case. She had discovered she was pregnant two years after Benny, and worried constantly about what she was facing. She lost weight when she should have been gaining; she found it difficult to sleep more than a few hours a night. After four months, she suffered a miscarriage. Gigi went into a deep depression. She and Tim doubled their efforts to avoid another pregnancy. Lakeside was the one place where Gigi felt happy in those days, so they prioritized its expense in their annual budget, knowing how important it was for the whole family. Then in 1960, Gigi discovered, to her surprise, that she was expecting another baby. On the advice of her obstetrician, and with Tim's devotion, she was able to curtail her activities to the bare minimum - and carry the baby to term. Her doctor scheduled a Caesarian, which was standard practice after having had one previously, and Janie was born quickly and without undue discomfort, a healthy, chubby little girl. Gigi and Tim considered her birth to be a miracle. The boys adored her on sight; the pretty blond girl was a treasured child.

Gigi sighed and took a sip of iced tea. She had changed into clean shorts and had left her shirt untucked; her light brown hair had been pulled back into a ponytail, and her feet were bare. She closed her eyes and listened to the sounds of Lakeside. Gulls barking like dogs, children shouting in the distance, lawn mowers, laughter, a neighbor's transistor radio playing the Beach Boys. She could smell beef on someone's barbeque grill, freshly cut grass, and some kind of fuel, perhaps from an outboard motorboat. She anticipated with pleasure the ice cream cones they would walk to Walnut Avenue to get later, and the feel of Lake Erie water, bracingly cold, on her feet when they went to the pier to watch the boys swim. Maybe this will be the summer Janie learns to swim, or at least goes underwater, Gigi mused.

Her reverie was interrupted by a knock on the screen door. "Hello, Mrs. O'Reilly! May I interrupt your nap?"

Gigi opened her eyes to see Harriet Slade at the door, smiling. Harriet was wearing a white sleeveless shirt tucked into belted khaki slacks, and brilliantly white sneakers and socks. Her blond, tightly coiffed hairdo was covered by a colorful silk scarf, tied under her chin. She was carrying a large white patent leather purse which looked out of place with the rest of the outfit. Harriet was a short, squat woman who had only taken to wearing pants, or anything other than business-like dresses, recently, largely as a result of her retirement from the real estate business. Somehow, she always managed to look like she was a spinster schoolmarm or someone's widowed aunt, no matter what she wore.

"Miss Slade! So nice to see you again. Come in! I have iced tea. Will you join me?" Gigi sat up and beckoned Harriet to come in.

"Well, if it's no trouble, that would be nice. It is a hot one out there."

Gigi went to the kitchen and poured a glass of tea and put in lots of ice cubes. "Sugar?" she called from the kitchen.

"Oh, just a little, thanks."

Gigi took a moment to tuck her sleeveless, flowered camp shirt into her white shorts and stick her tanned feet into a pair of faded canvas shoes. On the porch, Harriet removed her scarf carefully and tucked it into her bag. She sat on the porch swing and smiled to herself as she did. Gigi returned to the porch. "I haven't sat on one of these in a while. I wish I had thought to put one in my porch when I remodeled. They are so relaxing," she said when Gigi handed her the tea and sat back down.

"They are. I think it's the best thing about this house. Have you been here before?"

"No, this is the first time I have seen this one. It's lovely. Nice and big for your family. I was surprised you had moved. I remember helping you find your other rental on Second Street."

"I know. We miss that house. But this summer we can't stay for two weeks. We're only here for the long weekend, so we had to find something else. This was the only place available with three bedrooms. It's more money than we wanted to spend but -- you know how we love it here, so we just bit the bullet and here we are! How are you, Miss Slade?"

"Oh, you know me. Just fine and dandy. I've taken to walking around town and looking at cottages. Can't help it. I just look and think about how much they would sell for, or what a good rental price would be, or what kind of family would fit best, things like that. Old habits die hard, don't they? This is the first time this summer I have been on this end of Fifth Street, and I was delighted to spot you on the porch. I hope I didn't wake you."

"No, I was just enjoying the peace and quiet. Tim is out with Janie, and Timmy and Benny are swimming, I guess. It's not usually like this. But I'm so glad to see you."

Gigi was about to continue when Tim appeared outside. He had been running, she could see.

"Honey? What's up? Where's Janie?"

Tim didn't bother to come in the porch. Panting for breath, bent over at the waist, hands on his thighs, he answered his wife. "I can't find Janie. I've been looking everywhere."

Gigi peered at him through the screen. There was a pause. "Tim O'Reilly, if you are joking, that isn't very funny."

"Not joking. Janie's missing."

Marianne Colby was walking as fast as she could, which wasn't easy with two children in tow, one holding each of her hands. "C'mon, kids, let's hurry now!" she urged them. Mark, the older, was actually pulling his mother, but the smaller blond girl was slowing down. "Where are we going?" she asked.

"Home, of course, sweetie. It's getting late and I have to start dinner," Marianne answered her, trying to sound normal and not panicky. But she hardly felt normal. She wasn't used to handling two children. Mark was enough of a handful, heaven knows, she thought. "Can you run and keep up with Mark? I bet you can run pretty fast!"

"Will Daddy be there?" asked the child, walking even more slowly. She tried to let go of Marianne's hand but the woman clasped her more tightly.

"He'll be there soon enough. As soon as he is finished talking to all his friends. He has a lot of friends, doesn't he?"

"I guess so....I want to find Daddy."

"He's coming, I promise, sugar. Now let's hurry, okay?"

Janie stopped walking. She wouldn't look at Marianne. She didn't want to be impolite but she didn't want to go any further without her father. He had drifted off earlier while she had been searching for her lost penny, and she had been surprised by Marianne, who knelt down next to her on the grass. "Did you lose something? Can I help you find it?" she asked kindly. Janie had smiled and looked the adult right in the eyes, as her father had taught her just moments before. "How do you do? My name is Janie," she said firmly.

"Hi, Janie, my name is Marianne. And this is my little boy, Mark," she gestured toward an overweight child who was fiddling with a button on his shirt. He had red hair and an extraordinarily large head, which made him look like one of the dwarfs in her Snow White book. She wasn't sure if he reminded her of one of the nice ones or not. But Marianne seemed nice. Janie couldn't bring herself to call this woman by her first name; her daddy had told her to use 'Missus' and 'Mister.' But she didn't know what else to say. The next thing she knew, Marianne had helped her stand up, taken her by the hand, and started to walk away from the picnic area, and her father. Janie didn't even have a chance to turn and look for him before the three of them had emerged onto a town street and were passing cottages she didn't recognize.

And now the child had simply refused to walk any more. "Janie, I don't have time for this!" Marianne scooped the small child up in her right arm and held her firmly by her side like a disobedient puppy. Janie kicked her feet and shut her eyes as tightly as she could. Marianne walked very fast now, following Mark, who clearly knew the way home. They turned into a small yard and went to the middle of the front screened porch where there was a door. As they entered the dilapidated little house, Janie found her voice, and yelled, "NO!" very shrilly. Marianne pulled the struggling child into the living room, and with her foot, slammed shut the wooden door between it and the porch. She turned the lock. Placing Janie gently on the couch, she went quickly from one window to the next, pulling the dusty bamboo slatted shades all the way down and securing them with a knot in the pull cord. Janie had started to cry and curled up in the corner of the couch, eyes shut and holding her arms around her head as if to protect it from oncoming danger. Mark ran upstairs and came back down with a box of toys. He sat on the rug in front of the couch and rummaged through the box, pulling out one object after another and holding them up for the unhappy child to see. She never looked at him; she didn't even know he was there. She kept her eyes shut against her fear and frustration. Tears escaped her eyes anyway, covering her red face. Marianne, dressed in faded capri pants and an oversized man's collared shirt, went quickly through the house, securing doors and windows, darkening the space until she had to turn on a lamp to be able to see.

"Mark, maybe Janie wants to read books! You have some books there on the table. I could read to you both, if you like!"

"She don't want to, Mommy," said Mark, the first words he had spoken since they had found Janie. "She's sad."

"I'm sure she won't be sad for long, honey. I will make you both a nice snack, how does that sound?"

"Peanut butter crackers?" the boy asked, brightening.

"All right, if that's what you want. And a nice big glass of Coke, okay?"

"Yay!" cried the boy.

They both looked at Janie and were disappointed to see no reaction, as if she hadn't heard. "Janie, aren't you a little hungry? Mark and I are going to have a snack, and we would like it if you joined us. Why don't we go in the kitchen?" But the small girl continued to cry and pushed herself even further into the couch cushions, as if trying to disappear. Marianne noticed a stain on the couch from tears and mucus from the child's nose. Marianne ran to get a box of Kleenex. "Here, dear, wipe your face. You're making a mess." Janie remained unmoving. Marianne reached toward her with a tissue. "I have to wipe your nose, what a mess!" she said, a little louder. When her hand touched Janie's face, the child screamed and writhed away from her. She scrambled quickly to the opposite side of the couch and turned her back so that her face was completely hidden by the upholstery.

"Mommy, peanut butter crackers! Peanut butter crackers! Coke!" cried Mark, pulling on his mother's arm.

"Mark, just a minute! I'm trying to help Janie!" Marianne shrugged him off her arm. He began to intone in a loud voice, "PEANUT BUTTER CRACKERS PEANUT BUTTER CRACKERS PEANUT BUTTER CRACKERS PEANUT BUTTER CRACKERS." His mother stood, walked to the kitchen, covering her ears with both hands, against the noise in the living room. She turned on a glaring overhead light and sat at the worn white wooden table situated in the middle of the room. Two unmatched wooden chairs were pulled up to it. She thought, I must bring in another chair for meals. She heard Janie scream and sob. Mark was still chanting. She turned on the transistor radio and turned the volume level up.

The cottage next door to the Colby's was a summer rental but was rarely rented. It had only one real bedroom, a bathroom that had been tacked onto the back of the kitchen only five years earlier when outhouses had been officially banned in Lakeside, and its appearance was shabby and dark. However, it was affordable. Some might say cheap. The owner had moved to the southwest and hadn't been able to sell it, so he listed it with the Harriet Slade agency, whose realtors had been less than eager to show it, but sometimes it was all a client could afford. This week was one of the few this summer in which it was rented, probably because of the holiday. The tenants were an elderly woman named Bea Lindquist and her son, Andy. Andy was a large man, bald and with a blotchy, red-cheeked complexion, who worked in the Sandusky US Post Office, making just enough money to pay the rent on his small downtown apartment. He was forced to share it with his mother, whose Social Security checks made the difference between eating or not. And Andy did a lot of eating. This was their first vacation together and so far, they had found a lot to complain about in Lakeside.

There were no cabs, for instance, and they were hardly interested in riding bicycles. So getting to town for groceries or an ice cream cone was a long and difficult walk for Andy. His mother stayed on the screened porch and watched her neighbors come and go. She thought they were unfriendly or downright rude, badly dressed or showing off, neglectful parents or saddled with bratty children. The weather was beastly hot and the porch caught no breezes at all. She preferred a queen sized bed but the bedroom had only a double. Andy was either gone too long or in the cottage too much. This day, he sat on the living room couch that doubled as his bed, reading one of the cowboy stories he had found in the cottage, and she was left alone on the porch with no one to talk to, again. She was becoming aware of a lot of noise coming from the cottage next door. It sounded as though a child were crying inconsolably, and the mother – Bea knew her name was Marianne – was yelling. But the windows were covered with blinds and no one was on the porch. Bea always thought there was something "off" about that woman. And that child of hers! Either he didn't speak at all, or he screamed one word over and over until Bea thought she would lose her mind.

Bea called out to Andy in the living room, "Why don't you go next door and find out what all the racket is about? A body can't rest in this neighborhood at all these days. What if I wanted to take a nap?"

"You never nap, Mother," said Andy, from behind his book.

"Well, now, how would you know? You're never home with me. I'm alone all day, what am I supposed to do? A nap fills the time. If I want to nap, I should be able to without telling you all about it."

"Right."

"Well, are you going over there or do I have to do everything?"

"Where?"

"Next door! Don't you ever listen to me?"

"Mother, if her son is crying, I can't just order her to shut him up."

"Well, if she knew she was bothering her neighbors, she would find a way. She'd give him a cookie or something. It's just so loud!"

"I wouldn't know what to say to her. I don't want to intrude."

"Oh, all right. I'll do it myself. Just like I always do around here."

"No, Mother," Andy said wearily, "I will go and ask if I can bring them something from Jenny's when I go to town later. I'll try to find a way to mention that you need some peace and quiet for your, well, your naps. If she doesn't get the hint, we are leaving the subject alone. You can't tell other people how to live."

"She'll get the hint if you are clear. Speak up, son, don't mumble. You always mumble."

"No one else thinks so. I think you need a hearing aid."

"Well, that shows what you know. If I needed a hearing aid, how could I be so aware of that child screaming next door? You just go over there and you make it stop." Bea picked up her knitting, a gesture of dismissal.

Andy sighed, heaved his considerable bulk off the couch, and slipped on a pair of rubber sandals. He walked slowly out through the porch and approached the house next door. He went to the porch door and knocked. There was no response. He could hear loud voices and one of them a child's voice seemingly repeating the same words over and over, but Andy couldn't make out the words themselves. He called out, "Hello? Is anything wrong? It's Andy from next door!" Again, no response. He walked around to the side of the cottage but all the windows he could see were covered with closed blinds. There was a chain link fence preventing him from entering the weed-choked back yard. He gave up, with no small measure of relief. He decided not to go back but to walk to the downtown, and maybe get an ice cream cone, maybe watch some shuffleboard. Within just a few minutes, Andy was out of shouting range of his chronically dissatisfied mother. He had forgotten to ask what groceries she might want from Jenny's.

Harriet Slade decided not to sit on the O'Reilly's porch while Tim and Gigi flew into action, determined to find their lost child. Tim had run to the local police office, staffed as it was with volunteers and a daily visit from the Port Clinton Police Department. Gigi had turned to the phone.

110

There were many people in Lakeside who didn't have a phone at all in their cottages, and those that did rarely used them, preferring to walk to neighbors' homes, and send postcards to friends and family back home. But a few of Gigi's friends had phones, and she knew the hardware store in town had one, too. She called every number she knew in Lakeside, but in most cases the phones just rang and rang. It was a sunny day over the Fourth of July weekend; most people were at the lake or playing miniature golf or tennis, not in their cottages answering a ringing phone. She did get an answer from Big Lou, the owner of Lakeside Hardware Store, however, and he listened to her urgent message and turned to the few customers in the store, calling out, "Hey, everybody, there's a missing little girl, probably in the woods near the wishing well. Anybody willing to go over there and search?" Two men who were looking for barbeque tools and charcoal for tonight's cookout put their things on the counter and asked him for directions to the picnic area, then took off on a run toward the south end of town.

But Harriet decided the way she could be most helpful was to take a walk in the neighborhood near Tim and Gigi's rental. The wishing well and picnic area were only two blocks south and one block east; it was a small area, and one she knew well, having been renting and selling these cottages for decades. She decided to call out to anyone she knew and ask if they had seen the child or if they knew of a group of children playing nearby – all the while walking toward the picnic area where Janie had last been seen. Harriet moved more swiftly than her usual stroll, her white sneakers carrying her round body efficiently. She didn't stop to talk to people she saw. Instead, she called out to them while continuing to move. Few people were home that afternoon. Of the people she did see, no one had noticed a 5-year-old blond child anywhere nearby. She turned finally onto Seventh Street and walked toward the picnic area. She saw Bea Lindquist sitting on the screened porch, knitting.

"Hello! I'm looking for a lost child named Janie. She was at the wishing well with her father earlier. Any chance you've seen a little blond girl?" Harriet called out to Bea.

"Who are you?" answered the old woman on the porch.

"Harriet Slade. I don't believe we have met. I would stop and chat but I am worried about little Janie."

"Harriet Slade? I rented this cottage from Harriet Slade, didn't I?"

"Oh, that is my former agency. I am retired now. But yes, you probably did. We have handled this cottage for many years. I hope you are comfortable here. But I really must move on," Harriet said as she turned to go into the wooded area.

"Do you handle all these houses? Even the one next door?" The old woman was peering at Harriet through slitted eyes. "There are children next door. They make a terrible racket. I can't rest at all."

"I don't know who is in there this year," said Harriet, distracted. "As I said, I retired a couple of years ago."

"Well, my lazy son was supposed to get them to pipe down but I bet he just went to get ice cream instead. Maybe you could find out what all the noise is about. They said Lakeside would be a sleepy little town. I didn't pay for all this craziness."

Harriet turned back to Bea. "Children? Next door? I'm sorry, what did you say?"

"Can't you hear it?" shouted the old woman, thinking this fat lady with the white shoes must be deaf.

Harriet stopped and listened, turning her attention to the cottage she had assumed was vacant, since its windows were covered and there was no sign of people on the porch or the small yard. Then she heard a child yelling something repeatedly. She thought it was something about crackers. There was crying and then the unmistakable sound of a slap. More screaming, higher pitched this time. There was definitely somebody inside and they were having a terrible time of it. Harriet decided to knock on the porch door.

"Hello? It's Harriet Slade. Are you all right in there? Can I help? Hello?"

There was no response. Harriet knocked louder. "Is everything all right?" She was about to back away from the door when the interior wooden door opened, and a slender woman of perhaps forty slipped carefully through it and closed it tightly behind her. Her man-tailored shirt looked stained.

"I am so sorry if we are bothering anyone in the neighborhood. My son is having a tantrum. He does that sometimes. It happens in all families, right? There's really nothing you can do. I do appreciate your concern, but please, go away, I can handle him okay. I have to go back in." She seemed nervous and looked back over her shoulder a couple of times. "We'll be fine, really." She turned to open the door, but as she did so, a small blond head followed by a squirming girl's body pushed out into the porch. Her face was streaked with tears. The young woman lunged for her, gasping, but the child wrestled away.

Harriet spoke quickly. "Janie?" she called to the little girl.

"I want to go home," shouted Janie.

"You are home, sweetie," the young woman said loudly, reaching for Janie. But Janie was trying to open the latch. Harriet stepped up on the concrete block in front of the house and with surprising speed and strength, opened the screen door and grabbed little Janie.

"There seems to be a problem here," said Harriet quietly, holding the trembling child.

At that moment, Andy Lindquist turned onto the street. He noticed the people at the house next door to his and heard Marianne Colby shout, "There is no problem! I told you my child was having a tantrum! I don't need you to interfere in my life! Put my child down immediately!"

Janie clung even more tightly to Harriet who was unaccustomed to holding children, but she held her ground. "You said your child was a boy. This is a little girl. I believe her name is Janie O'Reilly. Is that right, honey?" Janie nodded slightly which Harriet could feel against her neck. She could hear the child say again, this time in a whisper, "I want to go home."

Andy spoke up. "What's going on here?" He looked over at his cottage and could see his mother standing at the end of her porch that was closest to the Colby home. She had abandoned her knitting, finding the drama next door irresistible. "I am taking Janie O'Reilly home to her parents," said Harriet. "She got lost but everything is all right now." Harriet tried to put Janie down on the ground, but the child would not let go of her neck. Harriet hefted her higher on her hip. "Would you please hand me my purse? It's the white one over there," she said to Andy. He handed it to her. "Are you all right?" he asked Marianne Colby who was sitting on the front step of her cottage. As he asked, the front door of the cottage opened and a chubby, red-headed boy peered out. "Mommy?" he asked. "Peanut butter crackers?" Seeing that Marianne wasn't answering, Andy spoke kindly to the child. "I can find them for you, if you want. Would that be all right?" The boy didn't answer him but he held the door to the living room open wider and stared at the big man. Andy walked into the darkened house slowly.

Harriet had already walked away from Seventh Street and was moving as quickly as she could, considering she had a child clinging to her side. When she turned onto Fifth Street, a neighbor spotted her and cried out "She's got Janie! Janie's home!" Gigi O'Reilly appeared at the door of her cottage and ran to take Janie out of Harriet's arms. The child fairly leaped into her mother's embrace. Both of them were crying, this time with relief. Harriet straightened her blouse and patted at her hair. She felt a little unsure of what to say or do, and decided to remain silent for a while as mother and daughter regained their composure. As she waited, Tim O'Reilly turned the corner, leading a uniformed police officer.

"Janie! Monkeyface! Oh, kid, am I ever glad to see you! Thank God!" Tim cried, gathering his wife and daughter into a bear hug. Moments later, Timmy and Benny O'Reilly rode their bikes onto the street. "What's going on?" asked Benny, wide-eyed at the presence of a policeman standing with his parents and sister.

Since no one answered his question, Harriet said, "Janie got lost while she was playing near the wishing well. Everybody's been looking for her. She's okay but she was scared and she's just glad to be back home. No harm done, I'd say."

"Who are you?" asked Timmy.

"My name is Harriet Slade. The last time I saw you two was a few years ago when I came to check on your cottage rental. I helped your parents find it."

"Oh, yeah, I remember," said, Timmy, satisfied.

"Harriet, what happened to Janie?" asked Gigi.

"Well, now, I don't know about you, but I think maybe you want to take your little girl inside and give her a snack or something. Then we can talk. Okay?"

Tim said, "I'll take her." He and his daughter went in the porch and then into the house, holding hands.

"She's a darling, isn't she?" asked Harriet, watching them. "Why don't we take a walk, Mrs. O'Reilly? And Officer, perhaps you could join us?"

Repairing Lakeside
1968

One early May morning, Big Lou sat down on a folding chair behind the counter at the Lakeside Hardware Store, closed his eyes, sighed audibly, and died. When asked about it later, no one at the store, employee or customer alike, could remember ever seeing Big Lou sit down as long as the store was open. Instead, he was opening boxes, filling shelves, taking inventory, ringing up sales at the old hand-operated cash register, answering the endless questions posed by vacationers who really didn't know what they were doing while fighting losing battles against antique cottages. Big Lou's real name was Luigi but there were only a handful of Lakeside residents who knew that. Luigi Antonielli, originally from Detroit, was one of the few year-round Lakeside residents. There wasn't much to do in the little Chatauqua community in the off-season. Big Lou took advantage of the quiet to re-paint the ancient hardwood floor of the store, refinish the worn counters, dust the inventory, clean the old light fixtures hanging from the tin ceilings, design new signs for the windows, and order products typically purchased by homeowners in the spring, so they could freshen up their weather-beaten cottages in preparation for the tenants who began to fill up the little town around Memorial Day.

Big Lou didn't take vacations. His wife, Donna, could attest to that. She had given up waiting for family vacations decades ago, so she took opportunities each year to spend a week with her sister, sometimes at her Boston home, and sometimes at a rented condo in Vero Beach, Florida. Donna loved Big Lou but she saw little of him. It seemed to her that he barely noticed when she was gone. Still, after his death, the size of the hole created by his absence was a shock to her. She could not imagine her life as a widow. She found the questions posed to her – where will you live? Will you sell the store? Do you have life insurance? – overwhelming. She supposed she would have to rely on their son, Tony, to help. She sometimes questioned whether her tall, large-boned, clumsy son had the wherewithal to be of much assistance. He had always been a good son, and he had finished high school with better than a C average. He had a steady job in Sandusky, loading trucks for an interstate trucking company, and occasionally driving. He had even been married, for a while, but that hadn't worked out, and there were no grandchildren to delight Donna in her sudden widowhood. She knew she needed a new focus for herself, but she had no idea how to find it.

The people of Lakeside were devastated by Big Lou's demise. No one could remember the town without him. He had been closely involved with every home improvement project in Lakeside, seemingly since the town's establishment. Although Big Lou wasn't the founder of Lakeside Hardware, no one could remember anything about the previous owner. The store shared a building with the post office, so everyone who stayed in Lakeside for more than a week or two had reason to drop into the store. It was a popular spot for conversation and gossip. And now, to the consternation of the whole town, it was for sale.

Donna knew very little about the hardware business and in fact knew very little about finances of any kind. She and Big Lou had lived as comfortably as many middle class couples in the mid-1960s, in a modest house on Third Street in Lakeside. It was one of the few houses in town with central heat, insulation, a working fireplace, and wall to wall carpeting. They had moved to Lakeside permanently after their son graduated. Tony got a job and an apartment in Sandusky, where they had raised him while Big Lou worked long hours in Lakeside. Donna had been a fourth grade teacher before she got married, but was a stay-at-home wife and mother after that, and had never gone back to work. Her many friends and she loved to play bridge and garden. She was a wonderful cook and prided herself on treating her husband and son to carefully planned dinners that often featured her husband's favorite Italian recipes. Many of her baked goods appeared at local bake sales for charity, especially for the PTA of Sandusky. She made homemade applesauce, jellies and jams, pickles, fudge, and her special cranberry-orange relish at Thanksgiving. After Tony left home, she continued to supply him with much of the food he ate; she didn't know what else to do with the leftovers. Two people can only eat so much for dinner.

Donna was not well prepared to be a widow. She had always left the bill paying to her husband, and bigger decisions regarding money, like investing and insurance and mortgages, were of little interest to her. It took months after the funeral for her to realize how much trouble she was in. It turned out that Big Lou was a poor money manager, and his business was not lucrative. He had taken out a second mortgage on their Lakeside home to finance some crucial repairs on the antiquated building that housed the store, yet he still struggled with plumbing issues that became evident every time there was a heavy rainstorm. Keeping his prices low to be competitive with city hardware stores meant he was barely covering costs. He had borrowed against his life insurance and neglected to pay it back. He was in his early sixties when he died and, as Donna soon learned, his affairs were hardly what one would call "in order."

Donna was friendly with a Sandusky banker and his wife, and she brought all the paperwork she could find to him. He assigned her an associate who specialized in estate management and he was the one who delivered the bad news. He advised her to sell the house and store as soon as possible. He put her in touch with a broker who could handle selling the inventory, but when he suggested the name of a real estate agent, she balked. "I will call Harriet Slade. She will sell the house and the store," she stated firmly.

"Miss Slade, it's Donna Antonielli. How are you?" Donna said on the phone the same day.

"Mrs. Antonielli, how are you doing? I want to say again how sorry I am that you lost your charming husband. We will miss him so much here. I don't know how we will manage without him. He was such a friendly man," Harriet answered.

"Yes, he was. Thank you for your kindness. I certainly enjoyed the cookies you brought over."

"Oh, it was the least I could do. How can I help you now?"

"Miss Slade, I need your help with selling my house and the hardware store," Donna said.

"Oh, I am sorry to hear that. I was hoping your son might take the business over and keep it in the family."

"He really doesn't know too much about hardware stores. He has a good job in Sandusky. I'm afraid Lou kept most of the details of the business pretty much to himself."

"And the house? I hope you aren't moving away."

Donna hesitated, not wanting to over-state her financial problems. "I am thinking it might be a good idea to move to Boston to live with my sister. She never married, and we have always enjoyed each other's company. I find I don't much like living alone."

"Well, I hope that turns out well for you. Wouldn't your son miss you, though?" asked Harriet.

"He keeps busy with his job and his friends. We would stay in touch, certainly."

"Well, Mrs. Antonielli, you may not know that I have retired."

"Oh! No, I didn't know that. I still see your For Sale signs around town."

"Yes, the company still exists, under my name, but I have been officially retired for about six months now. However, I still have my real estate license, and I would like to help you get started, at least. I like to keep my hand in now and then. Old habits die hard, don't you agree?" Harriet laughed a little.

"I guess I should have put two and two together when you moved here to Lakeside. I've walked by your cottage. It looks as if you have made quite a few improvements. I loved Cree Fox, but she was letting that place fall down around her ears. I used to worry about her. By the way, have you heard how she is doing?"

"She is in a nursing home on the west side of Cleveland, near her son's home in Rocky River, I believe. I see him from time to time. I think she is slipping, but he tells me she is as dignified as ever."

"I miss her. What an extraordinary woman. Can you feel her presence in the cottage?"

"Yes, I can. I like to think she would approve of the changes I have made."

"Oh, I'm sure she would. Miss Slade, do you know anything about hardware stores?"

"Well, not specifically, but I know who to ask. We'll get the store and the house listed as soon as possible. I will need to meet you at the store to walk around and take some notes – and the same thing with your house. The market is strong right now and I am sure we can sell your house quickly. It is one of the few winterized places in town, isn't it?"

"Yes, that's right. I wonder if it might be sold to someone who is looking for year-round ownership here. It is not really a summer cottage at all."

"I understand. Let's meet this week. When would be convenient?"

Donna and Harriet met a few days later and spent the morning touring both the shuttered hardware store and the house. Harriet had invited a broker she knew in Sandusky who specialized in sales of retail businesses, and his advice was very helpful. He also had some ideas about people who might actually be interested in buying. He and Harriet had already talked at length about the unique qualities of life in an antique summer community on the shores of Lake Erie, where cars were forbidden on the town's streets and people got around on foot or by bicycle. Such a community posed real limitations on a traditional hardware business. On the other hand, homeowners and renters alike were often in need of the small things that the store offered, like nails and screws, WD40, patch kits for inner tubes, small kitchen implements, children's toys, beach chairs, and the like. Handled well, the store had real potential for a particular kind of buyer.

The house was in excellent condition. Big Lou had been conscientious in keeping up with repairs and renovations as they were needed. It was unusual in the town because it had a lawn and mature plantings and even a driveway. There was a small but well laid-out living room, a dining room and a small but efficient kitchen, and down the hall, two bedrooms and a bathroom. Off the kitchen was a screened-in porch, practically a requirement in Lakeside. Upstairs, Lou had never finished the one large room, but it provided plenty of storage.

When Harriet had seen enough, she suggested that Donna come to her home on Fourth Street to sign the necessary papers. They met after lunch on Harriet's comfortable porch.

"Oh, this has certainly changed. It's downright civilized!" exclaimed Donna, enjoying the space that was now filled with a long harvest table along the street side of the porch, an attractive redwood patio set with thick green cushions on the couch and two matching chairs, and a large sisal rug on the refinished wooden floor. Everything was spotlessly clean and the effect was fresh and welcoming.

"Thank you. It has been a labor of love for me to make it my own."

"May I see the rest?" asked Donna.

"Oh, I would love to show it to you," answered Harriet, blushing a little with pleasure.

Donna and Harriet walked through the small cottage, upstairs and down. Donna wondered silently how much money Harriet must have spent to accomplish all that she had – shoring up the foundation, making the fireplace functional, refinishing floors, installing an entirely new kitchen and bathroom, rebuilding the stairs to make them safer and re-wiring the whole house. Not to mention new furniture throughout, all of which was stylish and high end. Why didn't she just tear it down and start over, Donna wondered, or find one of the last empty lots and build new? The real estate business must be better paying than I would have thought, especially since Harriet seems to specialize mostly in summer rentals. She didn't say she sold the business, she said she retired. She's about my age. I should have kept teaching. I wouldn't be in the position I'm in now if I had.

"Oh, Miss Slade, it's wonderful. You must be so happy here."

"This is the best time of my life, Mrs. Antonielli. I love living here in the summers. I am actually thinking about selling my Sandusky home. I'm not sure about that, but it's a possibility."

"And live here year-round? Lakeside is really quiet in the winter. I tend to spend my days in Sandusky or Toledo, or at least Port Clinton, with friends, as much as I can. It can get downright creepy."

"Oh, I don't think I will stay here in the winter, but it's good to know I can come when I want to and not freeze! I plan to do some more traveling this winter." Harriet said.

"How exciting! Where will you go this time?"

"Poland. I have family there. It is a lifelong dream. I plan to be gone at least a month, maybe two."

"Oh, how fascinating!"

"I know! And I can hardly speak Polish anymore. It should be amusing! Shall we sit down and get to these pesky papers? The tea is ready, and I made some lemon pound cake this morning. How would you like a slice?" At Donna's smile, Harriet went to the kitchen to fill a tray with her silver tea set and a plate of cake. Donna sat down on one of the cushioned side chairs. As she did so, the screen door opened and Ida Green came in, calling to Harriet.

"I'm home! Sorry to be la….." she stopped when she saw Donna. "Donna! What a surprise! I'm sorry, I didn't mean to interrupt."

"Ida, how are you? I haven't seen you yet this summer. When did you arrive?" asked Donna.

"Oh, I've been in Lakeside since early May. I would have come in April but I was in Boston with my daughter, visiting the grandchildren. I've just been so busy with one thing and another, I haven't seen a lot of people. But I haven't had the chance to tell you how sorry I was to hear of Lou's death. What a shock that must have been to you. Are you doing all right? Is there anything I can do for you?"

"Thank you, dear. I think I am doing pretty well under the circumstances. But I have decided to sell the house and the business and move to Boston. It sounds like you can give me some advice about that, since you just came back from there."

Harriet came into the porch and smiled at Ida. "Just in time to join us for tea and lemon pound cake. And then you have to skedaddle, because Mrs. Antonielli is here on business and I need to do some paperwork with her," she said, fondly. They both sat on the couch and Harriet placed the tea tray on the small table in front of them. She poured for everyone and passed around the cake.

Ida peppered Donna with questions, but she did it with good cheer and listened carefully to the answers. Donna finally changed the subject.

"Miss Slade, I am feeling guilty that you are coming out of retirement for me. Is there someone else I should be talking to, to let you off the hook?"

"Well, I will be transferring the papers to an associate of mine, yes. But no one at the office knows Lakeside as well as I do, so I am happy to get things started for you. But then I am going to bow out. I have a trip to plan!" With that, she smiled happily at Ida.

"Yes, you said you are going to Poland. I would love to hear more about that."

Ida filled her in. "Well, Harriet has been doing some genealogical research on her family's history in Poland. Her parents were immigrants, you know. And Harriet has never visited. There are some amazing stories of the families that stayed. We're going to meet some of them. One family has even offered us a room in their house! We can't wait!"

"Will you be flying over this time?"

"Oh, yes. There is so much to see and do, we don't want to waste time getting there. We plan to visit Austria as well. I've been reading about the pastries and wine there. I plan to taste everything!" said Harriet. "You'll have to keep an eye on me – I don't want to get as big as a house!" She was looking at Ida, eyes sparkling with anticipation.

"Now don't be saddling me with that responsibility. I want you to have as much fun as you want. We can walk the pastries off when we get home," smiled Ida, patting Harriet's knee affectionately.

Donna looked from one to the other and realized she was alone in the room; they occupied a different, private space. There was a rather long silence as she wondered what she was witnessing.

"Oh, I am sorry. Mrs. Antonielli is here to sign papers. We must get down to business," said Harriet, turning finally to Donna.

"I am just leaving. Grocery shopping - and I have to put down some mulch in my garden. It was lovely to see you, Donna. Sorry if my interruption held you up," said Ida, rising to leave.

"No, I was happy to run into you, Ida. I would love to stop by someday soon to see your beautiful garden. I wish I had your green thumb."

"Nonsense, there's no such thing. You just give plants some food and a comfy bed, just like people. And they need plenty of water. Besides, you have a lovely garden of your own. I don't know about you, but I like to putter around a little every day, and it rewards me with such color and texture, it's totally worth the effort. Well, I'm off. Come over when you're finished, my dear," she called to Harriet.

"Naturally!"

Later that same week, Donna Antonielli went grocery shopping at Jenny's. She was having her first small dinner party since Big Lou died. She invited three of her best women friends in Lakeside, with the promise of a homemade dinner and a bridge game. She had decided to make a big chicken salad and homemade corn bread for dinner and bake a cherry pie for dessert. It was too warm in early July to eat a hot dinner, and cherries had just come into season, so the menu seemed just right to her. Since Lou had been gone, she had been eating eggs and cereal, or toast and tea, and the occasional hamburger, when she got hungry. It was time, she thought, to eat a real meal. Jenny's had cherries, she knew, so she didn't have to go to Port Clinton to shop. She ran into several friends and former customers of Lou's while she filled her cart.

"Donna, how great to see you, and looking so well!" said a large elderly woman with white hair. "I do miss Big Lou, though. We lost a good friend to Lakeside when Lou died."

"Thank you, Mrs. Hooper. I know, it just seems so different now."

"Harder for you, I am sure. I shouldn't complain." Mrs. Hooper laid a comforting hand on Donna's arm. "Will you be selling the store?"

"Yes, we hope to. It may take a while, though. Harriet Slade is helping me with that."

"Oh, really. I thought she retired." Mrs. Hooper's voice changed slightly, Donna thought.

"Yes, she has, but she agreed to get the ball rolling for me. I really appreciate her help. She knows Lakeside better than anyone in real estate."

"That may be so. But I would think you would hire someone who knows how to sell a hardware store. I doubt very much that the Slade woman would have any experience with that."

Donna saw a neighbor coming into Jenny's at that moment. "Nice to see you, Mrs. Hooper. Say hello to your son for me."

"I will. Goodbye, Donna."

Donna chatted for a minute with her neighbor, and finished her shopping. She went home and made the pie. While it cooled, she roasted chicken breasts in the oven and prepared her famous cornbread recipe. That went into the oven while the chicken cooled. She set the dining room table with a fresh cloth and a bowl of hydrangeas she had picked up at the last minute at Jenny's. That afternoon, with the TV tuned to her favorite soap operas, Donna made the chicken salad with green grapes and celery, cooling the finished salad in the refrigerator. She was surprised by a mid-afternoon phone call. Although most all the cottages in Lakeside had phones, they were rarely used. Most people preferred to talk face to face during their summer idyll.

"Donna, it's Nancy Fox," the caller said.

"Hi, Nancy, I hope you're not calling to cancel."

"No, I'll be there at six. I called to ask a question."

"Ok, what's up?" asked Donna.

"You hired Harriet Slade to help you with the store, right?"

"Yes. And the house."

"You're selling the house, too? I didn't know that. Are you leaving us?"

"I'm moving to Boston to live with my sister. It seems like the right thing to do," answered Donna.

"Well, that's not good news. But you have to do what's best for you. Anyway, I was wondering about Harriet."

"What about her?"

"Did you notice anything, well, peculiar about her? You've known her for a long time, right?"

"Yes, I've known her for years, but not well. She only moved into town last summer."

"But does she seem, I don't know, different to you?"

"I really don't know what you're getting at."

"Do you know Ida Green?"

"Of course. She and Harriet live next door to each other. They are good friends."

"Yes, but how good?" Nancy persisted.

"Nancy, what are you suggesting?"

"Just that their friendship is brand new but they always seem to be together now. Always."

"Well, Ida lost her husband, what, five years ago? And Harriet never married. I think it's nice they have found each other and can travel together."

"They are going to travel together?"

"Yes, they are going to Poland this fall, I think. They are really excited about it. Last year they went to the south of France and Italy. I would have thought Ida had done a lot of traveling with her husband, but it all seems quite new to them both."

"I would love to be a fly on the wall during that trip," said Nancy with a chuckle.

"I have no idea what you mean. Nancy, my oven is beeping. I need to check on my cornbread." Donna was stretching the truth – the cornbread was long since finished. She wanted to end this uncomfortable gossip session.

"Yum. I love your cornbread. I will see you later. Looking forward to it."

The dinner party went well, and Donna was surprised at how much she enjoyed entertaining. She and Big Lou had rarely had many friendships with other couples, but she had been active during the day with activities and clubs that brought her numerous women friends, whose socializing usually involved going to someone's house for lunch or tea, with card games or some kind of service project. Dinners were almost always at home with Big Lou and Tony, no one else. Restaurant meals were rare. During the summer, Donna and her friends met at the pier, which was the favored meeting spot for women to work on their tans, read, and share gossip with other summer residents. This was the first time in years that Donna had invited friends over for a summer dinner. Summer people were uniformly casual, so the women walked to her house wearing Bermuda shorts, sleeveless blouses, and sandals. Summer vacationers or not, they enjoyed being treated to some of Donna's wonderful food in a real dining room with carpeting on the floor. It was a nice change from the regulation barbequed hamburgers and hot dogs eaten at a picnic table in the yard or on the porch table.

Before Donna served dessert, they moved to the porch where she had set up a card table and prepared it for a game of bridge.

"Nancy, I want to be your partner this time. I never hold any cards when you're my opponent," said Betty McCarthy, who had been spending the month of July in Lakeside since she was a teenager.

"Oh great, so Donna and I won't get any cards. Thanks a bunch," teased Hoddie Wellman. Hoddie was a third generation Lakesider and couldn't remember a summer that didn't include at least six weeks in the cottage her family owned. She and her brother split the available weeks between their two families, and always spent Labor Day weekend together in the big old Victorian-era house.

Nancy Fox was married to Phil, whose mother, Cree, had until recently owned the cottage that Harriet Slade had bought, a few blocks away from his. He had been coming to Lakeside since 1928, as a boy. He had fond memories of the 1930s, his teens, when on every Saturday night at the hotel there was a dance. Many of the young people of those days were still vacationing in Lakeside or coming for the occasional weekend.

When he was dating Nancy, he brought her to Lakeside for a weekend and watched carefully to see if she could adapt to the old-fashioned town and its eccentric people. Her instant love of the place meant she passed a kind of test she didn't know she was taking.

The four old friends enjoyed bridge and often played on the pier. Hoddie was by far the best player of the group and was sometimes impatient with the constant conversation which made her deliberations difficult. This night was no exception; being in Donna's house prompted a lot of conversation about decorating. None of the others' cottages were anything like this; they had crumbling sisal rugs instead of carpeting, they had mismatched furniture, most of which was designed to be used outdoors, they had cast-off linens and cookware, even though their winter homes were all lovely. Lakeside was for fishing and swimming, cookouts and picnics, band concerts at the gazebo, biking and miniature golf and shuffleboard. Lakeside was for shorts and t-shirts, bathing suits and sneakers, suntan lotion and Noxema. Donna in her winterized year-round house was the exception.

"Did I see a For Sale sign at the store, Donna?" asked Betty, lighting a cigarette from the stub of the last one. The ash tray next to her was filling already, Donna noticed.

"Yup. If you know anyone who wants a crazy, unprofitable, dusty store, let me know."

"Is Harriet Slade's company handling it for you?"

"Harriet herself, as a matter of fact. At least for a while."

"Really? I'm surprised," said Hoddie.

"Why? She knows Lakeside better than anyone," said Donna.

"I didn't think she'd want to work anymore. She's kind of trying out another, shall we say, lifestyle."

"Lifestyle? What do you mean?" asked Betty.

"Oh, come on. Don't tell me you haven't seen her and Ida Green on the pier. Or at the hotel. Or taking walks at the lake. Or at Jenny's."

"So? They're friends. They're both alone, why shouldn't they do things together?"

"Do things together? I hate to think of the things they do together. Ladies, they are more than friends. Watch them look at each other. That's love. No question."

Donna had been following the discussion while she refilled coffee cups at the kitchen counter.

"Love? What do you mean?" asked Donna, raising her voice so she could be heard on the porch.

"Donna, they're together. I mean together. Like living together. It's what I was telling you earlier," called Nancy, with a knowing wink.

Donna sat down at the card table and picked up her bridge hand. "They aren't living together. They're next-door neighbors, best friends. I've been to Harriet's cottage, Nancy, she has done amazing things with Cree's house. You wouldn't recognize it."

"Well, I'm not likely to go there. That sort of thing makes me feel sick."

"Me, too. It's just too gross to think about. I think it doesn't belong in Lakeside. I was sort of hoping they would go to Europe and stay there. It's supposed to be more – what, progressive – than here. That kind of 'progressive' I can do without, frankly," said Hoddie.

"Really?" asked Betty, her head wreathed in cigarette smoke. "You really think they're – lovers? That's disgusting. I can't believe it. Maybe you're wrong."

"I don't think so. It's only a matter of time until you see them kissing, you mark my word."

"Oh, Hoddie, you're exaggerating," said Donna who was becoming uncomfortable with the topic. "Let's let them alone. They're not bothering anybody. Besides, I've always liked Ida. She's been coming here for years. I think she and Bill were very much in love. They were a lovely couple. Can someone just turn from loving men to loving women overnight?" She directed her question to Nancy, who was the only one of the four of them with a college degree and who worked outside the home.

"If a certain woman comes along who has a certain kind of power, they can. People can be very susceptible to suggestion when they're grieving. I think Harriet took advantage of Ida's loneliness. And all that work she had done on Cree's cottage, it's just inappropriate here. Who does she think she is, anyway?" Nancy was warming to her subject, becoming more animated each minute the conversation continued. "There had to be all kinds of trucks driving all over this town while she had the work done. We don't do that here. She should know that."

Hoddie nodded. "She made it look like a year-round house. Doesn't go with any other cottages nearby. That's going to have a negative effect on the real estate market, you'll see."

"Have you been inside?" asked Donna.

"No, but I walk by it almost every day. I live down the street, remember."

"So you've peeked."

"Sure, who wouldn't? It's like out of a magazine. Who does that in Lakeside?"

Donna sat up straighter and looked directly at Hoddie. "Well, I sorta think I did. Lou and I. I hope we're not having a negative effect on real estate because we winterized. And also, Harriet made sure all the work was done in the spring. After the summer people arrived, she made the workers walk. Come on, everybody, let's change the subject."

"How about we play bridge? I opened with one no trump about an hour ago...." said Hoddie.

Harriet and Ida took a walk to the lakefront. It was a particularly bright early summer morning and the lake was uncharacteristically blue, sparkling as if diamond dust had been sprinkled on top of the waves. It was just past sunrise, and the large lawn in front of the hotel was uninhabited at the moment. The shadows of last night's revelers still sang and danced in the gazebo and surrounded the town's bell that hung in a stone cage-like enclosure at water's edge. The pavilion stood white and pink, reflecting the sun's infant rays, and the sand at the waterfront was textured with layer upon layer of footprints, some child-sized, some larger, leading to the shallow water lapping the shore. Colorful plantings of petunias and snapdragons shook off their dewy coatings like fairies after a cool dip. Ida and Harriet noticed it all and shared the wonder of a perfect summer morning, hand in hand, heart joined to heart. Ida carried her Keds in her other hand; Harriet wore a straw hat whose brim was decorated with a bright, floral band. Words were unnecessary; they walked in silence.

"Ida?" The single word interrupted their quiet communion.

Ida turned around to see a tall, slender man, wearing jeans, a long sleeved shirt, and a multi-pocketed vest. He was carrying a fishing rod and a tackle box. "Larry? What on earth are you doing here, and at this hour?"

"I should think that was obvious. Fishing. You're up early, too," he said, looking quizzically at Harriet.

"The birds woke me. The morning was too amazing to miss. I don't know if you have met my friend, Harriet Slade." Ida had let go of Harriet's hand. "Harriet, this is Larry McCarthy."

Larry smiled and said, "Nice to meet you. Your name sounds familiar."

"I have been doing real estate work in Lakeside for forty years. Perhaps you have seen my sign," said Harriet, smiling slightly.

"Oh, yes, I have. I did hear you had moved to town. Well, I don't want to ruin your nice walk. It's so unusual to be here with other people. I usually try to get to the pier when it's still dark and I'm alone. I actually overslept this morning."

"Is Betty in town?" Ida asked.

"Sure. She's sleeping in. I'm sure you'll run into each other soon."

"Tell her I said hello, and I will look for her on the pier."

"Will do. Nice to see you both." Larry turned and headed down the long concrete pier.

"Shall we continue?" asked Harriet to Ida.

"No, let's go back. I'm hungry," said Ida.

Harriet and Ida walked to the cottage on Fourth Street, saying little, Ida a little ahead of Harriet on the street.

"You okay?" asked Harriet when they went inside her newly remodeled house and headed for the kitchen.

"Sure. Why?"

"You seemed preoccupied. And the day started so well. Was it running into Larry – what's his last name?" Harriet took bacon and eggs out of the refrigerator.

"McCarthy. He and Betty have been coming here for years. Bill and I used to see them socially sometimes. I haven't seen him lately, not for over a year, I think. He isn't my favorite person."

"Why not?"

Ida busied herself with making a pot of coffee in the percolator. "Oh, it's hard to pin down. It has something to do with the way he and Betty are together. I wonder if they're happy - or just faking it."

"Isn't he good to her?"

"Not really. She keeps trying to impress him, I think. It's like she's all dressed up for a date and he just doesn't even notice. I don't know, I'm probably wrong. There was this one night…."

"What happened?""

"I'm not sure, but I had the impression that he was flirting with me. Right in front of Bill and Betty. It was embarrassing. Maybe I imagined it, but you know, after a while, you start to trust your instincts. And my antennae were picking something up from him."

"Were you flattered, at least?"

"No, I was very uncomfortable. He had a lot of cocktails in him, and all I could think of was how to get them to go home. Bill didn't seem to notice anything and we never mentioned it afterwards, but I've never forgotten. I sort of avoided them after that. I'm wondering what he thinks now. After running into us this morning, I mean."

"We were holding hands," Harriet said quietly. She had her back to Ida, frying bacon at the stove.

"Yes. I have no idea how that will sit with him, or Betty, either, for that matter."

"How does it sit with you?"

"With me? You know. I've never been happier. But, dearheart, the rumor mill in this town takes about a day to cover everybody. All he has to do is mention our encounter to Betty and we'll be the talk of the town by sundown. I don't know if you're ready for that. I know what a private person you are."

"I'm fine." Harriet turned from the stove and took Ida's hands in both of hers. "I have nothing to hide; nothing to be ashamed of. I don't care who knows how I feel about you. But I haven't been living in this town for decades, like you. I don't have a popular late husband. I don't play bridge with the women on the pier. You're the one with roots here, not me. I'll be your best friend in public if that's what you ask me to do. It's up to you."

"You are so sweet. But, you know, at this point in my life, pretending doesn't appeal to me at all. I say let's be ourselves, indoors and out, and let the rumors fly. We don't have the luxury of time. If people decide we're not their type, what do we care? Okay?"

"Okay." Harriet held Ida's hands, stroking the long fingers with her thumbs, as they smiled at each other. Then, closing her eyes, she drew the taller woman to her and enveloped her with her arms, holding tightly and breathing in the scent of sunshine and wind in her hair. Ida returned the hug warmly. They swayed a little from side to side. When Harriet opened her eyes, she noticed there was someone looking in on them from the kitchen door. It was Donna Antonielli.

"Oh, I am so sorry. I went out for a walk and I saw your lights were on, so I thought I would just check in. I didn't mean to – I mean, I should have knocked – oh, dear, I am sorry." Donna's face was red with embarrassment.

"No, it's fine," said Harriet. "Please come in, Mrs. Atonielli. We were just sitting down to bacon and eggs. There's plenty. Will you join us?"

"Oh, I couldn't. I just wanted to know if you have listed the house yet. But it can wait until later. I can come over after lunch. When you're not busy."

"Please, join us, Donna," said Ida. "Harriet always cooks too much and we really can't save scrambled eggs, they just get thrown out. Honestly. Coffee's fresh, too."

"Well, maybe for just a few minutes. Thank you. I actually haven't had any breakfast," said Donna.

Donna and Ida sat down at the small kitchen table. Harriet piled eggs and bacon onto three plates and served them. She brought the percolator to the table and produced three heavy coffee mugs.

"Cream and sugar?" she asked Donna.

"Black is fine, thank you."

"Just like us! It's so much easier to serve coffee if you don't have to add stuff to it," said Ida.

"I never tasted it with cream and sugar because my parents drank it black," said Donna. "So I don't know what I'm missing."

Harriet sat down at the table after pulling up an extra chair. "Well, I know what I'm missing. But Ida is encouraging me to cut down on calories. So I am learning to appreciate coffee without cream. But if I could...'

"You may drink your coffee any way you like it, dear, you know that," said Ida, smiling. "It's just that I want you to live for decades."

"Decades without cream. Not entirely appealing," muttered Harriet.

Donna laughed. "We might be the only three people in Lakeside awake this early. I find I can't sleep as well without Lou. I wake up before the sun. I never used to."

"Larry McCarthy is awake. We ran into him at the pavilion. He was going fishing," said Ida.

"Well, I can pretty much guarantee that Betty wasn't up, seeing him off. She sleeps late when she can," said Donna.

"That's what he said, too."

"Miss Slade, when would you like to talk about my house?" asked Donna, changing the subject.

"I think if you are going to sit with us at the break of dawn and share bacon and eggs, you should be able to call me Harriet, don't you agree?"

"Then you must call me Donna."

"I would be delighted. And we can talk real estate as soon as we clear up these dishes, how's that?"

Harriet finally understood the urgency of Donna's financial situation, and called her agency in Sandusky as soon as the office was open that morning. She spoke to her associate who promised her to put the Antonielli property, both house and store, on top of the pile. He said he would be ready to show the house in a week, and advised Donna to do everything she could to clear personal items out so the house would show well. Harriet explained that buyers want to be able to see themselves living in the house and can't do that if someone else's family photographs and memorabilia are filling the space. Donna looked worried.

"You have a week, Donna. It's amazing how much you can accomplish. You'll see."

"But where shall I put it all? There isn't a garage or a shed. And I only have a little car."

"I tell you what. My upstairs bedrooms are never used. I had such fun decorating them, hoping that friends and family would visit and enjoy Lakeside with me, until I remembered I don't have any friends who visit me, and my family and I have never been close. For such a small cottage, it's still more than I need. Why don't you get some boxes from Jenny's, fill them, and bring them here? I would be happy to help you. It will be fun."

"Oh, I couldn't impose," protested Donna.

"Don't be silly. I told you, I retired. My associate is taking over your listing and doing all the work on that end. I don't have much else to do but sit in the sun and read. I would actually welcome the diversion. And Ida has a big handcart that she uses in the garden sometimes. We can fill it with boxes and pull it back and forth. We'll stop when we get tired and have lunch or whatever. Really. Let me help you."

"Well, all right then! Thank you so much! I will go home now and start taking things off the shelves and off the walls, and make some piles. Tony will help, too. Tomorrow's his day off, I'm sure he'll come. He can get the boxes for us."

Donna's house went on the market the next week. It was a difficult house to sell because it was a winterized, year-round home in a town that advertised itself to be a summer vacation getaway. Even so, there was enough interest in the property to bring several potential buyers to look around. Two of them were long-time renters in Lakeside who wondered if they might consider having a second home that could be used in any season. Donna waited anxiously for news from the Slade Agency.

"Have you had any offers yet?" asked Betty McCarthy one afternoon as they sat on the pier with Hoddie and Nancy.

"No. But there has been lots of interest. Harriet assures me it won't be much longer."

"Harriet? Is she working or retired?" asked Nancy, looking up from her paperback.

"Retired. But she has been such a help to me, I can't tell you. Her agency is handling the sale and she keeps in touch with them every day for me. I even stored my extra stuff in her cottage. Ida and she came over every day for three days while Tony and I stripped the place of everything except basic furniture and moved it to Fourth Street. I can't thank them enough."

"Really. How sweet. Do you honestly like hanging out with those two?" asked Hoddie, lighting a cigarette.

"They're lovely. I really like them. Yes, I do," answered Donna, nodding her head emphatically.

"Everybody's talking about them. I notice they don't come here very much anymore. For a while, they swam a little and lay out in the sun, but lately, I haven't seen them. I told you, didn't I, that Larry ran into them really early one morning when he went fishing? They were holding hands?" Betty lowered her voice, but not very much.

"So what? Who cares who holds hands with who? It's none of our business, or Larry's, either," said Donna.

"Well, we just don't go for that sort of thing in our family," said Nancy. "It bothers Phil no end that they're in his mother's house. If he had known, he never would have sold to Harriet," said Nancy.

"I can't imagine anyone else would have renovated it so nicely. I think Cree would be proud and delighted," answered Donna.

"Donna, I know my mother-in-law better than you, and trust me, she would not be proud and delighted that that kind of woman lives in her house." Nancy picked the paperback up and started to read, basically announcing that she had said her piece.

"I agree with Nancy. This is a family town, run by a church. These are good Americans here, and they just do not want people like that to spoil things. They should go live in a big city where there are other women like them. They'd be much more comfortable, and so would we," said Hoddie. "Listen, I hate to break this party up, but we're having a family cookout tonight and I have to go into Port Clinton and shop. I should have left hours ago but I just couldn't resist the sun today. Are we on for bridge on Tuesday?" She stood, folded her aluminum lawn chair, and picked up her canvas tote bag.

"I'm not sure I can make it. I'll have to let you know," said Donna.

"Oh, Donna, don't get all huffy, just because we don't like your new friends. You know you love to play bridge with us," said Betty.

"Bridge is one thing, unkindness is another. I want to think about it. I have to go now, too. I'll see you tomorrow, probably."

Donna did play bridge with Hoddie, Nancy, and Betty on Tuesday evening, at Nancy's cottage. She considered saying no, but her friends would have known she had no other place to be that night, and would have taken her snub personally. She reasoned that she would be living in

Boston soon and could start over making friends whose values she shared. Meanwhile, she really enjoyed bridge.

The game over, she went home and watched the television news, followed by Johnny Carson on *The Tonight Show*. Donna was reluctant to go to bed; sleep had been eluding her lately and she found herself worrying about money most of the night. Eventually, she undressed, turned on a fan for relief from the summer heat, and climbed into her bed, staring at the ceiling and calculating for the hundredth time how long she could live off her savings account. She just had to sell this house, she thought. Dozing occasionally, Donna became aware of a sound coming through the open windows of her bedroom. Once she was fully awake, she recognized loud bells, ringing regularly. She knew what it meant: fire.

Donna put on the slacks she had worn for the bridge game and a sleeveless blouse that had been tossed carelessly on the bedroom chair. She slipped into a pair of loafers and went out onto Third Street. Walking quickly toward the lake, she became aware of an acrid smell that was reminiscent of something familiar. Despite the cloud cover on that summer night, she could see billows of gray and white smoke blowing straight up until it was caught by the wind. She knew where it was coming from: the hardware store. It only took a few minutes to reach it, and to know that it was a total loss. Already there was a small crowd watching from across the street. Harriet spotted Donna as soon as she turned the corner, and hurried to be with her.

"Oh, Donna, we are just so sorry." Harriet put a comforting arm around Donna's shoulder.

"When did it start? How?" Donna gazed on the scene with a blank expression.

"We were down by the water and happened to see the smoke. We hurried as quickly as we could to the O'Reilly's cottage, where we could see lights were on. They called the fire department. We were told it was the store. We hurried here, but you could tell it was too late to save it. We thought about how we could be useful, and Ida went home and put on coffee. She is calling you now, and I was instructed to wait here in case you appeared. And here you are. Did she reach you?"

"No, my phone is in the kitchen and sometimes I can't hear it when the fan is on. I heard the commotion outside, though. That's odd, isn't it?" Donna seemed almost to be talking in her sleep.

"I think you are accustomed to listening for your husband. And something ties you to the store. Anyway, here you are – and here is Ida." Harriet was patiently trying to bring her friend back into reality.

Ida hugged Donna and peered into her face with concern. "I am so relieved to see the fire department is here. We can't help them; as a matter of fact, we're probably in the way. Let's see if we can help some of these people." She raised her voice above the commotion. "Everybody, there is plenty of hot coffee and sandwich makings on Fourth Street. Number 411. Maybe some of you would like to come over and sit down for a little while," she called to the assembled residents.

Harriet, Donna, and Ida left the grisly spectacle and walked the two blocks to Ida's cottage. One of them kept a hand on Donna's back or arm as she seemed partially unaware of her surroundings. Harriet said, "I'll make another pot and heat up some soup. People can come to my house, too. Spread the word."

It took a while, but slowly, residents began to come into both Harriet's and Ida's cottages, grateful for the coffee and the food. Jenny Jones, who owned the only grocery store in town, opened her store and carried bread, peanut butter, milk, and cookies to Harriet's kitchen. She and Harriet and Ida stayed in their kitchens for the next two hours, making more sandwiches and starting new pots of coffee. It seemed everybody in Lakeside stopped in for a snack, a bathroom break, or a quiet conversation before heading back to the scene of the fire, and eventually, home to bed. Everyone took a moment to sympathize with Donna, who sat in Ida's living room, dazed and unable to process. By the time a pink and blue striped dawn was visible through the east side of the screened porch, two visibly tired firefighters turned up at Ida's house. They gratefully accepted a sandwich and a cup of coffee and told Donna what they knew about the fire.

"It's hard to say exactly, but it seemed like the fire started in the back of the store, near the back door," said one of them. "There was a lot of trash back there and some empty drums that smell of some kind of accelerant. I'm afraid the store is a total loss, but we were able to contain it so it didn't spread to any houses nearby. We were lucky that it wasn't windy last night. We will have a state inspector coming in a day or two, when everything is cooled off, to try to figure it out. He's pretty good at it. I bet we'll get an answer. Do you know whether anyone was in there yesterday?

"No, it was boarded up and locked. We had managed to sell most of the merchandise just last week, to some kind of broker. And the post office moved to Jim Benicke's house. But the building was up for sale. It was abandoned." Donna was beginning to sound like herself again.

"What about the drums out back?" the other firefighter asked, finishing his coffee.

"I don't know anything about that. My husband sold all kinds of stuff like paint and mineral spirits - kerosene - turpentine. I'm sorry, I wasn't very involved in the business. I don't think I can be of much help," Donna said.

"Well, there's nothing anyone can do now. It's still a little hot and no one should get close. We have a barricade set up around it." They stood up to go, and the younger man added, "I've never been to this town before. It's pretty cute. No one drives, huh?"

"No, you leave your car outside the gate and walk in. Or bicycle. It's pretty old fashioned. But we like it that way," said Ida. "I think I would like to see if Donna can get some rest now, if you don't mind."

"That's fine. Nothing to be done now anyway. I'm sure our inspector will be in touch. Thanks for the coffee."

When the Lakeside Hardware Store burned down, several things changed in town. The most obvious was that there was little chance of the store re-opening, and two gift shops in town expanded their merchandise to include some of the small necessities of life that the hardware store had provided. Two teenagers, first-time summer visitors, admitted that they had set the fire. That night, they sneaked out of their cottages, met at the store, smoked cigarettes stolen from their parents and threw the still-burning butts into what they thought was an empty kerosene can. They narrowly escaped serious injury, and everyone agreed that the wrath of their fathers was punishment enough. Donna Antonielli was completely surprised by a phone call she received from the agent who was handling the sale of the store. He told her that he had discovered a large insurance policy that Big Lou, wary of fire, had taken out on it. Donna was the sole beneficiary of the policy. When she finally got the check, she was able to give a quarter of it to her son, Tony, and still be able to face a retirement, if not in wealth, at least free from fear. Donna's house sold just a week after the fire, to a young couple with plans to start a coffee shop and gift shop on Second Street. They planned to stay open from Easter to Thanksgiving every year. Donna liked them and trusted them with her house. There was also a change in the attitude of long-time residents to Harriet Slade and Ida Green. Their insomnia that hot Tuesday night had elevated them to near-hero status, since they had seen smoke and gotten to a phone within minutes. They had also provided the kind of simple hospitality that is the special talent of small town residents, and it had resulted in many casual acquaintances feeling closer to each other than ever before. Larry McCarthy began to call Harriet "Chief" whenever he saw her, which she took as an affectionate nickname – and it was.

Soon after the fire, Harriet rented her Sandusky home to her associate in the company and his new bride. They were thrilled with the tastefully decorated Victorian home, near the office, and she stopped worrying about its upkeep. Over Labor Day weekend, Ida welcomed her daughter, Laura, and her family to Lakeside, the first time she had been there since the death of her father. Ida was nervous about Laura's reaction to the part Harriet played in her mother's life.

"There is one thing I haven't told you, dear," Ida began with Laura, after the children had gone to bed. Laura's husband had gone for a walk. The two women were sharing a bottle of Chardonnay.

"What?"

"You met Harriet this afternoon."

"Yes, it was nice that she brought over that cake. The kids liked her. So did I. Did she just move into Cree's house?"

"Last summer. She completely remodeled it. I hope you get a chance to see what she has done. It's gorgeous," said Ida.

"What do you want to tell me?" said Laura.

"Harriet and I are - very close. I am very happy that I met her. Very, very happy."

"How close is close?"

Ida took her daughter's hand in hers and gazed into her eyes. "I am in love with her, dear. She is my life now. I hope you can understand."

Laura sat for a moment, looking at her mother. Releasing her hand, she stood and lit a cigarette. There was no view out the kitchen window in the dark but when she opened the back door to let in the cool night air, she could hear the ceaseless string section of the cricket orchestra. She stood in the doorway, smelling the town – a mixture of lake water, mud, grass clippings, and the perfume of flowers. Ida sat quietly, waiting, hardly daring to breathe. "Mom, what I understand is that you are relaxed, smiling all the time, singing in the kitchen, playing with the kids. I noticed it in Boston when you came to see us. You were different, you were like - twenty years younger." Laura turned and faced her mother with a smile. "All I see is that you are truly happy. Why would I have a problem with that? If you love Harriet, then I love Harriet. Why isn't she here right now?"

Ida returned her daughter's smile. "She is sitting on her porch, waiting for me to wave to her. I'll go get her."

"I'll get another wine glass. And let's get into that cake."

Returning to Lakeside
2014

This is all wrong, I thought; everyone knows you can't drive into Lakeside. You walk, or you rent a bike. But the sign read "$20 Visitor's Day Pass." There was no mention of parking and walking. Nevertheless, we paid the friendly lady at the gate house and drove our mid-sized sedan onto the narrow town streets, where it seemed our car was so huge that we could reach out of the open windows and touch the porches of the cottages on either side of the street. Where the crunching of our tires would surely wake anyone napping on a hammock. Where the smell of gasoline fuel would offend the gulls. There were cars parked on what passed for a front lawn or beside a cottage, wherever space could be found. Whenever the street was wide enough to permit street parking, we saw no empty spaces, unless accompanied by a sign reading "resident parking only." There were even, and this surprised me even more, parking lots dotted around, filled to capacity with cars. I was quite sure there were no parking lots in Lakeside in the 60s when I was here as a girl. No need for them. No cars allowed. I had hoped nothing had changed.

Once I got used to the cars - because my mind simply erased them from view - I relaxed enough to discover that the pock-marked and sandy streets were still narrow, lined on both sides with mostly small Victorian-era cottages of varied sizes and designs and colors, many faded and in need of paint. The screened porches were still here, the bikes leaning on them, the fishing poles and clothes lines still visible, the children in flip-flops walking along the edge of the road in twos and threes, sometimes with adults, sometimes not. There was a group of teenagers, over twenty of them, gathered on a lawn in front of a church or civic building of some kind, fooling around, all talking at once, and wearing identical t-shirts that identified them as a religious youth group of unclear origin. There were older people strolling along a road – Second Street – that had a few shops and restaurants on it. There was a hardware store, a food market, two gift shops, a summer boutique with women's sundresses in the window, an ice cream shop, and a breakfast/lunch café. Turning down Montgomery Street, there was the Hotel Lakeside.

The hotel. It was still there. It looked – the same. Old, weathered, sagging in places. That huge screened porch on two sides – the narrow side of the long building, and the side facing the lake over the huge expanse of lawn. White with green shutters, some hanging a little crookedly, for want of a nail. Three floors of windows, representing three floors of small, serviceable guest rooms, some, perhaps many, with shared baths and iron double beds. And on the main floor, a large cafeteria, open to the Lakeside community, the only restaurant in town that served dinner. I bet there is still pot roast, Salisbury steak, roast chicken, and fish sticks to choose from every night. And slices of pumpkin pie or Jello with whipped cream for dessert.

"Can you park anywhere around here?" I asked my husband. I had almost forgotten he was with me, but there he was beside me, slowly navigating the narrow streets, avoiding the dozens of cyclists and pedestrians, and following my directions, without comment, allowing me to gape out the window at my childhood haunt. "I doubt it, but I'll try," he answered, eventually settling on a space marked for temporary standing, not parking. This allowed me to get out of the car and leave him inside, engine idling, ready to move as soon as someone asked him to. I stepped onto the hotel's huge front lawn. Its focal point was a freshly painted white bandstand, surrounded on all sides by deep granite steps, and on the next level, below concentric stone circles, low shrubbery, broken several times with concrete pathways radiating outward. Facing the bandstand on one side were at least ten rows of inexpensive, standard-issue white plastic folding chairs, arranged, it seemed, for a concert or perhaps a wedding. Outlining the lawn were carefully tended flower beds, filled on this June day with a colorful assortment of low-growing, long-lasting annual flowers: red petunias, yellow snapdragons, blue ageratum and white alyssum. Dotted over the expanse were enormous trees, probably, I thought, elms, beeches, and oaks, but I have never been good at identifying trees. I just knew they had stood in their assigned spots for long enough to have witnessed countless politicians, lecturers, preachers, lovers, unattended children, and aging couples whose every summer had been spent in this very place. I looked up at their thick green and black canopies, and I thought I heard whispers from long ago.

Walking away from the hotel, I approached Lake Erie, whose water today was almost blue but dotted with whitecaps, a reminder that even on a calm summer day like this one, weather patterns hundreds of miles away, perhaps in Canada, can be felt in Ohio. I saw the pavilion, a large white gateway to the waterfront which stretched perhaps fifty yards from left to right, with an arched opening at the mid-point. As I looked, the teenagers we had seen earlier burst through the opening, coming toward me in their matching t-shirts; tall, short, black, white, male and female alike, they were following an older man who was enthusiastically playing a guitar. He was leading them in song, a well-harmonized and surprisingly well-sung arrangement of *Sinner Man*, a rousing spiritual I recognized. I smiled as they passed me. Once I had been a folk-singing teenager, happily learning to harmonize with my friends, accompanied by their guitars. That was more than fifty years ago, I realized. As usual, I pushed the thought away.

I went through the gateway they had used, to see the waterfront, one of my favorite childhood playgrounds. It hadn't changed. There was an enormously long concrete pier jutting out into the lake, taking a 90 degree turn to the left maybe 100 yards or more away from shore. A few fishermen dotted the edge. Closer in, there was a swimming area, delineated with ropes attached to buoys and a sandy beach where the smallest children, accompanied by adults, splashed and dug in the sand. Older children jumped off the pier into the deeper water. The shore on the eastern side of the pier was filled with enormous boulders, suggesting the daunting work involved in creating the swimming area on the western side. But judging from the number of people taking advantage of this bright, warm summer day at the Lakeside pier, it had been worth the struggle. I had checked on line before we came, and had learned enough about the town to know it had been welcoming swimmers and fishermen to its pier since the late 1800s.

I was reluctant to leave the sight but I was feeling guilty about my husband in the idling car. Turning toward the parking area,

I saw a Lakeside landmark I had forgotten: a large bronze bell was suspended from a bronze framework, which was in turn surrounded by a stone enclosure, allowing one to look at, but not touch, the bell. The monument was surrounded by more fastidiously tended flower beds, this time filled with riotous red geraniums. Next to it was an Ohio state historical marker, explaining the history of Lakeside as a pioneer of the American Chatauqua Movement, and one of the few that remain. It explained that each summer, the late Victorian community "provides spiritual, cultural, intellectual and recreational programs designed to nurture the mind, body and spirit." It had certainly done that for me, I mused, as I looked for and found our car, still idling where I had left it.

"Where to now?" asked my patient husband.

"I wish I could find Auntie Cree's cottage," I said, "but I have absolutely no idea where it was. I was just a kid. But – wait a minute – something tells me it was on Fourth Street." Where I came up with that, I didn't know, but there it was. Connor obligingly began to drive up Montgomery, away from the water, until he reached Fourth Street. "Which way?" he asked.

"I don't know. Pick one. I doubt I'll recognize it, and it might even have been torn down. It was ancient then. And it's been over fifty years. But I do know that it had a screen door on the side of the porch; I can picture that door. Auntie Cree always yelled 'Don't slam the door!' whenever we walked through it. My dad finally bought her a hydraulic door closer and installed it for her. She adored him from that day on."

"Okay. I'm turning left." And we crawled along the narrow street, looking at block after block of old weather-beaten cottages. And then, I saw it. Yellow, with geranium-filled window boxes all along the screened porch which was as wide as the cottage. Filigreed screen door, on the side. An overgrown rhododendron bush on one corner, an American flag blowing in the afternoon breeze. It was still there. It looked well taken care of and loved. If the roof sagged a little above the second floor, the porch roof was straight. And I could just make out a clothes tree in the back, with flapping towels. "This is it! Stop!" I called out. Connor pulled the car over to the side of the street, blocking an unoccupied driveway, and I got out, cell phone in hand. I had to take some pictures. It was hard to believe I had recognized Auntie Cree's cottage, yet I was certain this was the one. As I took a series of pictures, changing the angle each time, I disappeared into memories for a moment. I was barefoot, hair still wet from swimming the afternoon away, towel dragging behind me, hurrying onto the porch, grabbing the door just in time to prevent its slamming.

"Excuse me, can I help you find something?" a voice interrupted my momentary daydream. An elderly woman, small of stature, wearing a large-brimmed white canvas hat and sunglasses, was approaching me.

"Oh, hello. I'm sorry, I was just taking a picture of the cottage across the street, the yellow one. I used to come here when I was a child, to visit. I haven't been here in a really long time and I was excited that I recognized the place. I didn't mean to disturb anyone." I spoke rapidly.

"Oh, my dear, you haven't disturbed me. It's not often that anyone finds my house worth noticing."

"Your house? How long have you lived here?" I asked, then blushed. "I am so sorry, that's none of my business. I was just wondering if anyone in town remembers my Auntie Cree. But it's not likely."

"Cree Fox was your aunt?" the woman asked.

"Not exactly, we just called her that. Did you know her?"

"Yes, my mother lived in the cottage next door. That one," she said, pointing to the somewhat larger white house on the east side. "I grew up coming here every summer. I remember Cree very fondly. It is so nice to think of her again, it has been years. I am glad I ran into you."

"I am, too! My name is Claire McKay. I was Claire Benson in those days. My Auntie Cree was my grandmother's best friend. We used to drive her here from Cleveland to visit Cree."

"And what was your grandmother's name?" said the small woman.

"Marguerite Wickham."

"Yes, of course. I remember her, too. How extraordinary."

"You remember my grandmother? Really? She and Cree both died in the 1960s."

"Yes, my dear, but I was well into my thirties by then. I had been coming to Lakeside for more than twenty years. I have not lost my memory. Actually, my memories of the 60s are clearer than my memories of last week, strange to say. I do wish you would come inside and have a glass of iced tea with me." She gestured toward the yellow house, smiling.

"Oh, we wouldn't want to intrude. My husband is here with me," I said, pointing to the car. He smiled at the woman.

"He is welcome as well. My name is Laura Taylor. Please do come in."

"But there is nowhere to park," I said.

"You can park right where you are. The people across the street are not here this week. You aren't blocking anyone. Please. It would be such a pleasure for me to show you Cree's cottage. You won't recognize it."

Connor parked the car, moving it as far off the street as he could without hitting a building, and we followed Laura to the screened porch door. It had a somewhat rusted hydraulic door closer attached to it.

"My father installed that," I smiled, pointing to the door closer. I could picture him standing on a chair, with Cree watching his every move from her big chair on the porch.

"Bless his heart. A lot of the doors around here just slam shut," said Laura.

Later, Connor, Laura, and I sat comfortably on the screened porch, watching pedestrians and bikers pass by, along with the occasional car or sometimes a golf cart moving slowly. Sometimes a person would call out a greeting to Laura and she smiled and waved. We had iced tea and Girl Scout cookies – Thin Mints – on a plate in front of us on the big harvest-style table that dominated the room. The cottage was absolutely lovely, I thought, and much more attractive than I remembered. "Well, my dear, when Harriet bought this place, it was in rather sorry shape, I remember. Your Auntie Cree wasn't much interested in how the place looked, and nothing had changed or even been cleaned for decades. Harriet tore it apart and basically started over. I've had to replace the stove a couple of times and sometimes I've needed help with plumbing or whatever, but really I just like it the way it is."

"I'm sorry," I said, "But I don't know who Harriet is."

"Oh, no, of course you don't. Harriet Slade bought the cottage after Cree stopped coming to Lakeside. Harriet and my mother became very close friends, and I spent quite a bit of time in this house before Harriet died. My mother and I wanted to keep the house in the family, so to speak, so I bought it from Harriet's estate.

142

I haven't changed much of what she did, except for a good cleaning once a season."

"Is the house next door still in your family, too?"

"No, that one was bought by a lovely family with small children. You know, I never want to live where I can't hear the noise that children make. Of course, they are all grown up now, but there are still lots of little ones in the neighborhood. Tell me, what do you remember of your visits to Lakeside?"

"My grandmother and Auntie Cree were best friends for most of their adult lives, I think. By the time I was born, my grandfather had died, and my grandmother never learned to drive, so she needed us to bring her to see Cree. My grandmother lived with us for about six years, while I was quite young. We lived outside Cleveland. Driving her to Lakeside was the highlight of my summers, but we didn't stay more than a day or two, I don't think. Even when my grandmother moved to Michigan, we still visited Auntie Cree for a couple of years. We stayed in this cottage, upstairs. I remember the smell of the dresser drawers up there, isn't that weird?"

"Moth balls?" asked Laura.

"Yes! You remember, too!"

"Oh, everybody's drawers smelled of moth balls in those days. Blankets and sweaters were made of real wool then, and the moths fed on them all winter while we were away. You did what you could to protect your things, but the fact is, most of us just tolerated the little holes."

Connor interrupted: "Honey, I think, if you don't mind, I'll take a little walk and check this town out. Is there something you need, Laura?"

"You know, there is. On Second Street, you will find a small market called Jenny's. We could use some cheese and even a bottle of wine, don't you think? And if you like, you could be my guests for dinner at the hotel tonight," said Laura, smiling broadly.

"Oh, Laura, that isn't necessary," I protested.

"I know it isn't. But I am enjoying this conversation more than you know, and I will try to keep you here as long as I can. Where are you staying, by the way?"

"Actually, we are visiting Bellevue, which was my grandmother's home town. I realized yesterday that we were only half an hour from Lakeside, so I persuaded Connor to make this day trip. I never expected to meet a new friend, but - here we are."

"So you can have dinner with me and still get back to your motel at a reasonable hour," persisted Laura.

"I suppose so. Is that ok with you, honey?"

"Of course. What kind of wine do you like, Laura?" he said.

I turned to Laura, with excitement. It had been so long since I had spent time with anyone who had anything to do with my childhood. My family had all moved away from the Cleveland area, and most had ended up in California, and I had moved to New England where no one from my family lived. My parents had both been dead for many years and I had no siblings. Laura seemed to me to be some kind of link, even though she was not related to me. I wanted to cling to the moments and make them last as long as I could.

"Why are you visiting Bellevue?" she asked me. "Do you still have family there?"

"No. I guess I am reaching into the past. I don't really know why, but there seems to be something pulling me to look at Mamama's life. I might want to write a book about her. So I decided to start by going to Bellevue. She talked about it all the time."

"I remember she was very small, but she was funny. She and Cree together told the best stories; they kept us laughing for hours."

"I love that you said that. I thought she was funny, too, but I was only about ten when she left our house, so I don't trust my memories."

"Memories are the one thing you can trust, Claire. Hang onto them." Laura seemed wistful.

"I remember Cree and her son, Phil, and his family. You must have known them."

"Sure. Phil, Nancy and the children. They had a son close to your age, I bet. David?"

"Yeah, he was a couple of years older. We hung out together sometimes."

"He's kind of a hero around here, you know," said Laura.

"David? Why?"

"Well, that's kind of a long story."

"I have time. Is David still coming to Lakeside?" I prompted her, for fear she wouldn't tell the story.

"He still owns the cottage on Fourth Street that he grew up in. Now he spends August here with his wife, children and grandchildren. The Foxes are still a Lakeside family. They must know just about everybody here. Especially David."

"He rescued me from a bully once, at the waterfront. I've never forgotten that. I wish I could thank him myself," I said.

"Rescue, huh? Interesting choice of words. When David was about seventeen, I guess, a black family moved to Lakeside. They were the first. Since then, the town is more diverse, although I guess not as diverse as American society as a whole. Still, we've come a long way. Anyway, the Edwards, that was their name, they were a lovely family. They had two boys, I think, who liked baseball. There's always a pick-up game somewhere in town during the summer and sometimes they even organize themselves into a kind of league so they can play games and decide on a champion. It's just for fun."

"Sounds like fun," I added, for encouragement.

"I'm trying to remember how this went. There was another boy who used to spend most of the summer here, named – um – Gary, that was it. Gary Ferris. He was from kind of a strange family. Mostly we only saw the father. I wondered if the mother was sick or something. Gary and his Dad would show up at the hotel for dinner pretty often, just the two of them. The father was….oh, I'm not sure…..maybe Nick?"

Nick Ferris was pissed off. Gary hadn't taken the garbage out – again. You could still smell the oily mess they had thrown in the corner of the kitchen after last night's burgers and fries, laced with stale beer. Not a nice greeting when you come home from a long day of fishing. The grease had started to coat the brown paper bag they were using for garbage. That means grease is on the floor, too, Nick thought in annoyance. He propped his fishing gear against the back wall of the kitchen and washed his hands in the sink, which still had dishes left over from last night's dinner and this morning's breakfast. A half-empty box of Corn Flakes was standing open on the counter and a bowl with a few flakes and milk had been tossed in the sink. Nick could tell it had been there for several hours, because the milk had congealed into a kind of blue-white pasty ring on the sides of the plastic bowl. That must be adding to the smell in here, he thought, as he walked into the living room and then up the narrow, slightly sloping staircase.

"You awake?" he called out in the direction of a closed bedroom door. There was no response. He hadn't expected one, anyway.

"Hey? Have you had anything to eat? Want me to make you a sandwich or something?" he said as he pulled off his waders and fishing vest, leaving them in a heap on the hall floor. He opened the bedroom door. There was barely any light, since the windows of the run-down cottage faced east and the pull-down shades were drawn, anyway. The windows were shut in the July heat. Nick stood for a minute, letting his eyes become adjusted to the dimness, and then he saw his wife, lying on the bed. She was wearing a faded slip, nothing more, so thin that he could see different colors, waxy cream and brown, on her narrow body through the wrinkled fabric. Her brown hair was damp and lank. One pale arm hung off the side of the bed. The narrow shoulder strap of her slip had fallen to the middle of her arm. Her eyes were closed, but he spoke to her anyway.

"Hey, do you know where the kid is? He was supposed to clean up this morning. I gotta figure out something to teach him a lesson. I'm sick of yelling at him. I don't think it works." Nick was rummaging in the crowded dresser drawer, trying to find a clean undershirt. "Want to come down? There's some cold Coke. It's a scorcher out. I can't believe you haven't opened the windows. It's a steam bath in here. Ok if I open them?" Nick pulled on a short sleeved white undershirt and turned to his wife. She hadn't moved. He stared at her small, almost child-like form for a minute, then slowly walked over to the bed.

"Hey?" he said more gently. He focused for a moment on her full lips, now shaped like a flower just ready to open. He reached out to touch her. Running the back of his fingers down her cheek, he recoiled from the touch. She was freezing cold.

"Jesus! Wake up! Frannie!" he called out. He leaned over her body and put his ear on her left breast, listening. "Frannie! What the hell! Wake up! He took her by the shoulders and shook her. He pulled the top half of her thin frame up off the mattress, but her head, unsupported, fell backwards. "God damn it, woman! Wake up!" There was no response. Nick dropped her on the bed and ran down the stairs, two at a time. He ran out the front door, calling out, "Help! I need some help here! My wife!"

Although it didn't seem so to him, it was less than a minute before neighbors began to appear on their lawns. "I'll call the clinic!" called his next door neighbor, turning to run back inside. "Do you need help carrying her?" asked an elderly man who happened to be walking down Third Street.

"I need a doctor, for Christ's sake! Get a doctor!"

"Where is she?" asked a tall, soft-spoken black man who had just turned onto the street. He was almost running toward Nick.

"Who the hell are you?" asked Nick.

"Mitchell Edwards. We live on Second Street. I heard you yelling. Can I help?"

"You ain't no doctor. I need a doctor. Jesus!"

Edwards didn't hesitate. "I have medical training. In the service. Where is your wife?"

"Upstairs. But stay away from her."

"Let's see if we can get her downstairs so it'll be easier to get her to the clinic. I'll call my wife and have her bring our car. May I use your phone?"

"Man, you aren't listening. I said stay away from my wife!"

But Mitchell Edwards was already inside, racing up the stairs. He found Frannie and gathered her up in his arms, and as quickly as he could with his awkward burden, carried her down to the living room couch. Placing her gently, he picked up the phone, only to have it pulled from his grasp by Nick Ferris.

"I can do it," Nick snarled.

"I'll get the car." And Edwards deftly sidestepped Nick and ran out the front door.

Dr. Hartman from the clinic arrived some ten minutes later. Nick was sitting with Frannie, holding her cold hand and staring at her immobile face, which was surprisingly young looking, as it was when she slept. He tried to smooth her hair the way she liked it. Sometimes he rubbed her arms to warm her. He arranged her slip so her naked body wouldn't be so visible through the worn fabric. He reluctantly stepped aside for the doctor, but the truth was clear to them both: Frannie Ferris was dead. Mitchell Edwards came in the room just as Dr. Hartman said, "I'm sorry, Nick. I'm afraid we are too late. There's nothing anyone could have done."

147

There was a small group of neighbors that had gathered on the street in front of the cottage. They murmured to each other, and they turned in sympathy when one of them said, "Oh, here's Gary."

Gary Ferris was a narrow-framed teenager, whose legs and arms had outgrown the rest of his body, giving him an unwieldy appearance, like a street performer on stilts for a Fourth of July parade. His skin had erupted in bumps of various sizes and degrees of infection, all over his greasy face and upper chest and back. His hair was equally greasy. He was dressed that warm July day in drooping jeans, above which one could see the top of gray underpants; on his feet were red Converse sneakers, and he had a torn and faded blue t-shirt. He walked onto his front lawn, glancing from one concerned neighbor's face to another.

"What?" he asked.

"It's your Mom, Gary."

"Where is she?"

"Inside, with your Dad."

"What happened?"

"You better go in. Let me know if I can help, ok?" asked Carol Hawthorne, who had known the Ferrises since they bought the cottage two doors down from hers in the early 1950s. Gary was only a little boy then.

"Dad? What's going on?" Gary said as he banged through the screen door to the dim living room.

"It's your mother. Where've you been?" Nick was kneeling on the floor, holding his dead wife's hands in his. He didn't look up at his son.

"What's wrong with her?"

"Christ! Can't you see? She's dead, for crying out loud!"

Gary stopped moving forward. "Dead?" he asked.

"And where were you, anyway? Why weren't you here with her? I didn't think she would be alone all afternoon."

"I didn't know I was babysitting today," Gary answered, under his breath. But his father heard.

"Shut your damn mouth!" Nick jumped up to his feet and lunged at his son. "What's the matter with you? You can't stay home for your mother? She was sick, you knew that. You were supposed to clean up and bring her some lunch. And now she's dead. How's that feel, you little shit?"

148

Gary avoided his father's flailing arms and crossed the room, stopping behind a large upholstered armchair, in a guarded posture, ready to strike out if he had to. Just at that moment, the porch door opened and Mitchell Edwards came in the living room.

"Mr. Ferris? Can I help you? Is there anything we can do? The men from the clinic are outside. They can take Mrs. Ferris now."

"What the hell is he doing here?" shouted Gary.

"I don't know. We can handle this, Edwards. My boy and me. Get out."

A new voice chimed in from just outside the screened door. "Dad? Do you need more help?"Mitchell Edwards turned toward the door. "No, thanks, son, we're okay. You better head on home now."

"Oh my God, now it's Jason. Why don't you go to batting practice. We don't want you here," sneered Gary. Volunteers from the clinic in Lakeside opened the screen door and gently lifted Frannie Ferris' body onto a stretcher. Nick stood and watched them go. Gary watched his father warily. Mitchell Edwards still stood in the living room.

"We could bring you some supper for tonight, Mr. Ferris, if you think you'll have some appetite."

"No. Don't need it. Just go."

"All right, I'll go. I'll check back tomorrow, just to see how you're getting on."

"Leave us alone," said Nick, who was walking toward the back of the house and the small, dirty kitchen.

Mitchell and Jason Edwards left, the neighbors quietly dispersed, the truck carrying Frannie Ferris made its way to the local funeral home – just outside the gates of the summer community. Lakeside was not set up for death, although that hadn't stopped it from visiting occasionally. Nick found a beer in the refrigerator, opened it, and drank a long draft thirstily from the brown glass bottle. He reached for another before the first one was done. Gary, realizing his father would not be coming back in the living room anytime soon, slipped as quietly as he could out the front door to the yard, then walked more quickly toward the north, and finally broke into a run. He kept running until he got to the granite-enclosed bronze bell at the edge of the huge lake. He grabbed two of the stone pillars and put his face against them. Leaning in as far as he could, Gary let his body's weight be supported by the monument. He took several deep, uneven breaths. He felt the heat drain from his body until, in spite of the July heat, he was uncomfortably cold. He could see his mother's lifeless body on the couch, nearly naked. He realized, maybe for the first time, that she had been beautiful, lithe and graceful. He remembered scenes of her and him, in snatches. It had been a long time since she and he had gone anywhere together, but he still remembered going to movies, with her in a pretty light dress, on Saturday afternoons, and ice cream sundaes afterwards. He felt proud when people smiled at her. He remembered the two of them lying on the grass of their back yard in Willoughby, looking up at the clouds. He could still feel the thin fabric of her dress and smell her shampoo. He remembered helping her make corn bread, the good kind with lots of sugar in it. She had let him stand on a chair to reach the counter and she let him lick the spoon after the batter had gone into the square baking pan. She always wore a stained white bib-style apron over her clothes when she cooked. He remembered the gentle low sound of her voice when she spoke so only he could hear, and the throaty sound of her laugh. He hadn't heard that in years, he realized. He didn't know when everything went wrong, but it was a long time ago, he was sure of that. He noticed tears on his cheeks, dripping off his chin.

"Hey, Gary, how you doin', man?" asked Jason Edwards, behind him. Gary tried to ignore him.

"Hey, Jason told me. I'm really sorry. Anything we can do?.... Do you feel like throwing a ball for a while?" asked David Fox, who was with Jason.

"Go away," said Gary.

"Ok. Just checkin' in....hey, man, I'm sorry. It totally stinks."

After a moment of hesitation, the boys walked away. Gary froze in place, waiting for them to disappear into the ball fields or swimming pavilion or shuffleboard courts. He stared at the Lakeside bell for a long time, until his legs wouldn't hold him up any longer. He slid to the ground and leaned his back against the cold stone enclosure. The summer people finished their afternoon's recreation in the area all around him, swimming, playing tennis, sitting on park benches, throwing Frisbees, talking and laughing. Gary hardly noticed. His thoughts were so jumbled that he couldn't really have said what they were that afternoon. He felt numb and exhausted. It felt easy to just sit – getting up didn't seem appealing to him. The air cooled as the sun dropped lower over the horizon. Most people ambled away, presumably to their cottages and hotel rooms, for the dinner hour. Some went into the Hotel Lakeside for a cafeteria-style supper. Sitting far away from them next to the water, he could hear the murmurings of their voices and the tinkling of tableware on china, but it was muffled. Clouds gathered remarkably quickly as a lake storm came in on the evening breeze. Still Gary sat with his back against the Lakeside bell. He became aware of fat raindrops landing on his head and legs. Still he sat, immobile. And then it was dark, darker than a usual summer night because of the thick cloud cover. And people closed the bamboo shades or canvas drapes on their summer cottage porches and gathered around fireplaces or under quilts to read or play cards until the summer storm passed. And still Gary sat.

And then Gary pulled himself up, unsteadily at first, and he turned toward the lake. Staring at the gray water, dappled with big raindrops, with a surface that looked solid and impenetrable like mottled granite, he began to speak to his mother. He knew there was no one who could hear him, but he didn't care.

"Why, Mom? What'd I do? I know I wasn't that good at school and stuff, but I tried. What did you want from me? Why'd you stop talking to me? Why? I guess you just didn't like me very much. Nobody else does, either, you know. I'm an asshole. Everybody says so."

Gary began to walk toward the huge boulders gathered at the shoreline on the east side of the long fishing pier. He climbed out on the first of them, his worn Converse sneakers losing their traction as he slowly picked his way from one huge rock to another, ever closer to the swirling, sucking water. "Why?" he asked repeatedly. "What'd I do?" Another slip, then he righted himself, bumping his elbow on a jagged stone. "Jesus Christ, Mom. Wasn't there an easier way to get away from me? Didja have to *die*?" His right foot slipped into the cold water. A shiver went through his body from ankle to skull. The other foot followed. He couldn't find a good foothold on the rocky surface under the water and now he couldn't see a thing, so each step was slow and halting, as he became slowly engulfed by the big lake. Sneakers, jeans, t-shirt, all were under water. He kept his arms on the surface for balance as long as he could but they slipped under the surface, too, and then he was floating. And shivering. And crying, loud this time and without checking himself.

"Why? What else could I do? Where have you been? What the hell did I do? I loved you, for Christ's sake! Fuck! Fuck! Fuck!" And his face began to slip into the water, filling his open mouth with cold, sandy foam. He coughed and spit and began to swim, just enough to stay afloat. But his clothes, especially his jeans, were heavy and dragging him down. He kicked off his shoes. He was aware of being very, very cold and weirdly unaware of his surroundings. There was no sound that he noticed beyond the sound of his own voice screaming in his brain. He no longer knew whether the screams were vocalized or imagined. He no longer knew why he was in the water or where it would take him. He no longer knew what he was doing. He slipped under the surface for a moment, then bobbed up, sputtering and shaking his head. He heard screaming and didn't realize it was his own. He slipped under again.

A hand grabbed him around the rib cage and pulled his head up out of the water. Gary began to struggle against the intrusion. His legs churned wildly. Water filled his eyes and he couldn't see what had happened. There was suddenly a great deal of noise and frothing of water, more hands, more kicking feet, voices shouting. He became aware of a light. He tried to shove his assailant away but couldn't find a body to push. He plucked ineffectively at the arm around his chest. Suddenly a wooden club appeared in front of his eyes, he tried to push it away in alarm but he couldn't control his arms. His head plunged into the water, then was pulled up again. He bumped up against a huge wooden wall of some kind and more hands grabbed him. Then someone pulled his t-shirt up and someone else pushed his ass up at the same time and he was shoved roughly into what turned out to be a rowboat. His leg bumped hard against the rub rail and was scraped by the oar lock. Finally, he lay huddled on the floor of the boat, coughing, spitting and blinking the water out of his eyes. Other arms and feet surrounded him, voices assaulted his ears, the light made him squint. After a moment, he roared with pain and rage and thrashed about in the boat. Two hands suddenly held down his shoulders against the floorboards while two others pushed down on his knees. He stopped struggling.

"Jesus! Gary, what the hell were you trying to do?" asked David Fox, panting while holding his shoulders and peering down at him. "Did you fall? What were you doing in the lake in a storm? What the fuck is the matter with you?"

Jason Edwards was holding Gary's knees. "Man, you scared the hell out of us."

"How did...why...." Gary tried to talk but kept coughing up more lake water.

"I went to your cottage to see if you guys were okay. Your dad said you had run out in the afternoon and he hadn't seen you since. I only knew you had been here in the afternoon so I came to look. I almost didn't see you, but then I saw your shoe on the rocks. Jason's cottage is just over there so that's where I went to get the boat. Man, I thought you were gonna pull me down with you," sputtered David.

Gary gave up the fight and went limp in the floor of the boat, staring at the sky, while Jason rowed back to his family's dock. His father was standing on the dock as they approached and helped pull the boat in, tying its line to a cleat quickly. David and Jason started to help Gary out but he pulled free of their hands and got out on his own power.

"You okay?" asked Mitchell Edwards. He could see the boy was soaked to the skin and shivering. If it had been daylight, he would have seen purple lips and fingernails, and bruises. Gary was barefoot. He pushed aside any offer of help, however, and lurched off the dock onto dry land.

"Come inside and get warm," said Jason.

"No way," said Gary, in a surprisingly strong voice.

"You can't walk home like that, boy. Let's get you dry at least," said Mitchell.

"I ain't goin' in your house. Leave me alone."

And with that, Gary disappeared into the dark town, swallowed by the diminishing storm.

Laura paused. I was aware time had passed but I didn't know how much. I looked at the clock on the porch wall, shaped like a ship's wheel, with wooden spokes. "Oh! I had no idea it was so late," I said. "You must be sick of talking to us." I took a sip of my wine. Connor had been acting as host: he had poured wine and refreshed our glasses, especially mine, since Laura began her tale, and he had created a very attractive platter of cheese, crackers and grapes for us to snack on. Somehow the normal dinner hour had gotten away from us. I looked at Laura, aware of her age, and worried that we were upsetting her routine.

"Please, I want to finish my story. I'm fine. "

"Are you sure we're not imposing?"

"On what? My other evening plans? My dear, I no longer go out at night very often, and your visit is a very welcome surprise."

Connor said, "I noticed some cold barbeque chicken in the refrigerator. From Jenny's, I think? Should I bring some out here?"

"You are a darling. Yes, that would be great. I was going to take you to the hotel as my guests, wasn't I?"

"Oh, if we have chicken on top of our cocktail snacks, we'll be fine," I assured her. "Besides, I don't think I can wait to hear the ending. I hope it's a happy one. Unless you're too tired."

"Don't be silly. I love having visitors, and they are all too rare these days. And I haven't thought about the Ferrises for years. It's good for an old lady to have to remember. You're doing me a favor."

"All right, if you're sure. I do need to take a break, however. Be right back." I knew very well where the small bathroom was located off the kitchen.

When I returned, Laura and Connor were talking about the concerts that were presented on the lawn in Lakeside every week. "Oh, you're back. Good. Where did I leave off?"

"Don't you need a break?" I asked, patting her knee.

"No, my dear, I'm fine. Let's see…"

Gary had nowhere else to go than home, but as he approached his cottage, his pace slowed. He was afraid to walk in. He didn't know what he would be facing. But he was really cold; his teeth were chattering and he had chills. He was more and more aware of a cut on his leg that was bleeding, and it hurt. He hoped his father was asleep, or more likely, passed out from beer. He could see a light on in the cottage. He walked in the front door, hoping to avoid seeing Nick altogether. But Nick was in the kitchen, standing at the sink, and he turned when he heard the door open and shut. Neither of them spoke for a minute.

"What happened to you?" asked Nick, squinting at his son.

"Doesn't matter. I gotta take a shower." Gary moved toward the small bathroom in the back, off the kitchen.

"Hold it." The tone of Nick's voice was enough to stop Gary in his tracks.

"What?"

"You look like hell. You been in the lake? Didja fall in?"

"Yeah. I'm really cold, I need a shower."

"What were you doin' at the lake in the middle of a storm?"

"Nothing. Just thinking. Can I go?"

"Yeah. And when you're clean, we're gonna talk. You want something to eat?"

"I'm not hungry."

"I'll make you a sandwich. I could use one, too. Go."

When Gary was clean, he went into to the living room. He had on clean jeans and a sweatshirt of his father's. He was pulling on a pair of woolen socks as he sat down. Nick, who had been picking up trash, turned on a second lamp and peered at his son's face.

"You still look like hell. Is that a bruise on your face?" He grabbed his son's head and turned it toward the light. Gary offered no resistance. His expression was unreadable. He was still shivering.

"Christ, put this blanket around you," said Nick, grabbing an old Navy blanket that was draped over the back of the couch. He stood up, too upset to sit still. "Anybody would think you got no sense. Runnin' around in the rain, in the dark, during a storm, nobody knows where you got to, falling into a lake that's so big you can't miss it. Wait - shit, *did* you fall? Did you? Tell me!" Nick was standing behind the couch, behind his son, where neither one of them could see the other's face. He had his big hands on Gary's shoulders.

Gary ignored the near-panic in his father's voice. "Forget it. I just want to go to bed." Gary started to get up. Nick took hold of his shoulders and pushed him down.

"You eat that sandwich," he said more quietly, indicating a plate on the coffee table. "It ain't bad. Mrs. Hawthorne brought over some meatloaf. And somebody left potato salad on the porch when I was – well, I wasn't paying attention. Look, boy, this has been the worst day of my life. Yours, too, I guess. We gotta talk about it. There's stuff to do tomorrow and the day after that, and we gotta be ready. I gotta know where you went. I gotta know. We gotta talk. I know we ain't too good at that, but we gotta start. Now. You're gonna talk to me."

Gary sat, silent and unmoving for a long time, staring at nothing in particular in the room. Then he reached out for the sandwich and began to slowly eat. The first two bites made him cough, but after that, the food began to taste good and he ate it eagerly. He realized that a bowl of Corn Flakes at about seven that morning was the last time he had eaten anything. The warm, heavy blanket was doing its work and his body was responding. He had the sense he was waking up from a nightmare. Satisfied, he leaned back on the couch and closed his eyes.

There was a soft knock on the porch door. Nick called out, "Yeah?"

David Fox came just inside the door. "Hi. Just wanted to know if you guys are okay."

Gary opened his eyes and looked at David for a second, then closed them again.

"We're okay. You can stop following me around."

"I'm really sorry about Mrs. Ferris... um, Mom wants to know if I can bring over some muffins in the morning. She makes great banana muffins and there's only three of us here right now, so we have too many. I'll just leave them on the porch, you don't even have to answer the door. Okay?"

"Sure, that's okay, thanks," said Nick. "You want to sit down or something?"

"No, that's ok, I'll go. Oh, I forgot. Mrs. Edwards told me she dropped off some potato salad. Did you find it?"

"Edwards? That was from them?"

"Yeah. So you got it. I'll let them know. They told me to tell you they're happy to help if you need them. Um, I gotta go." David left, letting the screen door slam.

Nick didn't know how to start talking with his son. There was a long, uncomfortable silence.

"Look, Dad, I'm really tired. Let's talk tomorrow."

"No. Tonight. Your mom is gone, boy. I'm all you got now. We have to learn how to talk. Start by telling me where you went."

Nick sat down on the armchair that faced the couch and waited. It was a long time before Gary spoke.

"I needed some air. I couldn't talk to the neighbors. They all hate me anyway. Just because my mom d---I mean, passed, they're gonna be my new best friends? No way. I had to get outta here. And you were, well, you were drinking. They had taken Mom's - she was gone, I didn't want to stick around so I went for a walk. I went down to the lake and did some thinking, I guess. Maybe I slept, I'm not sure. It started to rain but I didn't care. Then I fell in and hero-boy saw me and pulled me out. End of story. Okay?"

"What was David doing down there in the storm?"

"How should I know? He's always pokin' his nose into my business."

"Sounds to me like he saved your life. You think you might owe him a thank you?"

"Hell, he couldn't even do it by himself. He had to get help from that spook."

"Shut up, kid. Don't say that anymore."

"Why not? You say it all the time."

"Look, listen to me. I got something to say," Nick took hold of Gary's chin and forced his son to look at him. "Your mom died today. I guess I shoulda seen it comin' but I just didn't want to face it. She's been sick for a long time. She got a lot of doctors to feel sorry for her, and she's been filling prescriptions at different drug stores in the state for years. I didn't know, I swear." Nick let go of his son and stared at the floor as he continued. "I found the bottles tonight while you were gone and read the dates. She's been keepin' 'em, gettin' ready. Lots of doctors, lots of downers. She must have swallowed them all this morning. I was going to be fishing all day and you were God knows where, and nobody visits no more, and she knew she had enough time. She's been planning this for a while. God. I had no idea. Where have I been?" Tears were welling up in Nick's eyes. One or two spilled over before he swiped roughly at his face. Gary hunched over, looking at the floor, hands between his knees.

"I loved that woman, you know. When I met her, I thought I had hit the life jackpot. And the best day of them all, you were born. We used to lie on the bed with you between us, with you kickin' your feet and kind of bubbling, and I'd look at her and you and I'd think, this is it. This is the best. I don't deserve this but I got it..... And then, I don't know, she didn't seem happy after a while, and I thought I was a big disappointment to her, and I couldn't look at her, I was so ashamed. And she stopped talkin' much to me, but she was still real crazy about you. You two was like best friends, and I couldn't figure out how to be part of that. So I started workin' late and then comin' home and drinkin' beer. There was a lot of beer, boy. She'd be asleep and you'd be asleep, too, and I'd be drinkin', thinkin' about you two upstairs and not knowin' how to push my way in. I got real mad. I'd yell sometimes and sometimes I'd just run out and drive around...... And I got passed over for a promotion I wanted at work and they gave the job to a black guy who'd been with the company for less than a year, and I blamed him. I got real mad at him and I called him a lotta names he didn't deserve. I got fired, which I guess I had comin' to me."

Gary looked at his father. "Was his name Fletcher?"

"That's him. Good worker, actually. Never yelled back at me. I don't think I coulda done that..... Anyway, when your grandfather left this dump of a cottage to her, we took it, and I thought maybe we could have some good times here, you know, away from town and everything. We almost made it, too. That first summer, that was fun. We had cookouts and we took walks and we played shuffleboard, even. We even talked to the neighbors and they were nice to us. But then we had to go back and your mom got sick again and, I don't know, it hasn't been fun here since then. But we kept comin' back and I thought you might be havin' some fun, playin' ball, swimming, hoops, and you got a job at the gas station, and you were gettin' lots of outside time. But you and I, we never clicked. And she, she just kinda left us. Always sleepin' or readin' or just starin' out the window. It was the same here and in town..... I guess you been kinda raisin' yourself the last few years, huh? I guess I ain't been around much. I let you down, I think. I feel bad about it, kid."

"Whatever. I'm okay."

"No, kid, I don't think you are. I don't never see you with any of the guys. You're always by yourself, and there's been a coupla times when I got called to pull you out of a scrape you got in. Seems like you're always pissed off at somebody. Look, I had some time to think tonight. I didn't do nothing else. I started to drink, and then, I don't know, I thought about your mom and you, and I just stopped. Then I cleaned up the kitchen and the rest of the place. I opened all the windows. I took the trash out. I even washed a load of laundry and hung it outside. And all the time, I'm thinkin' about you. And while I'm here thinkin', you're in fuckin' *Lake Erie* and two guys you've known for a few years pull you out and save your goddam life, and you ain't even grateful, and I think, man, this is my fault. I shoulda told you this stuff before. Don't matter if one of them is black, he's a kid who helped you. He and his family have been helpin' me all day. I tried to throw that Edwards guy out and he just ignored me and kept on helpin'. Didn't yell back. But he didn't leave, neither. That guy is okay. Men is men and boys is boys. Black, white, purple, green, people is people - and sometimes they stink, but mostly they're all tryin' to get through just like me and you."

Nick stopped, took a deep breath. He hadn't spoken this many words in years. "We're gonna bury your mom tomorrow, and I swear to God, Gary, you and I are gonna make a promise on her grave, to find some good in this life, starting with each other, including folks who have been good to us whether we deserved it or not. You hear me, boy?"

Gary looked up from his usual slouch. What he saw on his father's face he couldn't have put into words, but it was raw, human emotion, guilt mixed with resolve and even optimism. And it registered in some primal place in his gut that this man loved him. That he was part of a family. But, after a full minute of silence, all he said was, "I hear you."

The sky over Lakeside was starting to brighten as the hour approached dawn. Nick and Gary stripped the beds, opened upstairs windows, swept the floors, filled brown paper grocery bags with trash and carried them to the alley behind the cottage. They said little, but they worked side by side.

"You mean to tell me, Gary was a nice kid after that?" I asked Laura. The old woman was still sitting on the porch rocking chair, wrapped up in a shawl, her voice still strong and her memory amazing.

"Well, no, it wasn't quite that easy. But I did see him and his dad together a lot more, and the cottage yard was cleaner. They sold the place a couple of years later and I lost track of them, sorry to say.

I heard Nick got a pretty good job in Willoughby, but they didn't want him taking a month or two off in the summer, and Gary went to a vocational school in Cleveland. I hope he's found some friends and a decent job, at least.... David and Jason are still friends. Matter of fact, Jason and his family come for a visit every summer. "

"You said David was kind of a hero here. How did everyone find out about him pulling Gary out of the lake?"

"Gary wrote a little article for the town newspaper. The *Lakeside Gazette* comes out once a week, and it's mostly just full of ads for the shops and weather forecasts, and announcements of upcoming concerts and lectures and whatnot. But now and then someone in town writes a little article. Everybody reads the silly thing, you know. We pick it up at Jenny's when we buy groceries. And one day a couple of weeks or so after poor Mrs. Ferris died, there was an article right on the front page, something like "How David Fox Saved My Life" by Gary Ferris. It was kind of sweet, kind of like something you might write for your 8th grade English class the first week of September, you know? David was embarrassed but he didn't deny it, only he was quick to include Jason Edwards in the glory. Really, they were all nice boys. Gary was a little rough around the edges, but he probably got better as he got older. I hope so, anyway."

"Laura, I can't believe you sat here until 10:00 telling me that story. You have to go to bed and we have to drive back to Bellevue. Thank you so much. This has been amazing," I said, rising stiffly to my feet. Connor had been dozing a little, but I thought he was a dear to wait so patiently for me.

"It has been my pleasure. Please come back. I'll still be here."

"I will never forget this evening."

"Nor will I, my dears."

As we climbed into our car and pulled slowly out into the sleeping street, I could see Laura waving from her screened porch, and turning out the little lamp that was attached to the wall. And I could hear the sound of the lake, lapping gently on the rocky shore.

Finding Lakeside
1970

Cree wondered why everyone was crowding around her bed when she was just trying to get a good night's sleep. She tried crying out "leave me alone! don't touch me! what is that? what did that man say? where is Phil?" and other protestations, but she found she couldn't form the sounds. It felt as if she could shape her lips correctly but the air wasn't coming up through her larynx to make sound possible. The frustration was terrifying. "Just go away. Leave it. I'm tired." But she didn't say any of it, just closed her eyes and pursed her lips together and willed it to stop. I need Phil, she thought. He would make them stop. He would yell; he was good at that. Better than I am. Yell at all these strange people to leave me alone and go away. Then he would lie down next to me and I would put my head in the hollow of his big shoulder and he would stroke my arm, and I would finally be able to sleep. I could always sleep when he was next to me. Always. Somewhere in the cacophony in her room, she could make out a familiar voice. "Mother? Can you hear me? I'm here, now." Phil. My Phil. He came after all. I should have known he would. He would never leave me alone and unprotected. He will yell at them now. It's going to be all right. A smile played on her closed lips and her neck muscles relaxed.

She let her mind wander back to youthful times when Phil and she were strong and straight-backed and healthy – they were a formidable couple in those days. They met at a dance in 1906. It was a house party in her

Cleveland Heights neighborhood. It was one of those self-conscious winter dances that her former school friends were always giving, in their huge houses with lots of food and wine and cigar smoke and a small orchestra hired for the evening. The young women wore long gowns with trains, short sleeves, scooped necklines, and an impossible amount of lace. Their arms were covered in long gloves with hundreds of tiny buttons, and in their hair they wore feathers or jeweled clips. They vied with each other to wear the most elaborate and eye-catching fashion. The young bachelors wore tails with top hats and white gloves which they left at the door when they entered. Servants carried coats and gloves to upstairs bedrooms and passed trays of canapés and champagne.

Cree arrived punctually, as usual, and thus was the first guest to be welcomed. She had a new dress for the occasion, made of silver satin and adorned with gray lace panels, which stretched out behind her in a short train. She wore long grey suede gloves that covered her elbows and had two silver combs in her thick hair. It was the most elegant costume she had ever owned and it made her feel unusually feminine and - dare she think it – alluring. She sat in the drawing room with her hostess, the mother of a girl Cree had gone to school with, and made polite conversation about the weather and the other social events planned for the season in Cleveland society. They exclaimed over the recently held Bachelor's Ball, given traditionally on New Year's Eve in the elegant Renaissance Hotel. Cree had actually found the affair tedious but she didn't say so to her hostess. As they sat and chatted, a servant announced the arrival of two more guests, Benjamin Wickham and Philip Fox. Cree looked up to see two young men she had not met before. One, a blond, blue-eyed man, was wearing a gray military-style uniform with a high, tight collar and a sash draped diagonally across his chest. The other was darker and taller than his companion, and was wearing black tie and tails. His posture was extraordinary, Cree noticed, and his dark eyes seemed to take in everything in the overly decorated room, including its overly decorated occupants. Mrs. Vance, their hostess, greeted the men warmly and introduced Cree to

162

them both. Servants began to rush to the double front doors, greeting large numbers of guests who all seemed to arrive at once. Cree, Benjamin, and Philip moved to the dining room, greeted friends and were formally introduced to strangers.

Later, as the guests moved slowly and gracefully to the ballroom on the third floor of the house, Cree found herself walking beside Philip Fox. His dark features were focused on her, which made her uncomfortable. "Is there something the matter, Mr. Fox? You seem to be studying me. I'm afraid I am not measuring up."

"You speak very directly, Miss Latimer. Well, so do I. You are the focus of my attention because I want to get to know you better. Do you think I could have the first dance tonight?" He smiled in an open way.

"I haven't even opened my dance card yet, so I suppose I am unattached - so far. You may have the first dance if you like," Cree answered. She was unaccustomed to flirting.

"Splendid. I don't really know many people here, since I am from the west side. My friend Ben wrangled an invitation for me. But he refused the first dance when I asked him," Phil grinned.

"Lucky for me. Is Mr. Wickham from the west side as well?"

"No, he is from Norwalk. But he is attending law school at Western Reserve so he is getting to know some people. I think young Vance is a classmate of Ben's. Do you live in Cleveland Heights?"

Cree and Phil had begun to dance. She was pleased to notice that he was taller than she, but not so tall that she couldn't converse with him face to face.

"Yes, not far from here. But in somewhat less elegant surroundings. I went to school with Katherine Vance. I don't understand why Mr. Wickham is in uniform if he is a law student."

"Oh, Ben teaches at Culver Military Academy to help pay his tuition at WRU. He thought he might make a good impression if he wore his uniform tonight. What do you say? Do you like to see a man in uniform?"

"I'm more interested in what he has to say than in what he wears," Cree said with a toss of her head. "What about you? Are you also a law student?" she asked Phil.

"No, I am a teacher. I just began in September at Hudson Academy, teaching history. "And what about you?"

"I am also a teacher. There is a public elementary school at the end of my street, and I have been teaching reading to some of the older children. I think I would like to be a librarian, however. I have started to look into classes I can take at WRU in library science."

"Well, that sounds like an ambitious plan."

"Do you disapprove of women working?"

"Good Lord, no. I can't imagine the idiocy of building a national economy by ignoring half the population. We can use all the talent we can get, I think."

Gordon James tapped Phil on the shoulder. "I wonder if I can get my name on Miss Latimer's dance card," he said to Phil.

"I think Miss Latimer is in a better position of answering that question than I am," said Phil, looking at Cree. "But if it were up to me, she would dance only with me tonight."

"I will do no such thing. However, I will ask you to escort me to the table for a glass of punch," said Cree. She walked away from them both, but Phil caught up quickly.

Cree and Phil spent the entire evening together, dancing, talking, laughing with friends of hers, and by the time the evening ended, she knew she would be seeing a great deal of Phil Fox, and she was delighted with the idea.

Thirsty. The overwhelming need to drink some water crowded out all other thoughts. Why can't I have a glass of water? Where is that young woman? Where is Phil? Why can't I move my hands? She began to feel the first tendrils of panic encircling her mind. Helplessness was never her style. She was competent, everyone said so. Cree Fox was a woman who could take care of herself. She was tall and straight and dignified. She was well educated and street smart all at the same time. Cree was a handsome woman, they said, with that spectacular white hair and the bluest eyes anyone had ever seen, but

164

she never seemed to capitalize on her beauty, almost as if she were unaware of it.

But when did things change? When did she lose the ability to get herself a drink of water? She was sure she couldn't do it but she couldn't remember why. I don't even know where I am, she thought in fear, but I know I can't move. She felt her pulse quickening, her heartbeat deafening in her skull. She tried to open her eyelids but they seemed to be weighted down with iron bars. Is this a dream? I want to wake up if it is. Her fingers began to twitch and her head moved from side to side as if in slow motion. A glistening thread of saliva dripped from the corner of her mouth and moistened the pillowcase. And then - relief - as water was rubbed onto her lips and her arms were massaged gently. Is Phil here? Did he come to take care of me? Will he lie down next to me? I wish I could ask him to, but my mouth just won't talk. Why not? Where is that water? I need more. I need more. Thirsty.

Cree arranged to meet Phil Fox at the Cleveland Public Library sometimes after school. They would sit together companionably as they read, she taking notes in a black notebook, he reading quietly. Later they would walk to a small, inexpensive restaurant and eat soup and bread for a simple supper. She would dress conservatively in a suit much like his, except hers included a long skirt and high boots. She rarely wore a hat, unlike most of her contemporaries. Cree's one extravagance was her hair, which she kept very long, and twisted it into elaborate braids which she piled on her head in various ways each day. Her hair was a rich reddish brown and it was thick, wavy, and luxurious. She knew that Phil occasionally looked up from his book to stare at her hair, and she enjoyed knowing it.

One late March Friday they met at the library as usual at 4:00 in the afternoon. She had been looking forward to seeing him all week and had washed her hair the night before, mixing in a pine-scented pomade which she had purchased for the occasion. The weather was pleasant, and the sun was shining later and later every day as the year moved toward the spring. Sitting near a partially opened window, Cree could smell the delightful scent of mud mixed with grass and stretched in pleasure at the library table.

"Finished reading?" asked Phil, looking up and smiling at her.

"I can't concentrate. I can smell spring, I really can. It's been such a beastly winter. I can't wait for crocuses to come up."

"I know what you mean. At school today, the students were more restless than usual. I think I need to take them outside for lessons next week if this keeps up."

"Let's leave and walk a bit. Do you think we might try that new café that opened at the hotel?"

"Um, actually, I have to make this an early evening. I have, um, plans later. With my family. I really am so sorry. I would much rather spend the time with you, honestly." Phil appeared to struggle.

"Oh, well, that's perfectly all right. Maybe I will go now and catch the next train home."

"You're angry. Don't be."

"I'm not, really. I just don't want to be cooped up in this library right now. I feel the need to be outside." The librarian was looking at the two of them with a warning in her glance. "Oh, my, look at her," Cree giggled behind her hand. "She's actually glaring at us. I swear I will never be that kind of librarian. I will be modern and kind and understanding, if two people are talking." She stood and put on her jacket.

"Cree, maybe you would like to spend this evening with me and my family, after all," Phil said as he gathered up his books.

"Oh, no, I don't want to intrude. I will see you next week some time, all right?"

"Cree, let's go and get a cup of coffee. I want to tell you something."

"My parents and my sister are meeting me tonight to attend services. Usually they don't come downtown, but they haven't seen me for weeks, and they are making a special trip," said Phil over their coffee.

"Services?" asked Cree.

"We are Jewish, Cree. We attend services on Friday night. Our family temple is in Rocky River but tonight we are going to Park Synagogue for Shabbat services. I would love to bring you with me. You might really enjoy it. The service can be quite beautiful. It's mostly in Hebrew, but I can translate it for you."

"I can translate it myself. I was raised in the Green Road Temple in Cleveland Heights," said Cree, quietly.

"You're Jewish?" asked Phil, his eyes widening.

"Yes, although I admit it has been a long time since I attended services. A very long time."

"I can't believe it. I never thought I would meet a Jewish girl at the Vance home in Cleveland Heights. Do your friends know?"

"I don't know. If they do, it's not because I have told them. My father is a judge, you know, and so he is sort of affected by politics. He has found it wise to not speak of his religion. He hasn't been to temple in, well, in years and years. And Mother is not especially devout, so she has gone along with his wishes. I was raised going to Hebrew school once a week but when they enrolled me at Hathaway Brown School, that part of my education ended. I missed it for a while; I liked learning Hebrew. I guess I just like learning languages. But I miss…. there is such poignancy in our heritage, don't you agree?"

"I do. But like you, I don't talk about this very much. I'm not sure Hudson Academy would have hired me if they had known. How long has your family been in America?"

"My father's father was a Russian Jew. He fled the pogroms and came to New York. But he found it unwelcoming, so he moved his family to Ohio and worked hard to erase his accent. My father has always known relative prosperity and has been accepted by Cleveland society. "

Phil's turn: "My grandfather was born in Latvia. He changed his name when he came here. He brought my father to Ohio when Papa was just a baby. His wife had died of scarlet fever and he wanted a fresh start in a rural setting. They settled in Bellevue and farmed. My Papa wanted a more urban life, so he moved to Rocky River. He owns a tire manufacturing business. He inherited his strong work ethic from his father. I guess I have it too, except for those magical times when I am sitting across from a special girl. Then I forget about work and religion and politics and all of it and just enjoy the moment – and the view."

Cree sat still and straight and looked at Phil. Neither of them broke the gaze. Her blue eyes filled with something he could not name but he knew he had caused it with his words. He silently vowed he would do everything in his power to keep that look in Cree's eyes for a very long time, indeed.

Finally Cree spoke. "I would be happy to go to services with your family tonight. But I absolutely am going to need something to eat, or my stomach will growl in the middle of the prayers."

Lucretia Latimer and Philip Fox were married two years later in a small ceremony in her parents' home, her father presiding. A family friend who was a retired rabbi offered a prayer and a blessing but there was no canopy. Guests included Ben Wickham and his young wife, Marguerite. Cree and Marguerite had become close friends almost the day they met. Marguerite was tiny and very dark in coloring, with large, almost protruding brown eyes and a Gibson Girl-style upswept hairdo pulled off her round face. She had a dry sense of humor and a deep intelligence that delighted Cree. They never tired of conversation, with or without their men, but the four of them were completely compatible as well. Ben Wickham had finished law school and had passed the Ohio bar.

Phil Fox had ambition beyond teaching at Hudson Academy, and he attended classes offered by Western Reserve at night to get his master's degree in history and education. He wanted to teach history at the college level. Cree continued her classes in library science during the day, and kept house and cooked, not very well at first, for her new husband. They lived in the University Circle neighborhood of Cleveland, and he commuted to school on the train. By the time he finished his graduate class work, it was often late in the evening before he came home. Cree and Phil would share stories of their classes and assignments over dinner and neither of them minded that the ham was dry or the pot roast was overcooked. After dinner, they would clean the kitchen and go to bed, where they learned together how to make tender love. These were the sweetest years either of them had experienced and few people broke into the velvet-lined nest they built for themselves. Occasionally, they allowed family members to visit, and more frequently, they entertained Ben and Marguerite.

Everything is so noisy here. People are talking, there's some kind of voice saying the same thing over and over. It doesn't sound human, is it a machine? I wish Marguerite would come and visit me. She could make this seem funny somehow. Maybe we could play cards. No. I can't move my hands. Why not? Where is she? Philip could go and pick her up and bring her. He's such a careful driver. I wish I could turn over on my side. I could reach for Phil and snuggle a little while. He is always so warm. Why am I so cold?

Phil graduated and was accepted onto the faculty of Baldwin Wallace College in Berea, Ohio, south of Cleveland and about an hour's train ride from his family in Rocky River. Ben and Marguerite had settled in Norwalk, also about an hour away by train, after they were married, and he established a law office there. Both Marguerite and Cree wanted children, but Cree found it difficult to conceive. During her Berea years, she acted as a favorite aunt to Marguerite's three sons, and worked as a librarian in the local public library. She and Phil never spoke of their disappointment that she was not pregnant.

One morning seven years after their wedding, Cree ate her usual breakfast and dressed for work. Their small New England-style house was within walking distance of the library and she enjoyed her morning walks to work in almost any weather. She was a familiar figure to Bereans: tall, broad-shouldered, and straight-backed, dressed in conservative but becoming skirts, shirtwaists, and coats, and rarely a hat. She set off at her usual brisk pace but after a few minutes, slowed and reached for a light pole to maintain her balance. She felt light-headed and nauseated.

After a moment, the feeling passed and she went to work. After hanging up her coat and taking her seat, Cree again felt ill. She excused herself to the bathroom recently installed on the same floor as the circulation desk, and just managed to lock the stall door before vomiting. Shaken, she told her assistant that she would have to go home. Cree barely made it to the house before she was wracked with abdominal pain and nausea. She managed to get to the bathroom but had not undressed when she fell to the tile floor and saw she was bleeding heavily. After a time, she was able to open the small window in the bathroom and call to her neighbor who was hanging laundry on the line in her back yard. Phil was summoned from school and Cree and he had to face the sad reality of the miscarriage of their first child.

Two years later, Cree again felt ill at work and knew what it meant. She hurried home and lay down, weak and shaking. This was the beginning of a three month siege which she learned soon enough was the first trimester of another pregnancy. Phil insisted she resign from the library, and his mother came to Berea to care for Cree and manage the house for the duration. Although Cree hated turning her chores over to someone else and resented the intrusion into her personal domain, she had to admit it was necessary. The second trimester went better for her but she was still weaker than she was accustomed to, and she spent most of the seventh and eighth months in bed or on a sofa, with weakness and headaches her chief complaint. Philip Fox, Junior, was born in the downstairs bedroom that had been specially set up for the momentous occasion, three weeks before he was expected, but he was strong and alert, and Cree fell hopelessly in love with his tiny red face and strong lungs. Her mother traveled from Cleveland Heights with a maid and took over the household from Phil's mother who was ready to go home by then. Phil and Cree and Baby Philip weren't really alone together in their home until the baby was four months old and sitting up. The two families had made sure that all the baby equipment, furniture, and supplies that the Foxes could possibly require were provided. Philip Junior was the best dressed boy in Berea for many years.

He was also a healthy boy. Cree believed every baby should spend at least one hour a day outdoors, regardless of the weather, and even though he was born in November, his pram could be spotted on the Foxes' front porch even during snowstorms. She bundled him up and took him for long walks and showed him nature as soon as he took the least interest. They learned the names of the birds, trees and plants, followed the east branch of Rocky River from its source in a local lake, to the place where it forked and became two smaller streams. She woke him at night to show him the stars and teach him the names of the constellations. She prepared nutritious meals and insisted he try a little of everything he was served. She read books to him as soon as he could sit in her lap and began to introduce the recognition of letters and numbers before he was three years old.

Young Philip's father was more interested in teaching his son sports and games. Philip became an enthusiastic athlete, and a chess player as well. Cree and Phil had long ago admitted to themselves that young Philip would be their only child, so they focused their considerable energy and love on him. The family did almost everything together, hiking and bicycle riding on weekends and tobogganing in the winter. They attended plays and concerts in Cleveland when they could. Philip was a sociable boy, with many friends and activities. He was a Boy Scout and worked hard at accumulating merit badges with plans to make Eagle Scout someday, if he could.

One January day in 1928, Philip came home from school – he was by this time in the eighth grade at Berea Junior High School – and told his mother he was going up to his room. She watched him go upstairs. She was in the kitchen baking bread at the time. Cree waited until the dough she was working on could be set out to rise, cleaned up her hands and the counter, and went upstairs to Philip's room. She knocked lightly on the closed door.

"Philip? Is everything all right?"

"Yes."

"May I come in?"

"All right."

Cree entered carefully. Her son was lying on his back on the chenille-covered bed, his hands laced behind his head, his eyes on the ceiling. Bookshelves lined one wall of the room and several trophies were displayed in a glass case. A collection of steel toy airplanes of all different types was on a table. A wooden desk and chair were set up in one corner with a small pile of books tossed there, and white bleached muslin curtains framed the winter scene out the front window. Cree turned the desk chair to face her son and sat down.

"What happened? Something is on your mind," she began.

"They told us today about the class trip to Washington, D.C. It's in March."

"Uh-huh. You've known that was coming."

"Sure."

"Well, is there a problem?"

"I need a roommate," said Philip.

"So are you supposed to ask a friend?"

"I already did."

"Really? Who? Do I know him?"

"Jack Ferguson."

"Oh, yes. I like Jack. He seems very intelligent to me, and his mother is a college graduate, I happen to know."

"Yes, well, he said no."

"Really? Does he already have a roommate?"

"No. He just doesn't want to room with me." Philip was still staring at the ceiling.

"I don't understand. You've known each other for quite a while. I thought you got along. What has happened?"

"I don't know," Philip said softly. Cree peered closely at him. He was usually so direct and honest. She had the distinct sense he was holding something back.

"Philip, what is it?"

"Oh, it's not important."

"What isn't important?"

"Well, yesterday in school, there was something written on my locker."

"What?"

"Try not to go crazy."

"What was written on your locker?"

"Kike."

Cree inhaled sharply. Her mind raced, looking for a way to shield her adored son from this poison. Too late, she knew. Too late.

"Oh, Philip, how dreadful. How absolutely dreadful. What is the matter with people? Oh, I hate that this happened to you. What did you do when you found it?"

Philip sat up and turned so he was facing his mother. His hands were clasped between his knees and he looked at them as if they held the key to knowledge. "Nothing. I just opened my locker and got my things. I guess the janitor cleaned it up because when I went back at the end of the day, it was gone."

"You didn't speak to anyone about this? Mr. Halliday, for instance?" she said, referring to the school principal.

"No."

"Don't you think you should have?"

"What good would it do? I don't know who did it."

"Well, I want to find out."

"Mother, I don't want you to do anything."

"But you think it has something to do with Jack Ferguson turning you down, don't you?"

"Everybody has been acting different in the last two days. Like I have the measles or something. Keeping their distance. I think they are laughing at me. Jack is friends with all of them. Who cares about religion, anyway? I hardly ever set foot in a temple, we aren't exactly observant, right? The only time I really think about being Jewish is when Dad's family and we do a seder on Passover. I never talk about it, so I guess my friends just didn't know. I'm still the same kid, aren't I?"

Cree moved to the bed, next to her son. She put her hand on his shoulder. "Yes, darling, you are still the same kid. And now you have been wounded by the world we live in. Your father and I hoped you would never be touched, but we knew that was unrealistic. This country brags about being welcoming to immigrants. You know, *bring these, the homeless, tempest-tossed to me.* But remember they are called the *wretched refuse of your teeming shore* first. And I am afraid that sometimes non-Christian, non-white people are still treated like wretched refuse, even in the land of the free and the home of the brave. Americans can be the worst kind of hypocrites."

"So what should I do?"

"Do?" Cree looked out the window at the peaceful winter scene in their comfortable neighborhood. A light snow had begun to fall and lights in the houses across the streets created a warm glow. "There's not much to do. Usually rising to the bait of a person so full of hatred that he would write an ugly word on someone's locker – or house – just gives him the satisfaction of knowing he got to you. You actually have already done the right thing, now that I think about it. You did nothing. You went on with your day. You must go on with your week, your school year. You must continue to be your sweet, friendly, curious self, and concentrate on your work. The kids who are worth being friends with will eventually come back, you'll see. Maybe not soon, but they'll be back. They like you, that's why. You'll see. Be strong and be pleasant to everybody. That's what you should do."

That night, while Philip was in his room doing homework, with the bedroom door closed, Cree and Phil talked quietly.

"I didn't see this coming," said Phil, rubbing his jaw.

"It has happened to you, too, hasn't it?" asked Cree.

"Not for years. But Cree, the things I hear people say at school. Not to me, but just in casual conversation. Such a distrust of Jews, such a desire to keep Jewish people out of the neighborhood, such fear that a daughter might bring a Jewish boy home for her parents' approval. You know, there were no Jewish students at Hudson Academy. I don't think the administration ever knew I was Jewish, but I am pretty sure if they had, I would have never gotten the job there."

174

"Are there other Jewish faculty at Baldwin Wallace?" asked Cree.

"Oh, yes. But it seems as if people know who is who. It's like there are two faculties, and they don't mesh too often. I seem to sail above it all. I feel dishonest a lot of the time. It's not as if I have lied about it, but I never say anything, and as far as I know, no one has guessed. I tell myself it's not a secret but maybe it is. I don't even know if I am glad they don't know. I don't know if we should expose Philip to his heritage more or less than we do. I just don't care about a person's religion so I don't talk about it. I'm really an atheist at heart, anyway. Why should this matter to anyone? It's nobody's business, don't you think?" Phil was struggling, Cree could see.

"I think we should follow our hearts and tell the truth. What else can anyone do?"

It was quieter now. Cree sensed that most of the people that had been hovering around her were gone. She wondered if she were alone. How can one tell? Then a low-pitched woman's voice began to sing, softly. It was an unfamiliar melody and the words made no sense. What was she singing? Why is she singing? Cree struggled to create context for this unexpected sound. She became gradually aware that someone was gently rubbing her arm and hand on one side, more or less in time with the music. The melody repeated over and over, becoming more familiar with each repetition. It seemed to exist beyond the normal structure of rhythm and meter, the notes floating for as long as the singer's breath held. The voice was low and throbbing, filled with air. Cree began to breathe in sync with the singer; long, slow breaths coming from deep within her belly. She felt as if her body were suddenly heavier and was sinking lower into the mattress. The notes began to come more slowly, the syllables didn't need to rush, the tones didn't need to maintain consistent pitch. The sensation of skin on skin began to spread all over her body, like being wrapped in a warm, hooded, fur-lined cloak. The heat spread into her organs and caressed her forehead and eyelids and scalp. The room became for Cree a lover's embrace of sound and touch, and she allowed herself to fall, fall, fall......

Before the school year ended, Cree, Phil, and Philip were invited to spend Decoration Day weekend at a friend's cottage. It was in a tiny Ohio town perched on a small peninsula jutting out into Lake Erie, about a two hour's drive from Berea. The town was aptly named Lakeside. Their host was a colleague of Phil's at the college by the name of Alfred Carpenter, a full professor of philosophy who had taken Phil under his wing from the very beginning of Phil's career at Baldwin Wallace. Alfred was a kind man with a sweet-natured wife named Marie. They were childless, and had always taken a special interest in young Philip. The Fox family packed lightweight clothes and bathing suits and drove up on Friday as soon as Philip got home from school. They reached the Lakeside gate about five o'clock in the afternoon, under a bright sun and a cloudless blue sky. The attendant at the gate charged them a small fee to enter the town, and pointed out where they might park their car.

"Can't we park at our hosts' house?" asked Phil.

"I'm sorry, but no cars are allowed inside the gate. You park out here and walk in. I'll be happy to direct you. The town isn't very large; you will be fine. If you prefer, you can rent bicycles," explained the middle-aged woman.

"I guess we'll walk," said Phil.

The family pulled out their suitcases and walked the four blocks to the Carpenter cottage. It was located on Third Street, three blocks south of the lakefront. Third Street was filled with small, unpretentious cottages built very close together. Each one had its own style and embellishments but they all appeared to have been built in an earlier age. The one characteristic they seemed to share was a large screened-in porch that usually faced the street. Clotheslines hung from railings to poles or trees, often festooned with bathing suits and beach towels. Toys were scattered about on the tiny yards, and fishing poles and tackle boxes were often resting against cottage walls. Bikes were parked in many yards. Even though the summer season was just getting underway, many of the cottages appeared to be occupied. Children played on all the streets, and people waved at the Foxes from their rocking chairs on the porches.

They had no trouble finding the Carpenter's cottage which was somewhat larger than most of its neighbors, and had four bedrooms. It was furnished with cast-off furniture and worn out rugs. The kitchen was small and old-fashioned, but there was an ice box that kept food cold as long as a block of ice was put inside it every few days. Ice was delivered in a horse-drawn wagon, much to Philip's delight.

The books in the living room were musty, the beds were simple and the mattresses filled with horsehair, but the linens were clean. There was a small bathroom off the kitchen, to Cree's relief. There were cards and puzzles, and the fishing, according to Alfred, was second to none. Phil found the place enchanting. Cree reserved judgment.

Early on Sunday morning, Phil and Alfred took their gear to the lakefront where there was a long concrete pier stretching several hundred feet into the lake, dotted with people in pocketed vests and wool caps, fishing. They found a spot near the end, and stood together companionably, while their lines waited in expectation of a bite from a hungry perch or bass.

"What do you think of our little corner of heaven, Fox?" asked Alfred.

"I love it here, Al. The simplicity of the place, it cancels out the stress of the week. Do you spend your whole summer here?"

"We do, and we love it. Kids are free to come and go as they please, it's safe and full of things to do. Marie doesn't worry so much about housework and cooking and she spends time on the pier with friends, playing cards and gossiping. And I fish almost every morning and I find I can write here in the afternoons. It's paradise."

"Sounds like it."

"Look, Phil, I'm on a committee here that is looking for new residents. Lakeside needs new families, young families, to come in and buy real estate if we're going to survive well into the twentieth century. I wondered about you and Cree. And young Philip. Do you think you might consider joining us in the summers?"

Phil squinted out at the brightly sparkling lake waters. The sun was beginning to warm his back. "It's awfully tempting, Al. But I don't make as much as you do, I'm not tenured yet."

"I can't guarantee anything, of course, Phil, but I happen to believe that problem will be solved at the end of the semester. You'll be looking at a substantial raise and some real security for your family."

Phil smiled with pleasure, but a minute later, his brows knitted together and the smile faded. "Al, explain one thing to me. Last night, sitting on your porch, a minister walked past the cottage and you and Marie put your cocktail glasses down where he couldn't see them. What was that all about?"

"This town was founded on the Chatauqua circuit by a group of Methodists as a place they could meet in the summer for lectures, concerts, tent revivals and that sort of thing. Families found the location so appealing that they began to build cottages for themselves so they could enjoy the lake whether they were involved in the church or not. The Methodists still have a corner on the religion market here, but it's no longer the only game in town."

"Al, I'm not a Methodist."

"You don't have to be Methodist! Marie and I were both raised in the Episcopal church. Nobody cares about that stuff. But everybody treats the pastor with deference. We play a little game about respecting, or appearing to respect, their rules about booze and tobacco and cards. They don't even want you drinking coffee or tea! We just keep the cocktails out of sight when Pastor walks by, just to be polite. Nothing to worry about."

"Al, Cree and I are Jewish," Phil said, not looking at his mentor.

Al was silent. They both looked out at the water and seemed to be paying close attention to their fishing rods, which so far had not produced so much as a nibble. It was several minutes before Al spoke.

Finally, Al spoke. "I didn't know that. I feel guilty. I thought I knew you pretty well."

"No reason to feel guilty. I don't talk about it much. At Hudson, it might have meant losing my job."

"Not at BWC," said Al.

"No, but it would change my relationship with the faculty. I'm not saying I keep it a secret; if anyone asked, I would tell the truth. But what do you think: would I be up for tenure this May if the board of regents knew?"

"I don't know."

"Well, I don't either. But I have my suspicions."

"Phil, I am not aware of any Jewish residents in Lakeside. Not to say there aren't any, but as I said, I'm not aware of it. But this isn't a country club, you don't have to pass some test by a membership committee or get a sponsor, or subject yourself to background checks. You just buy a little cottage and you move in."

"I would love to. I need to talk to Cree and Philip. You don't think our absence at Sunday services would cause folks to talk about us?"

"Nah. Lots of people don't go to services. I personally like the vacation from our Sunday morning routine. I just get up and go fishing. But you can't stop people from talking about you. That comes with the small town life. My guess is they're going to like you two just fine."

Images, memories, scenes, thoughts. Whatever they were, Cree was enjoying them. Like a movie whose editor threw pieces of film into the air, gathered them up from the floor, and spliced them together in completely random order. Philip leaving home for college that first time, dressed in a brown suit with freshly shined wingtip shoes and a fedora on his head. He looked so young and vulnerable with that grown-up outfit on him. Marguerite laughing, a cigarette in one hand and a martini in the other, riding on the cross-Canada train. How the four of them had enjoyed that adventure! Cree's mother, sitting at her vanity table, brushing her auburn hair, one hundred strokes every night, without fail. Cree loved to watch, even as a little girl. Phil, her darling Phil, crossing the room with his arms extended toward her, a small smile on his lips, his skin tan and uncreased. How she loved to sink into his embrace, how safe he made her feel, how adored. Shelves of books, bound in leather, organized first by subject matter and then by author. Cree loved the smell of books, the feeling of excitement when you took one down from the shelf, one you hadn't yet read, the anticipation of the wonders to be found inside the gilt-edged pages. The lakefront with the long concrete pier. The sound of children splashing in the water, laughing and calling out for their mothers to watch them do handstands, or to admire their form as they dived in. The long summer evenings on the broad lawn in front of Hotel Lakeside, the sound of thousands of cicadas chirping, starting and stopping their symphonies in perfect unison as if responding to an insect conductor, the lightning bugs flashing intermittently, adding a light show to the concert. Dogs barking in the distance, dim lights on the screened porches helping you find your own little cottage as you walked home from a trip to the ice cream stand. Dinner at Philip's and Nancy's house in Rocky River, with the grandchildren at the table, babbling about school and dances and sports. A grand party at a classmate's house in Cleveland Heights where she wore silver lace and danced all night with a tall, straight, dark-haired man who made her laugh. The music, the food on the long, elegant tables, the smoke that seemed to fill the air after a few hours, the shock of the winter night's fresh air on her face as she emerged on the dark man's arm from the house and into the waiting carriage, the look on his face as he watched her drive away that night. Oh, it has been wonderful. How lucky I have been. How beautiful it all was. How I have laughed. And learned. And loved. Mostly, loved.

About the Author

Beth Armstrong has made most of her living as a music educator and choral director. Currently residing in Rhode Island, she was raised in the Cleveland, Ohio, area, and lived for almost thirty years in New Hampshire. The mother of two and grandmother of five, she is married to a retired music educator and school administrator, Stewart Armstrong. This is her first novel.

Made in the USA
Middletown, DE
26 April 2017